Hero of the Titanic

Lilly Setterdahl

Midwest Writing Center Press, Davenport, IA

Published by the Midwest Writing Center Press
225 E. 2nd Street, Suite 303
Davenport, Iowa 52801
www.midwestwritingcenter.org

ISBN 978-0-9818089-7-0

Printed in the United States of America

For my sister Vivan

Lilly Setterdahl

Acknowledgments

This book has become a reality thanks to my publisher, the Midwest Writing Center Press. I am very grateful for its continued confidence in me as a fiction writer and for the assistance of its president, Susan Collins, and its board administrator, Lindsey Wheeler.

Cecilia Svensson Setterdahl created the art for the cover, and Daria Christenson kindly translated phrases to Italian. Thank you Cecilia and Daria.

Members of the board of the Midwest Writing Center took the time to read, evaluate, edit, and proofread the manuscript. Thank you, Julie Jensen McDonald, Rochelle Murray, and Dr. Trisha Nelson for doing this very important work. I am responsible for any remaining errors. I also want to thank John Norton for valuable help with the publicity of this book.

I have consulted many sources in my research of facts, among them *Almanac of World War I* by David F. Burg and L. Edward Purcell, University of Kentucky Press, 1998. I have chosen not to italicize the names of ships.

For information about my previous books, please consult my website:
www.authorlillysetterdahl.net

Lilly Setterdahl

From the Publisher

The Midwest Writing Center Press is pleased to present its newest publication, *Hero of the Titanic*, by Lilly Setterdahl. This novel is a sequel to Mrs. Setterdahl's successful intriguing novel, *Maiden of the Titanic*, published in 2007. We are confident that readers will find this new book just as compelling and desirable as the first.

The Midwest Writing Center Press, established in 2009, is the publishing arm of the Midwest Writing Center, a non-profit organization with the mission of "*Fostering appreciation of the written word, supporting, and educating its creators.*"

Founded over thirty years ago by authors David Collins and Evelyn Witter, the Midwest Writing Center offers opportunities for writers and readers alike throughout the Quad City region.

Our website serves as an information gateway to literary events and writing resources throughout eastern Iowa and western Illinois. Midwest Writing Center sponsors conferences, workshops, readings, book signings, contests, and many other literary events.

Susan Collins
Board President of the Midwest Writing Center
Midwest Writing Center
225 E. 2nd St., Suite 303, Davenport, Iowa 52801
www.midwestwritingcenter.org

Lilly Setterdahl

Prologue

In the early part of 1912, the wealthy Bostonian business tycoon, Mr. Henry G. Addison, took his wife and daughter Lydia on an extended tour of Europe. It was the third time that their Swedish lady's maid, Anna Olson, accompanied them. Endowed with a slender body, Anna dressed well in expensive clothes that Miss Lydia had given her.

Having enjoyed the winter in Genoa, Italy, and Cap-Martin, France, the party boarded the R.M.S. Titanic in Southampton, England, April 10 for its maiden voyage to New York. Mr. Addison and his wife occupied a stateroom in first class while their daughter and Anna were to share accommodations in second class, as requested by Lydia. Her boyfriend, Roberto Cosentino, had come from Genoa to board the Titanic. The two had met in Genoa while he worked as a lifeguard and sailing instructor for the luxurious hotel where the Addison party was staying.

Also boarding in Southampton was Anna's younger sister, Christina. Anna had left Sweden in her nineteenth year, and now it was Christina's turn. Both sisters were born in Boston, while their father worked as the gardener for the Addison family. Anna now told Christina that she had met a wonderful man in France, John Whitmore, a young American architect who was in Europe to study old-world architecture. When Anna left France, John had told her that he looked forward to seeing her again in the United States.

Before retiring for the day on the fateful night of April 14, Anna sat down by the desk in her cabin to make an entry in her journal. It was the fifth day of Titanic's maiden voyage. She had just finished writing, "There is word about icebergs ahead," when she felt a jolt and heard a scraping sound. The ink spilled on the page. Anna blotted it and looked at her watch. It was 11:40 p.m. She then went out in the corridor to inquire about what had caused the disturbance. A steward told her that the ship had scraped an iceberg, but that everything was all right. Lydia was supposed to be with her in the two-room cabin, but Anna knew that she preferred to be with Roberto. Not knowing what to do, Anna went back to her cabin and unpinned her hair.

That's when the call came. A steward knocked on her door and yelled, "Put on your lifejackets and come up on boat deck as soon as you can." Anna fumbled to put on her vest. She had experienced drills before, but not in the middle of the night. It must be serious. Passengers in first class would be cared for, but what about Christina? Anna forced her legs into motion. She had to find her sister. When she came to Third Class, the gate was locked. Angry passengers pounded on it from the inside. Anna found the key and unlocked the gate. The moment it opened, the passengers pushed their way out, knocking her to the floor and stepping on her. Christina was among the last ones trying to get out. Seeing her sister on the floor, she pulled her aside. Anna had a bump on her head and a sprained ankle. Leaning on Christina, she managed to climb the stairs to Second Class. Doors to empty cabins stood open. Seeing the closed door to Roberto's cabin, Anna knocked. Roberto and Lydia were in their night clothes. Anna told them to put on their lifejackets. It's an emergency," she said. "I saw the water seeping in below."

While Anna and Christina waited for Roberto and Lydia to get dressed, they went to Anna's cabin and wrapped her ankle. Anna's eyes fell on the journal that she had left on her desk. It was still open to the page with the ink blob. She quickly tucked the journal into her coat pocket. Perhaps she would have time to finish the entry later.

Roberto helped Anna hop along as the four of them entered the second-class elevator that was still running. Having reached the boat deck, Roberto and Lydia went to starboard to look for more lifeboats. Anna saw Mr. and Mrs. Addison on the port side and went up to them. She was surprised that Mrs. Addison hadn't been put into a lifeboat among the first. "I didn't want to go without Lydia," Mrs. Addison cried. The crew tried to release the last collapsible lifeboat. There was still hope for them. Anna's and Christina's eyes followed an emergency rocket go up from the ship. The floor leaned and the passengers on the deck started to slide forward. The two sisters glided apart.

The ship tilted and passengers hurled overboard. The bodies, clad in lifejackets, bounced like corks on the calm but bone-chilling waters of the North Atlantic. Roberto jumped overboard. Hitting the water felt like thousands of sharp needles penetrating his skin. Emerging at the surface among chunks of ice and debris, he watched in horror as the forward funnel came crashing down on deck. Hearing countless pleas for help from the people in the water, he called out the name of his sweetheart, Lydia. Then he saw her—the girl with the long blond hair. It was Anna, the maid. Being an experienced lifeguard, who had saved numerous lives in Genoa, Roberto knew what to do. He swam with Anna as quickly as he could to the closest lifeboat. Helping hands stretched to pull them aboard. Roberto blew air into Anna's lungs. With trembling fingers, he loosened her lifejacket and listened to her heart. *Grazie, Madonna.* It always felt good to have saved a life. But where was his dear Lydia?

All the lifeboats headed in the same direction. Roberto rowed to keep warm. Everyone in the boat watched the faltering Titanic. The lights on the giant ship went out as it sank into the sea, bow first. The heartbreaking screams of the victims echoed across the waters. Looking at the starlit sky, Roberto prayed, "*Madonna mia*, help my sweet Lydia. Help us all." The calls for help soon subsided. No one could live long in the icy waters.

The crew on the rescue ship Carpathia lowered a sling and hauled Anna aboard. Medical personnel stood by and took her to the makeshift sickbay. Roberto was among the last to climb up the rope ladder. For the rest of the day, he kept busy assisting other survivors. He had no time to visit sickbay. While handing out warm soup to the adults and hot chocolate to the children, he looked for Lydia. She did not seem to be among the survivors, nor were her parents. Was Anna the only one he knew on the ship? What about her sister, Christina? Could other ships have picked up passengers? At the end of the day, Roberto collapsed on a cot and fell asleep. In the morning, a fellow survivor told him that the Carpathia would bring them to New York and that it would take two days to get there. Trying to shake off his grogginess, Roberto stood up and accepted a cup of coffee.

In the make-shift sickbay, the nurse on duty told him that she had a patient by the name of Lydia Addison, but no Anna or Christina Olson. She took him to the cot marked Lydia Addison. "She is unresponsive, but we saw the label with her name sewed into her clothes," the nurse said. Roberto looked down at Anna's white oval face and realized what had happened. Lydia had given Anna the outfit she wore. The doctors had said that she might be in shock. Roberto struggled, but decided to go along with the mis-identification. He reasoned that she would be better off and so would he.

As the Carpathia docked at Pier 54 in New York on April 18, scores of reporters waited to get first-hand news from the Titanic survivors. Dressed in his wrinkled clothes, Roberto stood by Anna's stretcher and was among the first in line to disembark. A photographer snapped their picture. A reporter with a notebook in hand blocked their way and wanted to know who the lady on the stretcher was. "Miss Lydia Addison," Roberto answered. The reporter followed Roberto to the hospital and was not satisfied until he had had an interview with him. When he left, he told Roberto to look for his picture in the *Times* the next day.

Roberto spent the night at the Catholic Mission. Having gone to a store to buy shaving supplies his eyes fell on the *New York Times*. It had a picture of him on the first page showing his black beard and Anna on the stretcher looking pale and drawn. The headline read, "Italian lifeguard saves heiress." He picked up a paper and paid for it. Roberto knew the story and read it with ease. The article described his heroic act of saving the life of the heiress. Roberto noticed that there were several pages with coverage about the Titanic disaster and a list of survivors and missing passengers. He scanned the list and saw that Mr. and Mrs. Addison were among the missing. Anna and Christina were not listed at all. He and Lydia were listed as survivors. Roberto wondered how many other misidentifications there might be. He realized that Anna's and Christina's parents in Sweden must be frantic with worry. What he was doing to them was horrible, but he had cast the dice and had to live with it.

Roberto stood clean-shaven at Anna's hospital bed. He took her hand and brushed it against his chin. The hand felt limp. Her eyes remained closed. The doctor could not say when she would wake up. "From now on, I will call you darling," Roberto whispered. A man approached him and introduced himself as the Addison family lawyer, Frank Jones. He had read the article in the *Times* that same morning and had come to find out about the condition of his client's daughter. He told Roberto that he intended to take Miss Lydia home to Boston, but the doctor would not release the patient until she was conscious. To Roberto's surprise, Mr. Jones took him to the Ritz Carlton, signed him in and gave him spending money. The paper had stated that he was Miss Lydia's fiancé, and Mr. Jones said that she would need him when she found out that her parents had perished.

Roberto couldn't believe his luck. He had a nice room at a fancy hotel, and he didn't have to worry about finding a job. Sitting down to read the rest of the *Times'* coverage of the disaster, he learned that thousands of people had stood in Times Square until midnight waiting to learn more about the disaster. Captain Smith and the Titanic designer, Mr. Andrews, had gone down with the ship. But Mr. Ismay, the general manager of the White Star Line, had entered a lifeboat and survived. The majority of the survivors were women and children. The captain had followed the age-old rule of the sea, women and children first in the lifeboats. The Titanic had split in two when a boiler exploded, and two or three lifeboats had gone down in its wake. Many passengers who jumped too late, or were swept overboard, followed the ship into the depths. Of the hundreds who had life jackets on and didn't drown, only a few were taken aboard the lifeboats while the rest froze to death. A Canadian ship was on its way with coffins to pick up bodies. Roberto's eyes filled with tears as he prayed that they would find the bodies of Lydia, her parents, and Christina.

He learned that the Titanic had gone down at 2:20 in the morning, and that the first lifeboat had reached the Carpathia at 4:10 and the last at 8:30. At 8:50, the Carpathia headed back to New York with about 700 survivors.

In all, there were only sixteen lifeboats and four collapsible boats aboard the Titanic for more than two thousand passengers and crew. This was still above regulations, the White Star Line commented. The crew had lowered most lifeboats with less than a full load. The surviving officers said that they knew that the Titanic was sinking fast and that they didn't have time to wait for passengers to fill the boats.

As Roberto left Anna's side at the hospital that day, a nurse's aide came to him with a box in her arms. The box contained garments that supposedly had belonged to Lydia Addison. Roberto almost discarded the box, but on second thought, he opened it. When he lifted out the coat, he noticed something in one of the pockets. It was a small journal, still wet, but with legible writing.

Having awakened from her comatose state, but suffering from amnesia, Anna accepted that she was Lydia Addison and wanted to be called Liddy. When she was well enough, her private nurse, the lawyer, and Roberto accompanied her by train to Boston and the Addison home in Beacon Hill. The butler recognized her as Anna but kept it to himself. Roberto lived the good life at the mansion until Anna showed signs of regaining her memory. Knowing that she would be angry when she found out that he had lied to her, he left in the middle of the night, leaving Anna's diary and a letter to her in his room.

A few days before the funeral of the Addison Titanic victims, Anna learned that she was adopted by the gardener and his wife and the biological daughter of Mr. Addison. The butler had known it all along, but did not reveal the family secret until he was certain that Mr. and Mrs. Addison and Miss Lydia were deceased. As the only surviving daughter, Anna was declared the heir to two thirds of the estate.

John Whitmore knew that Anna was on the Titanic, and when her name did not appear on any survivor lists, he feared that she had perished. But when he returned to New York, he was much relieved to learn that she had survived. A short time later, Anna accepted his proposal.

Roberto read about Anna's inheritance and engagement in the papers and decided to ask her for a job at the mansion. After all, he had saved her life. But Anna knew that John would object to Roberto's presence, so she bought him a ticket back to Genoa. Both she and John believed that he had left until they were called to the lawyer's office to discuss an important matter. Roberto Cosentino had contested the Addison will, stating that he had married Lydia aboard the Titanic and was entitled to her share of the estate. The issue was resolved when one of the surviving Titanic officers gave a deposition stating that there were no weddings on the Titanic. But Roberto still had a card up his sleeve. He showed up uninvited at Anna's and John's wedding. John was ready to confront him, but Anna calmed him down, reminding him that they had Roberto to thank for their happiness. She made him forget about the troublemaker, but he had a suspicion that they had not seen the last of Roberto.

Will Roberto behave? And if not, will John keep his promise? Will Anna's newfound riches change her good-hearted personality?

Chapter 1

Roberto knew before he reached for his pocket that his wallet would be gone. He sensed the stink of garbage. A moan escaped from his lips as he touched a bump on his head. He felt the cold, hard ground beneath him. Cracking one eye open he saw his suitcase dangling from the hand of a rumpled, fleeing man dressed in a long, brown coat that looked too big for him. Dry leaves rustled around Roberto's feet as he tried to stand up by grabbing onto a garbage can. He had a thief to catch. The suitcase contained all his belongings—his Italian passport, shoes, clothes, and his shaving kit.

There were other bums in the alley, but Roberto took up the chase after the man in the brown coat. When the thief stopped behind a house to open the case, Roberto pounced on him. His muscles were strong from all the house painting he had done, and he soon had the bum on the ground. His hard knuckles hit the man's head, over and over again.

"That's my suitcase," he thundered.

"No, it's mine." The voice came from another, taller bum, who quickly grabbed the case and ran.

"That damned double-crosser," the bum on the ground hissed. His face bled and he wiped away the blood with the bottom of his coat sleeves. "We were supposed to share the loot." One of his eyes turned toward his nose.

Roberto looked at his bloody knuckles and walked away. A small crowd of homeless men had gathered, and he was afraid that they would gang up on him. As he left the scene, he felt worse than on that fateful day eight months ago when he had stepped ashore in New York with the rest of the Titanic survivors. Then he still had his passport and cash in his wallet. Now, he had nothing.

Roberto recognized the back alley in the seedy part of Boston where he had rented a cheap room for the past week. No one hired housepainters in late November. Out of work and hungry, he had been on his way to look for food and a cheaper place to live when the bum knocked him down. Shivering from the cold, he walked in the direction of the Salvation Army. He had seen the building many times and heard the officers standing on the street corner singing about salvation.

He knocked on the door and a uniformed man let him in. Roberto explained that he had been robbed and had no place to sleep. The kindly man looked at Roberto's bloody hand, and said, "I'm Captain Rose. Follow me."

When Roberto's hand had been cleaned and bandaged, a policeman came to the door and asked the captain questions that Roberto could not hear but suspected had to do with him. Captain Rose pointed to Roberto.

The police officer looked with disapproval at Roberto's week-long beard, swollen face, and bandaged right hand.

"It's obvious that you have been in a brawl," he said. "What's your name and address?"

Roberto gave his name, but what address would he use?

"I don't—I don't have an address right now. I was on my way to rent a room when I was robbed of all my money and belongings, sir."

"I'm here to arrest you for murder."

"Murder? I didn't murder anyone." Roberto's mouth dried up.

"There are witnesses saying that you beat up a man. That man is now dead."

"Dead? He was alive when I left him."

"You can talk when we get to the police station. Now, you have to come with me."

The officer handcuffed him and yanked on the chain. Roberto felt like a dog on a leash. This was the worst by far that had happened to him since he arrived in America. He wondered if Captain Rose would believe that he was innocent.

Having gone from the prospective husband of Lydia Addison, a Boston heiress, who perished in the Titanic disaster, to a hero for saving her lady's maid, to an out-of-work house painter accused of murder, Roberto had reached bottom.

Roberto braced himself for the interrogation. How could there be murder charges against him? The last he saw of the bum was that he was alert. He can't be dead.

"What do you have to say for yourself?" the police officer at the opposite side of the bare table asked. He sounded like an Irishman. Roberto stared at his brass buttons.

"I did not kill anyone," he said. "The man was alive and cussing when I left him. Someone else must have killed him." As calmly as he could he related the whole incident.

"You can explain it later to a judge. Until then, you will have to stay in jail, Dago. We know your kind. "

Roberto swallowed hard. He had been called Dago before, but not by an officer of the law. He thought about asking for permission to call Anna, but decided against it. It would be too embarrassing—and her husband would have yet another reason to despise him.

When the jail door snapped shut, Roberto was locked in with several intoxicated men, who pissed often in the urinal. The drunks soon went to sleep on the floor, but Roberto spent a sleepless night sitting in a corner as far away from the smelly urinal as possible.

In the early morning, all the sobered-up drunks were let out first.

"We'll get to you soon," the jailer told Roberto.

Once again, the door shut in front of him. To Roberto, the minutes felt like hours before the jailer returned and let him out.

"For now, we are releasing you to Captain Rose. He's here to take you back to the Salvation Army."

Roberto drew a long breath of relief as he greeted the captain and fell in step with him.

"Can you describe what the first robber looked like?" the captain asked.

"He was cross-eyed and wore a long, brown coat," Roberto said.

"That's Pete. I've seen him many times."

"The bum who took the suitcase from Pete was much taller. So if we find a tall bum, carrying my leather suitcase, we have found the murderer," Roberto said, sounding hopeful.

"If he still has the suitcase," the captain said. "Most likely he pawned it and bought whiskey with the money."

The bums made way for them as they walked through the alleys. Roberto felt safe with Captain Rose.

"You must have seen much misery on the Boston streets, Captain Rose," Roberto said.

"I have. We patrol day and night. I know many of the poor souls by name."

He stopped to greet one derelict. "God bless you, Burt. Have you seen a tall man carrying a suitcase?"

"Sure, I saw him yesterday. He carried a new suitcase. I don't know his real name, but we call him Bean Pole because he's so tall and thin. He was in a fight with Pete, and he might have killed him. Haven't seen Bean Pole today. He usually sleeps over there behind the garbage cans."

"We'll find him," Captain Rose said. "He's probably sleeping it off right now."

"I don't understand how anyone can sleep outside in this cold weather," Roberto said.

"They get used to it and sleep outside even after the snow comes."

Litter covered the ground. Dry leaves blew around and settled in the corners. Big rats scurried away. Dogs and cats snarled at Roberto and Captain Rose. The stink of rotting garbage polluted the air.

They saw his feet first, but Roberto was not prepared for what he saw next. The bum was on his back with vomit covering his face, neck, and chest. The rats sniffed the body. One arm was stretched to the side where an empty whiskey bottle had fallen out of his hand.

Roberto's knees threatened to buckle. The stink was almost unbearable. "Is he dead?" he asked Captain Rose.

"He must have choked on his own vomit." The captain reached out for the man's wrist to check for a pulse. When there was none, he mumbled a prayer for the deceased. He finished with "Amen."

After an appropriate pause, Roberto said, "My suitcase is gone. Someone must have taken it from him."

"A nice suitcase is a treasure trove to the homeless, especially if it has something in it. I'll stay here, if you would be so kind to go and fetch a police officer. Tell him to bring the coroner and transportation for the body."

"Yes, sir."

Roberto sprinted to the police station. Still panting, he reported the death. The officer asked him to lead the way to the victim.

As Captain Rose and Roberto walked back to the Salvation Army, Roberto felt remorse about having bought the leather suitcase in the first place. *Why didn't I buy a cardboard one instead? How much more misery could it cause? Two men were already dead, and the suitcase was still gone.*

"I wonder where my suitcase is now. I don't want it to cause another death," Roberto said.

"You could check at the pawnshop," Captain Rose said.

"I hope it's there, and not in the hands of another bum." Roberto couldn't stop thinking about the dead man.

"Captain Rose, if the victim can't be identified, how is the burial handled?" he asked.

"He'll be buried in the Pauper's Field. Only God knows his name. He may have relatives, but they will never know."

Chapter 2

Captain Rose conducted the burial service for Pete and the Bean Pole in the Paupers' Field and prayed for their souls. Roberto stood by his side. He hoped that the deceased men had known love in their lives, at least from their mothers. The cemetery workers stood waiting to cover the plain pine boxes. The cold wind made Roberto shiver. His thoughts wandered to his girlfriend's funeral. He had gone to pay his respect to Lydia after the other mourners had left. Everything had gone badly for him since he lost her. He wondered if he would ever be happy again.

Straightening out, he made a solemn promise to himself. He would never live in the alleys like Pete and the Bean Pole and he would never die like them.

The next day, Roberto went to the nearest pawnshop to ask if anyone had pawned a leather suitcase in the last few days.

The man behind the counter said, "Maybe. Why are you asking?"

"Because it was my suitcase and a bum stole it from me. If my passport is still in the case, I would like to have it back."

"The suitcase is empty."

"So it's here. Do you remember what the man looked like who pawned it?"

"He was very tall and unkempt. He sold the suitcase to me, so I can sell it back to you."

Roberto had no money to buy it, so he declined the offer and left.

To clear Roberto's name, Captain Rose suggested that they both go to the police station and report what the pawnbroker had said. "We'll take Burt with us," the captain said

The officer wrote down what Burt was telling him, but Roberto sensed that the deaths of two bums were not high on the agenda of the police.

"I'm still missing my suitcase, my passport, and my wallet," Roberto said. "They are important to me."

"You leave the investigation to us, but you are free to go," the officer said.

With those words echoing in his mind, Roberto considered his options. He couldn't stay much longer at the Salvation Army. He had tried living in a boarding house, where he had been infected with lice, and he was not willing to take that risk again. No, he had to swallow his pride and turn to the woman whose life he had saved on that tragic night that the Titanic went under. Anna could afford to help him. She had inherited a fortune and married well.

To gain access to Anna, Roberto must to go through the butler, Tom O'Donnell. Tom would recognize him as the man who had pretended that Anna was the look-alike Lydia and that he was her fiancé while he stayed at the mansion, but what else could he have done? He was destitute and had nowhere to go. Besides, the rescue ship had already identified Anna as Lydia. It wasn't his idea. He just went along with it. The deception worked as long as Anna had amnesia and believed that she was Lydia, but when she had regained her memory, he couldn't face her. That's why he had left the mansion in the middle of the night.

At the Salvation Army, Roberto worked for his keep. An officer, trained as a barber, gave him a haircut and shave. Standing in front of a mirror, Roberto inspected his face. He still had a bruise on his cheek, but he was thankful that his Romanesque nose was intact. Dressed in clean clothes, he was ready for his visit with Anna. He startled Captain Rose as he met him by the door. "I hardly recognized you. You look like a different man," he said.

"I feel much better," Roberto said with a smile. Captain Rose wished him good luck, and he was on his way.

He thought about the last time he had gone to the mansion to ask Anna for a job. She had probed him about what had happened to her that had caused her coma and subsequent amnesia. She also wanted to know what had happened to her sister, Christina. To Anna's great sorrow, Christina's body had never been found. He didn't have answers to all of Anna's questions, but he had filled a large gap in her memory and thought that he would be rewarded with more than a ticket back to Italy, a ticket that he did not use.

The butler answered the doorbell. "Mr. Cosentino, I'm surprised to see you again," he said.

"I'm here to congratulate Anna on her marriage," Roberto said, squaring his shoulders.

"I'll ask Mrs. Whitmore if she will see you then."

Sweating in his winter jacket, Roberto waited inside the door. He stuffed his cap in one of the pockets. The dog, Tramp, came up to him and licked his hands in recognition. Tramp didn't judge him for his actions.

"Mrs. Whitmore will see you in the library," the returning butler said. "May I take your coat?"

"Thank you, Tom." Roberto drew a quick breath of relief. Tom treated him like any other guest. The only difference was that he omitted "sir" at the end of his sentences. As the butler walked ahead of him to the library, Roberto noticed his gray, thinning hair. When Tom opened the double doors, he saw Anna behind the large desk. She wore her blond hair wrapped and pinned around her head.

Her oval face and attractive features reminded him of Lydia. Behind her were the glass-covered well-filled book cases that he remembered so well. He bowed and stepped forward.

"Please sit down, Roberto?" Anna said.

"I wanted to congratulate you on your marriage, Anna. John is a lucky man. I'm happy for both of you."

"I appreciate you saying that."

He could feel her blue eyes on his bruised face. His thick, black eyelashes covered his brown eyes as he looked down on his hands. "I wish I could have brought you a gift, but I'm somewhat down on my luck," he said. For a moment, he allowed himself to remember that they used to kiss. Now, he had to face reality. Clearing his throat, he began to tell her how he had been beaten and robbed of all his money, but omitting the part about the murders and that he had already been down on his luck before the robbery.

"It's so cold here in Boston," he complained, looking out the window. "I'm scared of the winter. No one hires housepainters during the cold season, and I can't find any other jobs either."

"You had saved some money, and now it's gone," Anna said.

"That's right, ma'am. Or should I call you Mrs. Whitmore?"

"You can continue to call me Anna. After all, we've known each other a long time."

"Thank you, Anna. I also want to give you Lydia's ring." He pulled it off his little finger and placed it on the desk.

"I saw you wearing it, and I thought it was Lydia's," she said as she picked it up and looked at it.

"I think you should have it." Roberto paused to search for the right words to ask her for help.

Anna understood and asked, "Do you need something, Roberto?"

"I was wondering… if you… or Mr. Whitmore… could find a job for me, so that I can survive the winter?"

"I'll talk to John about it," Anna said. She stood up and extended her hand like she was afraid that he would ask for something else. Roberto rose and met her gaze.

"I'd appreciate that very much." He folded both of his hands around hers.

"How can we let you know what we decide?" Anna asked.

"May I call you in a couple of days?"

"That would be all right. You remember our number, don't you?"

"Yes, I do. Thank you very much. I'll do anything to earn some money. Perhaps I could do some indoor painting in one of your buildings?"

"It will be up to John to decide. Do you have a place to live?"

"Only a temporary one." He just couldn't make himself say that he lived at the Salvation Army.

"All right then, I expect a telephone call from you the day after tomorrow, Roberto."

Anna walked him to the foyer where Tom opened the door for him.

"Goodbye, Anna. Thanks for seeing me—and my best to your husband," Roberto said.

He felt much better and hoped that Anna and John would come through with employment for him. As he looked back at Beacon Hill, he thought of how different it was from the area where he now lived. Anna could not imagine what life was like among the homeless.

John, who was thankful for the fact that Roberto had saved Anna's life, said that there were many apartments in their rental buildings that could use a fresh coat of paint. Anna's eyes softened as she walked into his outstretched arms. When a strand of his brown, wavy hair fell down on his forehead, she stretched to smooth it back in place and thanked her lucky star for having married this handsome, loving man.

When Roberto called Anna two days later, she had good news for him. He could start painting interiors the next day, and John had secured a small basement apartment for him in one of the buildings that the company owned.

Roberto hoped that the nightmares of the Titanic and the recent murders would ease as he got on his feet again.

Chapter 3

Outside it rained and the wind blew hard from the sea. In December, the rain mixed with snow. As it turned colder, the snow settled in a thin layer on the ground. Roberto looked in amazement at the white precipitation. He scooped up a handful and stared at it until it began to melt. Having lived in Genoa by the Mediterranean Sea before arriving in America, he had not seen or experienced snow until now. The kind folks at the Salvation Army had given him a cap, a warm winter coat, a sweater, pants, galoshes, overalls, and everything else he needed for work, but he had no good clothes.

Roberto tried out different restaurants every night for his dinner. He could cook pasta, eggs, and make sandwiches, but that's all. This evening, he had decided to go to a restaurant that served pizza. His eyes lit up as he saw the cute waitress coming to his table. Her name tag said Miss Julia.

"What do you recommend today, Miss Julia?" he asked as he looked up from the menu and into her hazel eyes. "I'm in the mood for pizza."

"All our pizzas are good, sir," she said.

"I'm sure they are, but do you have a favorite, Miss Julia?"

"This one has a delicious sauce that has simmered on the stove for hours," Julia said, pointing to a pizza on the menu.

"*Grazie,* that's what I'll have."

"Will there be anything else, sir?"

"*Un bicchiere di vino rosso, per favore.*"

"The bartender will bring you the wine, sir. Do you want it now or with your meal?"

"He can bring it now. I'm Roberto Cosentino, but please call me Roberto."

"We are not allowed to call our customers by first name, sir."

"I see."

"So you're Italian, Signor Cosentino. How long have you been in this country?"

"Since April."

"Oh, that's not long. Do you have relatives here?"

"No, I don't."

Roberto admired Julia's pleasing form as she walked away from the table. When she returned with a glass of water, he had another question ready for her.

"Do you know of any Italian clubs in town, Miss Julia?"

"Oh, yes. There are several."

"If you don't mind, I'd like to know where they are."

"I have a newspaper that advertises events, if you'd excuse me for a moment." She went to the back of the restaurant and returned with the paper. It surprised Roberto that it was printed in Italian and published in Boston.

"You don't want to go to the north side. The Italians there are poor," Julia said. "Please excuse me. I have to wait on other customers, and I think your pizza is ready."

Roberto opened the newspaper and turned to the advertisements. There were several events to choose from. When Julia returned with the pizza, he asked her which event would be the closest.

She pointed to one ad, "This one, signor, that's the one I go to. It's a cultural society."

"*Grazie mille.*"

Roberto enjoyed his wine and the pizza with the thin crispy crust, just the way he liked it. He waited until there were no other customers left in the restaurant before he called for the check.

"Here you are, Miss Julia," he said, leaving a generous tip. "You've been very helpful."

"Thank you, signor. I appreciate the gratuity. I work as a waitress to save money for college."

"That's very commendable. I'd like to take some classes myself, if only I could afford it."

"If you come to our Christmas party, my father could tell you how to take affordable classes. He's a teacher."

"I'm looking forward to seeing you then at the club, Miss Julia."

Roberto stood up and bowed to her before leaving. Walking home, he whistled a familiar Christmas carol, *Gloria in Terra* (Joy to the World). He looked forward to meeting countrymen who would not call him Dago and mistreat him.

He pulled the coat tighter around him as he walked home against the cold north wind. He thought about Lydia and how different his life would have turned out if she had lived, and they had married. Now, he had to count his pennies. He walked faster to ward off the chill.

On Saturday afternoon, he bought the least expensive suit he could find that fit his athletic body. He still felt like a million dollar man until he realized that he didn't have a top coat and fedora. Cursing the cold weather, he put on his winter jacket, the warm cap, and galoshes.

Roberto heard the music before he opened the door to the hall. Having shed his outerwear, he entered and looked for Julia. Dressed in an Italian folk costume, she stood by the table, pouring hot, spiced wine that she handed out as a welcome drink. Roberto lined up and smiled at Julia as it was his turn to take a glass. Julia smiled back. Oh my, how pretty she is, he thought.

"Hello, Julia," he said.

"*Come stai,* Roberto?"

"*Molto bene, grazie.*"

"That's all the Italian you'll get from me," Julia said. "My father speaks the language."

Roberto tasted the hot, spiced wine and scanned the room. There were people of all ages. A middle-aged gentleman came up to Julia, and she handed him a drink. He wore glasses and tilted his head forward like he was near-sighted. The white handkerchief peeking out of his breast pocket contrasted with the dark suit he wore.

"This is my papa," Julia said to Roberto. "Christopher Nicolo, and this is Roberto Cosentino. He's new here in Boston."

"*Piacere.*"

"*Piacere.*"

"Your charming daughter told me that you're a teacher, Signor Nicolo."

"Yes, I'm an elementary schoolteacher during the day, and in the evening I teach English to immigrants. What do you do for a living, Signor Cosentino?"

"I'm an interior decorator. It seems to be the only job I can get."

"Your English is excellent. I'm sure it won't be long before you can obtain a white-collar job, if that's what you desire."

"*Grazie*, but I could benefit from learning how to write better English, signor."

"We've classes for that, too."

"Are those classes expensive?"

"Not really. But I'm thinking that we might be able to use you as a teacher for evening classes in conversational English, Signor Cosentino. Then you could earn some money toward tuition."

"I'd like that very much. Do you really think I could teach?"

"I can't see why not. You do know both Italian and English."

"That's true."

"We've new classes coming up after New Year's. Would you like to give it a try?"

"Yes, I would."

"Judging from your speech, I presume you are from northern Italy."

"Yes, I'm from Genoa, signor."

"What do you know about the Italian immigration to the United States?"

"I know that there has been a mass exodus from Italy to America."

"Nearly fifteen million of us now live in America. One third of Boston's population is Italian. Most came in steerage and were badly treated on the ships and also after they arrived here."

"I was lucky in a way. I traveled second class. The unlucky part was that I sailed on the Titanic."

"Ah, but then you were lucky to have survived."

"Yes, I know, but I'm a good swimmer. As you know, the men were not allowed in the lifeboats, but I rescued a woman in distress in the water, and we were both taken aboard a lifeboat."

"And still there were so many lives lost. I hope it will never happen again."

"Oh, I think they learned a lot from the Titanic disaster and that sea travel will be much safer in the future."

"I hope so. I want to visit Italy some day and see my place of birth in Tuscany. I was so young when I came with my parents that I don't remember what it looked like."

"You said that the Italian immigrants were badly treated here. What do you mean by that, signor?"

"The Americans did not welcome Italians. They had forgotten that Christopher Columbus had discovered the continent and named it. People from southern Italy could not understand the dialect of the interpreters at Ellis Island, so the interpreters said that the Italians were illiterate and could not even speak their own language. Our countrymen were paid less than the colored people for menial jobs, and they were lynched and hanged for crimes they had not committed." Signor Nicolo spit out the words between uneven, yellowed teeth. "But enough of that, here is my daughter now. I think the program will start."

Roberto bowed to Julia, and asked, "What kind of program can we expect?"

"The children will be in a play, and then they'll sing Italian carols and dance folk dances."

"If you both will excuse me," Signor Nicolo said, "I see someone I want to greet."

"Your father is an interesting man," Roberto said to Julia. "He thinks that I could teach a class in conversational English to Italian immigrants."

"I'm sure you could."

"Do you know if they have any textbooks for those classes?"

"Yes, they do. I suppose that Papa could give you a book to study over the holidays. It's really elementary, such as 'What is your name? My name is... How are you? Thank you, please, and good bye." Julia spoke the words slowly and they both laughed.

A fresh Christmas tree and the traditional Italian *Albero di Natale* stood side by side. Wrapped in colored paper, the wooden pyramid had shelves for decorations, candles, and gilt pinecones. Small wrapped gifts were placed on the bottom shelf.

Roberto sat beside Julia and watched the children in a religious play portraying the nativity scene. They sang Christmas carols in both Italian and English. It surprised Roberto that all the carols he remembered from home also had English text. *Con I rami d'agrifoglio* was Deck the Halls, *Nella mangiatoia* was Away in a Manger, *Astro del ciel* was Silent Night. Next, the children began to perform folk dances dressed in Italian costumes. The girls wore wide skirts that swirled as they danced and the boys wore pants that were fastened below the knee. Roberto had worn pants like that as a boy.

He thought of his family and visualized his mother preparing for Christmas and Epiphany, *La Festa di San Nicola,* on January 6. He hoped that he would receive a letter from home soon. His parents must be waiting to hear from him. He would buy the most beautiful Christmas card he could find and enclose a letter. Now that he was on his feet again, he would be happy to tell his family how his life had turned out after Lydia.

During the coffee hour, Julia introduced Roberto to her friends. They sat around a table covered with a tablecloth embroidered with a Christmas theme. A long, lit taper stood in the center of the table surrounded by greens. The chocolate truffle cake melted in Roberto's mouth. The Italian Santa Claus, *Babbo Natale*, came and handed out gifts to the children.

Roberto enjoyed himself and felt at home with his own people. Although most of them were born in America, he considered them his people. He was one of them, and no one called him Dago. He and Julia raised a glass and wished each other Merry Christmas.

"It won't be merry for me," Roberto said. "I'll be all alone."

"You can't be alone at Christmas," Julia said, sounding perturbed.

"Well, I could attend church," he said in a forlorn voice. "It would give me some consolation."

"I'll ask my parents if we can invite you to our house. We usually have a few extra guests around our table."

"Oh, I couldn't impose. I haven't even met your mother."

"She's in the kitchen, cleaning up. She's a real Italian mama. You'll love her. I'll go and ask her now. Wait here."

Julia returned with her mother and introduced her to Roberto.

"Mama, this is Roberto Cosentino," Julia said. "He has met Papa, and he says that Roberto could teach conversational English to immigrants."

Roberto bent down and kissed the small, plump woman on the cheek.

"Signora Nicolo, *piacere*," he said, and bowed once more. Julia's mama smelled of soap and reminded him of his own mama back in Italy. She tucked in a strand of black hair that had escaped from her bun.

"Pleasure to meet you. I like polite young men."

She took his hand and said that he would be welcome to have Christmas dinner with them.

"It will be no trouble at all. We always have so much food that one more guest won't make a difference."

"How can I say no to such a gracious invitation?"

"Then say yes," Julia told him.

"Yes, I'll come then."

Mrs. Nicolo pressed Roberto's hand and then disappeared into the kitchen.

Roberto could hardly believe his luck. It was almost too good to be true. So much had changed since he was homeless, beaten, and robbed only a few weeks ago.

Chapter 4

Roberto brought a bottle of wine, and he was not the only one doing so. The corks popped all evening. He met Julia's aunts, uncles, and cousins. Everyone talked at the same time and laughed. They mixed Italian with English and enjoyed all the food. Roberto counted nine different entrees, all delicious. For dessert, they enjoyed creamy cheesecake and *crispelle*, dipped in honey and sprinkled with powdered sugar. After dinner, some of the men began to sing. First they sang Christmas carols in Italian, and Roberto joined in. Next, Signor Nicolo began to sing opera. The men sang their parts and the women theirs.

"Tremendous talent here," Roberto said to Julia.

"Oh, they all think they can sing like Enrico Caruso."

"How long will it go on?"

"Half the night, at least."

"Do you feel like going for a walk? " Roberto asked.

"I do," she said.

They walked side by side without touching.

Roberto asked, "When can I see you again?"

"There's a New Year's dance at the club."

"May I accompany you to that dance?"

Julia didn't answer right away.

"I had a chaperone until I was eighteen years old," she said. "But now that I've graduated from high school, I don't need one. It's still very important that the boys I go out with meet my parents first."

"I've met your parents, and I think they like me."

"Yes, I agree, but you still have to present yourself to them before we go to the dance."

"I wasn't planning on standing outside whistling for you, if that's what you think."

Julia laughed. "I just wanted you to know that my parents are rather strict."

"I understand. Now I need to go inside and say a proper goodbye to your parents, but first I want to thank you, Julia, for inviting me. Thanks to you, I didn't have to be alone on Christmas Day."

"And you don't have to be alone on New Year's Eve either."

Roberto gave Julia a light hug and a kiss on the cheek. As he was saying goodbye to her parents, her father gave him a copy of the small textbook that Roberto would use for his English class.

On his way home, he looked in the store windows for men's clothing. Perhaps he would splurge and buy a top coat and a fedora before New Year's. The snow had melted and if no more snow fell, he could leave the galoshes at home.

Roberto felt like a gentleman caller when he rang the door bell at Julia's home on New Year's Eve. Signor Nicolo answered the door.

"Good evening, Roberto. Julia will be down in a few minutes. Please come in and wait."

"Good evening, Signor Nicolo. Pleasant evening. Not as cold as before," Roberto said, removing his new fedora.

"The weather can change quickly here in Boston. But you're right. It feels warmer."

Julia came down the stairs looking marvelous in an ankle-long blue dress with a wide skirt. Having greeted Roberto, she went to the mirror and put on her hat. Her father helped her with her coat, and last she pulled on her gloves and picked up her purse.

"Well then, we're ready to go," she said. "Don't wait up, Papa."

"I'll see your daughter home after the dance," Roberto said as he bowed and opened the door for his date.

"You look lovely tonight, Julia," he said.

She looked at him with approval in her eyes, and Roberto slipped his arm around her back. He was almost sure that Mr. Nicolo stood in the window and watched them.

"Look at the star-lit sky," she said. "It's so beautiful." As Julia looked up, he wanted to kiss her, but it was too soon.

"Yes, it's beautiful, and the constellations are the same as at home in Italy," he said.

"It's strange, isn't it? When the stars are visible here, I suppose the sun is up in Italy?"

"That's true, and when they can see the moon, we see the sun."

"Papa is pleased that you accepted the teaching job," she said.

"I'm glad to get the opportunity, and I'll do my best because I want to get another job."

"What kind of job?"

"I was wondering if I could be a reporter for the Italian-language paper, *La Gazzetta*. Would that be too farfetched?"

"No, I don't think so. It might be too easy. Then you wouldn't learn any more English."

"That's true, but I'm not ready for an English-language paper."

"It might be good to learn some reporting skills at the Italian paper before you venture any further."

"That's what I was thinking," Roberto said, "but I don't know if they need any writers."

"It should be easy to find out although I doubt that they can pay you very much."

"The best part about my present job is that it includes an apartment. It's small, but it's furnished and a place of my own."

"That's a big advantage," Julia said.

When they entered the club on New Year's Eve, they had to raise their voices to be heard over the music. The bandleader paused and said that they would play the Boston waltz.

"What's the Boston waltz?" Roberto asked Julia.

"It's slower than the Viennese waltz," she said, "and we do three dips as we reverse, and then we do the walking step. Like this," she demonstrated, "Step, dip, point-dip, step-dip, step, dip, turn."

The bandleader looked at Julia and said, "Well, that's how we used to do it, but now we're introducing the Hesitation Waltz that was invented here in Boston this year. It has one step per measure, and then the stroll." The orchestra played, and the bandleader demonstrated the steps.

"In the second part, we do the Boston, turning to the right, four measures," he said.

"Well, that's a new one to me," Julia said with a smile. "Now, we're both novices."

Roberto and Julia and a few other couples practiced the steps and made some mistakes before they knew the moves.

"That's fun, don't you think?" Julia asked Roberto.

"Yes, it is. I like learning new things."

Dancing to great music in a friendly atmosphere suited Roberto. He danced with Julia and then with her girlfriends while she danced with other men, but he always came back to Julia. He drew her close and felt her curves and rounded breasts against his chest.

While the orchestra took a break, they all enjoyed *strufoli* sprinkled with confetti. At midnight, Roberto and Julia kissed and wished each other a happy new year. It was only a light kiss, but it made Roberto wish for more, and hoped that Julia did, too.

Walking Julia home, Roberto said, "I had a good time tonight, but I wish I could afford to take you to a concert or a play."

"Don't concern yourself about that, Roberto. Going to the club is fun, and it doesn't cost much." Roberto liked her common sense, but it was something that bothered him.

"Where will you attend college, out of town or here in Boston, Julia?" he asked.

"I haven't decided yet, but perhaps Boston College. Then I can live at home. But I also think that it would be fun to get out and live in other places before I settle down. Just think how far you have moved, Roberto."

"Well, that's true, but it means being away from family and friends. I miss them."

Julia squeezed his arm. "I understand," she said. "I would miss my family, too."

"But I don't regret coming here because I think it widens one's views to get out in the world."

"So why did you come?"

"A friend talked me into it."

"And where is that friend now?"

"She was one of the Titanic victims." Now he had said it.

"So it was a girl?"

"Yes, but I don't want to talk about the Titanic tonight," Roberto said.

Feeling attracted to Julia, he wondered why he hadn't really kissed her yet. He would definitely do it tonight if she would allow it. He had the feeling that he would have to move slowly with her and earn her trust. At her front door, he drew her close and kissed her gently on the forehead, which was level with his mouth. His lips went closer and closer to hers, and she didn't resist. When their lips met, she let it happen. Her face and lips were warm despite the cold air. Roberto felt the warmth penetrating his body.

"I like you, Julia," he whispered. "I like you very much."

"Hmm."

"When can I see you again?"

"I think I'm free next Saturday," she said.

"Would you go out to dinner with me?"

"Yes."

"We had fun tonight, but over dinner we'll have more time to talk."

"I agree."

"Another hug and a kiss, and I'll let you go." Julia parted her lips, and Roberto found it difficult to leave her.

"I have to go now," she said. "It's late. Papa might be watching us."

Roberto glanced at the front window and saw the drape closing.

"You're so wonderful. Thank you for tonight."

Roberto's heart sang as he walked home. Could he be in love again? It had been a long time since he loved someone. Lydia had been the one, but she was in heaven.

"Dear Lydia," he whispered to the star-lit sky. "I need to love again, but I'll never forget you."

Roberto enjoyed taking Julia to the restaurant for dinner and listening to her talk. She was a good conversationalist. He knew in his heart that she was a virgin and too good for him, but why did she flirt with him then? He couldn't help himself. That evening he tested the limits with her, and learned that it would take time to win her trust.

It was January, 1913. More snow had fallen and it was cold. Roberto had started to teach conversational English. He soon became bored with the limited vocabulary he could use, but wishing to make a good impression on Julia and her father and needing the extra money, he persevered.

When the beginner class was over, he got a class at the next level, and it became more interesting. He learned that all his pupils had menial jobs, such as dishwashers, broom pushers, and maids. Some worked in sweatshops. In comparison, Roberto realized that he had an advantage in being able to speak English, but still, he was far from satisfied.

He wanted to learn to write the language well, so he signed up for a class in grammar and composition. The class was held at Boston College, and the instructor was Signor Nicolo. Now, Roberto had to do his best.

"Don't expect much of me, Signor Nicolo. I have no practice in writing English composition," he said.

"That's why you're here. We'll start with spelling and easy sentences. You can use a *Webster's Dictionary*, and if you can't find the words there, you can consult an Italian-English dictionary."

While painting kitchens during the day, Roberto thought about the compositions he would write for the next class. Signor Nicolo had praised him for his writing. Roberto considered what he could do with all his new knowledge. Perhaps he would ask for a job as a reporter for the Italian-American newspaper. He recalled the *New York Times* reporter who had followed him after the Titanic tragedy, and imagined that he would interview people in English and write the stories in Italian.

Julia seemed to be proud of Roberto's accomplishments, but she was careful not to get close to him. When he invited her to his apartment, she declined as Roberto had expected.

"I'm going to college in the fall, and I don't want to jeopardize it in any way," she told him. He sensed that she was afraid of becoming attached to him. Still, it surprised him when one day she said, "I think it's best that we go our separate ways." Roberto felt a sting of disappointment.

"It saddens me, but I hope you will achieve your goal. Perhaps we'll meet again," he said.

Roberto realized that he had blown his chances by showing that he was physically attracted to her.

Chapter 5

To get his mind off Julia, Roberto decided to eat at a Dutch restaurant. Waiting on him was a tall waitress named Gretchel. Her blond hair was braided and wrapped around her head so that it formed a crown. Roberto asked her what the young Dutch people did for fun in the middle of the winter.

"We go skating at the indoor skating rink and attend the ice shows. Boston has one of the first indoor skating rinks in America," she said with pride in her voice.

"I would like to see it. Could I accompany you to one of those shows, perhaps?"

To his surprise, she agreed. For the show, Gretchel wore her hair in long curls that swirled around her face. Roberto liked that. After the show, he conceived the idea of writing an article about the Boston Ice Rink. He wrote it in Italian and sent it to the Italian newspaper, *La Gazzetta*. It would be the first article that he sent there, and he hoped it would get published. He could have written about the homeless bums in the alley, but would rather forget about that chapter in his life.

Roberto wanted to see Gretchel again, so he asked her what she was doing next weekend.

"The pond is perfect for skating, and I'll be going there," she said. After a moment's hesitation she asked, "Do you want to come with me?"

"I don't have any skates, and I don't know how to skate."

"You can borrow a pair. I'll teach you."

"Well, in that case I'll try, but I don't think I'll be able to skate," Roberto said.

On the cold but sunny day that they went to the pond, Gretchel wore her hair in pigtails with small, red bows tied to the ends. She had wrapped a red, knitted scarf around her neck and matched it with a red headband.

To Roberto's amazement small children with colorful stocking caps on their heads pirouetted on the ice like they were performing in a ballet. *If they can dance, I should be able to walk*, he thought. All the people on the ice looked like they were of Northern European stock. He was quite certain that he was the only Italian.

Gretchel thought that Roberto looked dapper and handsome with his tweed cap leaning to one side over his short black hair. She showed him how to strap on his skates. Standing up, he felt tall but uneasy. Slowly he moved one foot forward and then the other while Gretchel held on to his elbow.

"Bravo," she said, "Now, I have to put on my own skates." In the next moment, Roberto lost his balance and fell. To his embarrassment, he landed on his back with splayed legs.

"You shouldn't have said 'bravo,' Gretchel," he said. She took his hand and helped him up, and he hugged her to steady himself. Her cheeks were rosy pink and her lips red and tempting, but he had to concentrate on standing upright. They both laughed.

While Gretchel got ready, Roberto noticed that several couples skated hand in hand.

"Would you please take my hand Gretchel? I can't do this by myself," he said.

"Of course." With her mitten-covered hand, she reached out for Roberto's gloved one, and together they started out at what she called a 'snail's pace.'

"You're light on your feet. You must be a good dancer," she said.

"I love to dance, but this is much harder," Roberto said. They had managed to move half way round the ice when they heard a crashing sound and a high-pitched cry.

"A child has gone through the ice," Gretchel said with alarm in her voice. Roberto was the closest. A child was in danger of drowning. He had to help. He lay down on the ice and used the blades of his skates to propel himself forward. He saw the little girl waving her arms and trying to get a grip on the icy edge. A heart-wrenching cry came from her lips.

"Hold on to the edge, sweetheart. I'm coming," Roberto said in a calm voice. *Madonna mia,* please help her hold on, he prayed. The memory of saving Anna from amidst chunks of ice in the Atlantic flashed through his mind. *Grazie, Madonna*, now he saw the girl's hands above the edge. One of them was covered in a red mitten. The fissure widened. *I must reach the girl without causing more ice to break. The air in her clothing won't hold her up for long.* That's when he felt someone pushing on the bottom of his skates. He heard Gretchel's voice: "I'm behind you, and my friend is holding on to me," she said. Thanks to the push from Gretchel, he was instantly within reach of the frightened girl. Her blue eyes met Roberto's brown eyes as he took her hands. Her wet blond hair hung limp below her striped stocking cap. Her wide eyes showed how scared she was. "Don't be afraid. I got you," he said as he gripped her hands. He held his breath while pulling her out of the water. Not a sound could be heard from the other skaters. The only noise came from the cracking ice as Gretchel and her human chain pulled Roberto and the girl to safety. The people who had gathered at a distance applauded. Several yelled, "Bravo, bravo!" Gretchel looked at Roberto and said, "You did it. Thank God."

A man took off his coat and wrapped it around the soaked girl. "Thank you for saving my daughter's life," he said. A woman shook Roberto's hand. "I'm Olivia's mother," she said. "God bless you, sir, for being so brave."

"You're a hero." The words came from a man with a camera. "What's your name, sir?" he asked.

While Roberto took off his wet coat and wrung the water from the sleeves, Gretchel stepped up and introduced him. "Your hero's name is Roberto Cosentino," she said. "He's from Italy and has never seen a frozen lake before. Still he knew what to do."

"I just acted on instinct, but I did have help," he said, pointing to Gretchel and to the sky. His sweater was dry and warm enough, so he flung his jacket over one shoulder, doffed his cap, and flashed a smile to Olivia before turning around and skating away with Gretchel.

When Roberto's work partner Karl, the paperhanger, asked him if he wanted to go to a bar to have a drink and a bite to eat, Roberto accepted. He didn't have much food in his kitchen and very little money in his pocket.

The snow had been pushed to the side of the street and no longer looked white. As Karl led the way through the slush to the *Bierstube*, Roberto was thankful for the galoshes that the Salvation Army had given him.

Many of the customers at the bar spoke German or a mixture of German and English. When the bartender heard that Roberto was Italian, he turned to English. Roberto ordered a beer and tested the dark brew while scanning the men in the crowd.

"I don't see any women here," he said to Karl.

"I've asked two women to come here tonight, one for you and one for me. Here they come now," he said, pointing to the entrance.

Roberto looked at them and asked, "Which one is yours?"

"The tall one."

"All right. I appreciate that. She looks taller than me."

"Let's go and greet them."

"Ladies, so glad you could come," Karl said. "This is Mr. Cosentino. We work together, him and me."

Karl put his arm around the tall one. "This is Miss Helga Eckenberg and this is Miss Hilde Schroeder," he said, pointing to the shorter woman and winking at Roberto.

"Pleased to meet you both." Roberto bowed and kissed the women's hands.

The girls giggled, probably about the kiss, while Karl took their coats and hung them up. They kept their hats on. A waiter escorted them to a table, and Karl ordered a round of beer.

"I'd rather have a soda," Miss Schroeder said in a shy voice.

"Three beers and one soda then."

"Will there be food also?" the waiter asked.

"Yes, we'll order food later."

Roberto glanced at the brunette. She spoke without an accent, and she was definitely attractive. Miss Eckenberg spoke with the same accent as Karl. They make a good pair, he thought. Both are tall and sturdy.

"Miss Schroeder, I presume that you were born in America," Roberto said, looking at the brunette.

"I was two years old when my parents brought me here," she said. "What about you Mr. Cosentino?"

"I was on the Titanic." A statement like that always aroused curiosity and got the conversation going.

"Tell us about it. I haven't met anyone who was on the Titanic," Miss Eckenberg said.

"As you know we hit an iceberg.... At first, no one thought there was any danger at all. The Titanic was supposed to be unsinkable. But then it started to take in water, and the captain gave orders to lower the lifeboats. Women and children were to enter first, so I knew I wouldn't stand a chance. There weren't enough lifeboats for everybody, so I dove in and swam. I looked for my girlfriend in the water but couldn't find her. Then I saw a girl I knew, her head hanging down over her life jacket. She didn't respond to her name, but I swam with her to a lifeboat that was only half filled. They took us aboard, and I performed mouth-to-mouth on her until her heart beat had improved."

"What about your girlfriend?" Miss Schroeder asked.

"She did not survive."

"How difficult and sad that must have been for you."

"Yes, it was hard." He hoped that he hadn't said too much.

"Roberto has done something heroic here also," Karl said. "His picture was in the paper because he saved a little girl from drowning when the ice gave way underneath her."

"Oh, was that you?" Miss Eckenberg said. "I read that article. Weren't you afraid?"

"I didn't have time to think about my own safety," Roberto said. He could feel Miss Schroeder's eyes on him as he sipped his drink.

"I understand that you are an interior decorator, Mr. Cosentino," she said.

Roberto liked the description. It sounded more important than painter.

"What about you ladies? Are you in the working world?" Roberto asked.

Miss Eckenberg sighed. "We all have to work these days. I'm making my living as a seamstress."

"Nothing wrong with that. What about you, Miss Schroeder?"

"I'm a hairdresser."

Roberto couldn't see much of her hair under her big hat. Her perfect eyebrows arched when she talked. She smiled with both her mouth and her blue eyes. Roberto liked her.

Karl interrupted Roberto's thoughts. "Are we ready to eat? I'm starved. Hanging wallpaper all day makes a man hungry."

"Yes, I'm hungry, too. Let's get a menu," Roberto said.

"Oh, we don't need a menu," Karl said. "We know what we want. It's always meat and potatoes."

When the check came, Karl took up his wallet and paid. Roberto offered to pay half, but Karl refused. "You can pay next time," he said.

After dinner, Karl and Roberto helped the ladies with their coats before getting into their own.

"I'll walk Helga home, if you'll take Hilde?" Karl said.

"All right. Where do you live Miss Schroeder?"

"I came here on the streetcar, but I can walk if you come along."

Roberto offered her his arm. "I'll be glad to accompany you, Miss Schroeder. Walking will warm me up. I'm not used to this cold weather."

"You can call me Hilde," she said, and hooked arms with him. "It's easier."

"If you call me Roberto?"

"I will. I think it's a nice name."

Roberto walked her home, kissed her on her cheek, and said, "I had a good time. When can I see you again?"

"I don't know." She seemed to hesitate.

"Tomorrow is Saturday. Would you like to go dancing?" Roberto asked.

"The German Club has a dance tomorrow night. Helga and I usually go there."

"Is Karl coming?"

"I'm sure he is."

"Do they speak mostly German there?"

"Oh no. It's mostly English."

"They probably dance dances that I don't know."

"They dance some polkas, but also waltzes and tangos."

"I know the tango, and the waltz, too," Roberto said, sounding hopeful.

"I do, too."

"Well then, if Karl goes, I'll come with him."

Chapter 6

Roberto pulled his coat tighter around him as he walked home against the cold north wind. He was dating again, and it felt good, but his thoughts went to Julia and he missed her. He walked faster to ward off the chill. Tomorrow, he would meet Hilde again.

The coatroom at the German Club soon overflowed with winter clothes and overshoes. Roberto was glad to see Hilde without the big hat. Her hair was clean with every hair pinned in place. He would like to rough it up a little and see it hanging down on her shoulders. When the music played a tango, he was the first on the floor with Hilde. As Roberto and Hilde danced cheek-to-cheek, the men began to put their heads together and talk about the Italian newcomer. A former on-and-off German boyfriend of Hilde's seemed to have decided that the Italian held Hilde a bit too tight. As soon as the orchestra played a polka, he was quick on his feet and asked Hilde to dance. No one paid attention except Roberto, who didn't know how to dance the polka. He noted that the German's thick neck sat low on his broad frame. The floor boards rocked as the heavyweight stomped his feet in the dance, obviously to mark his territory. After the dance, he bought a soda for Hilde and then disappeared into the crowd with a determined look on his face.

Roberto saw the opportunity and asked Hilde if he could take her home. After a searching look around the room, she accepted. Roberto and Hilde locked arms and walked the short distance to her home. Roberto asked her if she had a jealous boyfriend that he should look out for.

"Oh, it's just that Reinhart. We used to go together, and now he's jealous of anyone I dance with."

"I suppose he resents that I'm Italian and not German," Roberto said.

"Could be, but I don't."

"That's good to hear, but I think someone is following us."

As Roberto looked over his shoulder, he saw a man disappearing behind a corner.

"Then you better come inside with me," Hilde said. "Reinhart is a boxer, and you don't want to experience his knock-out punch. We'll wait him out."

Roberto and Hilde enjoyed the wait on the couch, holding each other and kissing.

"Do you always go to that German Club?" Roberto asked.

"No, sometimes we go to the Turner Club, which is also founded by Germans, but besides having dances, it puts on plays and musicals. It has a big Gymnastic hall, and that's where Reinhart goes to box."

Roberto decided that he would stay away from that place.

After a while, he thought it would be safe to leave. No one could have waited that long for him, but he was wrong. As soon as he came outside the door, he heard, "Go home, Dago" and was knocked down. Hilde heard it and came outside. Roberto was out cold and Reinhart had disappeared. She went back inside for some water that she splashed on Roberto's face. He was still groggy when she dragged him inside.

"I'll get some ice to put on your cheek," she said. "Otherwise, you won't be able to see tomorrow."

Hilde came with a piece of ice wrapped in a handkerchief and held it on his cheek until the pain had subsided.

"I would defend myself against any man except a boxer," Roberto said. It was the second time he had been unprepared for an assault. At least he was not in an alley among the homeless.

"I'm sorry he hit you," Hilde said. "You can stay here until he leaves."

Reinhart made his presence known by throwing pebbles at Hilde's window. Roberto didn't dare to leave until dawn. By then, he had unpinned her hair and run his fingers through it. But he had a fearsome headache and when he looked in the mirror he saw that he had a black eye. He would not date Hilde again and he would stay away from German girls.

As he walked home he thought of the time he had been assaulted by the homeless man and lost his suitcase. He wondered if the pawnshop still had his suitcase. He now had the money to buy it back, but he would wait until his latest black eye had healed.

When Roberto asked about the suitcase, the pawnbroker looked it up in his record book.

"I'm sorry, but it has been sold," he said.

"Do you know who bought it?"

"It's not very often that women come into my shop, so I remember her. When they do, they usually want to pawn their rings. I can only tell you that the woman who bought your suitcase was blond and pregnant."

Roberto was relieved to hear that a woman had bought it. There won't be any more murders. He was close to the Salvation Army and decided to visit Captain Rose and give him a small donation for all the help he had received last winter. The captain appeared glad to see him and thanked him for the gift. Roberto told Captain Rose that the last owner of the suitcase was a woman. Captain Rose smiled and said, "She might not be the last owner."

As Roberto walked home, he remembered the slip of paper that he had tucked into one of the pockets in the suitcase. After his name, he had listed his address as c/o Whitmore, Beacon Hill. There was nothing he could do about it now. He could only hope that it wouldn't create a problem for Anna.

As spring approached, Roberto's fingers itched to write. If he could write for a living, it would be so much better than painting apartments. What could he write about next? He could write about the students in his class. They came from different backgrounds and they all had a story to tell. The French girl, Danielle, for instance, worked as a maid for a rich family He had helped her with her English lesson after class, and he had walked her home so that she would be safe at the late hour. Roberto decided to try to learn more about her experience as a maid.

Danielle pleased Roberto in more ways than one—her curves, her high breasts, her full lips, everything about her tempted him. He had to find a way to be alone with her. A walk in the park would sound innocent enough. On her next free afternoon, he would take time off so that they could celebrate the arrival of spring.

It was April and the wildflowers dotted the green lawns. Roberto had been in America one full year. He had interviewed several maids in his class about their work for American families, but he still wanted to ask questions about Danielle's voyage to America. He was surprised to find out that it had been uneventful. She said that she had been seasick on the first day, but after that she had enjoyed dancing her way to America. What a difference from his own experience.

When they came to a secluded place in the park, Roberto stopped and pressed Danielle's body against his. That was all he needed to know that he wanted more. As they came out of the park, he invented an excuse to go to his apartment.

"While you're here, why don't you come in and see my little abode?" he asked. When Danielle took a peek from the door opening, he pulled her in.

"I want to have a glass of wine. Why don't you join me?" he said. Knowing that French women were used to wine from a young age, he was not surprised that she accepted.

Their little party was interrupted by Mr. Whitmore who knocked hard on the door. Roberto had not expected him, so he had no time to hide Danielle or the wine glasses.

Mr. Whitmore sounded angry. "I went to the apartment that is supposed to be ready for new renters tomorrow and saw that you hadn't finished painting. The tarps are still on the floor." He placed one hand on each side of the door opening and didn't bother to tip his hat to the woman in the room.

"I didn't know ... it had to be finished tomorrow," Roberto stammered.

"You're not going to weasel your way out of this one," Mr. Whitmore said. "I'll dock one day's pay, and if it happens again, I'll dock a week's pay from your earnings. Is that understood?"

"Yes, sir."

"Now, go and finish the work. I'll come and inspect in the morning."

He slammed the door as he left. Danielle had turned beet red in her face. Her reputation was at stake.

"I hope that my employer doesn't find out about this?" she said, glaring at Roberto. "I never want to see you again. It's a good thing that my class is over."

"I'm sorry," he said, but he knew that there was no way he could make it up to her.

Now, he had to go and finish his work even if it took all night. It seemed to him that he had run out of luck with women. He had also jeopardized his job and perhaps also Danielle's, but worse than that, he had disappointed Mr. Whitmore and probably also Anna.

Chapter 7

Tom, the butler, approached Anna with a package.

"This came for you today, Mrs. Whitmore," he said.

"Thank you, Tom." She saw the foreign stamps on the package. It was from France.

What can this be? She tore off the wrapping and opened the carton. It contained a small evening purse that she recognized as Lydia's. She must have forgotten it at the hotel. There was a note in French attached to the purse. Anna knew the language and read that the hotel maid had found the purse on the top shelf in the wardrobe of the room that Miss Lydia had occupied last spring, and that the purse had Lydia's initials engraved on the outside. Anna opened the purse and saw that it contained an envelope also bearing Lydia's name. On the outside it said, "In case something should happen to me."

The envelope was sealed. Anna felt a lump in her throat. She and Lydia had been childhood playmates. The memories flooded her mind. She recognized Lydia's handwriting and had no doubt that she had written it. *Why did she have to die?* Anna fled upstairs as her tears began to flow.

Did Lydia have a premonition that something would happen to her? It was not like her to be so serious. What would the note say? It was almost like a message from beyond the grave.

Anna wanted to read what was inside the envelope, but decided to wait until John came home from work.

When John heard how distressed his wife sounded over the phone, he dropped what he was doing and came home at once. He didn't want Anna to be upset, especially not in her condition. She was six months pregnant and they expected their first child in July.

Anna stood by the door waiting for him.

"What's the matter, honey?" he asked. "You've been crying. Are you well?"

"Yes, it's nothing physical, but I have received a disturbing package. Come with me to the library, and I'll show you."

Anna translated the note written by the hotel clerk.

"You were right in not opening the envelope," John said. "Mr. Jones needs to be present."

He went to the phone and called their family attorney.

"Mr. Jones will come in a little while," he said.

"I'm so glad you're here, John. I couldn't handle this alone."

"You're in a delicate situation, honey, but whatever it is that Lydia wrote, I'll take care of it. I don't want you to worry about anything."

They went to sit on the couch, where John kissed Anna's tears away and stroked her back.

"Lydia and I were so close," Anna said. "We took French lessons and music lessons together at the mansion. And we went to school together."

"I know, and she even looked like you. I remember it so well when I first met the two of you at Cap Martin on that wonderful French Riviera. I thought you were sisters."

"And it turned out that we were half sisters, only we didn't know it."

John wanted Anna to think about something pleasant.

"But I liked you best. That's why I wanted to dance with you all evening."

"And then we went to the historic Roquebrune Chateau the next day... and we kissed. That's when I knew I was in love with you," Anna said. Her eyes had lit up and she smiled.

"And I had fallen in love with you at first sight."

"But then you made me suffer when you hugged your sister, and I thought she was your girlfriend."

"Oh, you mean in New York when you had come to meet me at the pier?"

"Yes. My whole world crashed at that moment. I was so anxious to meet you, and when I saw you hug and kiss another woman, I turned around and ran. I got lost and robbed of my purse in the slaughterhouse district. That was bad, but the worst part was that I thought I'd lost you."

"Well, I thought I'd lost you when the Titanic went under."

"But all that is behind us now."

"Yes, now we're married and we're going to have a baby. We'll be even happier when the baby comes."

"It gives me strength to face whatever else is in store for us. I need to freshen up before Mr. Jones comes."

"You do that, darling, and I'll go and meet him."

When the doorbell rang and Tom announced Mr. Jones's arrival, Anna had changed clothes and washed and powdered her face. She wore a loose-fitting dress and looked composed.

John invited Mr. Jones to come with them to the library and then closed the doors behind them. Mr. Jones opened the letter and read it aloud:

In case something unexpected should happen to me, my first wish is that the only property that I own, the beach house on Cape Cod, goes to the man I intend to marry, Mr. Roberto Cosentino. My second wish is that my jewelry goes to Miss Anna Olsson, who has been like a sister to me. I intend to live for many years, but accidents do happen. Mr. Cosentino will join me in Boston, following my stay here in France.

Cap-Martin, March, 1912.
Sincerely, Lydia Addison

"This is a will," Mr. Jones explained.

"But is it legal?" John asked.

"Do you recognize Miss Lydia's handwriting, Mrs. Whitmore?" the lawyer asked.

"Yes, I do, and I recognize her purse."

"Then there's no doubt that she has written the note. Informal wills can have validity. It will be up to the court to decide."

"But the court has already decided that my wife should inherit the beach house," John said. "You told us so on our wedding day."

"But that was before we knew that Lydia had a will."

"So Roberto might inherit Lydia's beach house?" John said in disbelief.

Mr. Jones placed the will in his briefcase and said that he would present it to Probate Court.

"I also have to notify Mr. Cosentino. He has the right to legal representation. Does anyone know where he lives?"

"He lives in one of our apartments," John said. "He works as an interior painter for the company." John gave the lawyer the address of the building.

"This will take time," Mr. Jones said, "so plan on enjoying your beach house for the first part of the season."

When Mr. Jones had left, John took Anna in his arms and asked how she felt.

"I already have so much," she said. "I shouldn't be upset about losing the beach house, but, but," she stammered, "I loved that place, and somehow, I don't trust Roberto to take care of it."

"If we lose it, I promise you to build another one on the Cape."

"But it won't be the same. Every summer I came there with the Addison family. Lydia and I used to go swimming together."

"Were you there as a child also, before you moved to Sweden with your parents?"

"Yes, I was invited to come along. I was only the gardener's daughter then, but when we were on the Cape, it didn't seem to matter. I got to play with Lydia's toys, and together we played with the neighbor's children."

"If the house means so much to you, we could buy it from Roberto. I can't see how he could afford to keep it. Knowing him, I think he'd rather take the money."

"I'm so lucky to have you, John."

"And you were lucky to inherit most of Mr. Addison's estate."

"I know."

"We're so blessed. I couldn't wish for more," John said.

"I remember how surprised I was to find out that I was adopted and that Mr. Addison was my father. It was thanks to Tom that it became known. And then I found my birth-mother, Brita, and learned that she had three younger children. It was a blessing."

"It certainly was. I like her and her entire family."

"It's ironic that I had three half siblings beside Lydia. I also had two sets of parents, one biological and one adopted, and I didn't know that either."

Chapter 8

Roberto could hardly believe that Lydia had listed him as her heir. Why had she written a will? Was it because she had nearly drowned that time in Genoa before he rescued her? She had written the will at Cap-Martin after they had become intimate. By writing the will, she had risked her parents' rage had they survived her. She must have loved him more than he realized.

He boasted to anyone who wanted to hear that he worked as an interior decorator for Addison Enterprises, that he taught English evening classes at Boston College, and freelanced for *La Gazzetta del Massachusetts*. Soon he hoped to be able to say that he owned a beach house on Cape Cod.

Delighted to see his name and story about the ice-skating rink in print, he bought three extra copies of the paper as he thought of Gretchel. She was like a big sister to him although she didn't look anything like his sisters in Italy. Gretchel was blonde and sturdy with freckles on her face and arms, and her smile was as sunny as a summer's day. Thank you, Gretchel, for giving me the material for my first article, he whispered. As a clipping, the article looked small and insignificant. It would be better to send the whole page to his parents in Italy. He was glad that he had brought home more than one paper. He took the page and folded it several times until it fit in the envelope. He pictured his father unfolding the page, asking, "Now, what is this?" It would be a surprise. Roberto enclosed a letter telling his family about Lydia's will and that he might become a property owner. He was sorry that he didn't have a copy of the newspaper article from *Boston Globe* that showed him having saved Olivia, but he wrote about it instead. The idea occurred to him that he should invite his younger brother to join him in America.

"It's going so well for me that I would like Antonio to come here. He can live with me, and I can get him a job as a painter. Since he has apprenticed for a Master Painter, I'm sure that he could teach me a thing or two," he wrote.

A month later, Roberto got a letter from Antonio saying that he was on his way to Boston. He checked the newspaper and saw that Antonio's ship would dock in Boston on Sunday.

"Welcome to America, brother," Roberto said as he thumped Antonio on the shoulders.

"I hope you still remember Italian?" Antonio said in their native tongue.

"Heck, I even write in Italian," Roberto said.

"So I've heard."

"You've grown," Roberto said, "I almost didn't recognize you."

"I'm 18 now." Antonio grinned and stretched. He was an inch or two taller than Roberto.

"Your shoulders are not as broad as mine," Roberto teased him. "I can probably beat you in wrestling."

"We'll see about that."

Roberto looked at his brother's Romanesque nose, so much like his own.

"How was your voyage?" he asked.

"It was good. I was afraid of those icebergs though. Saw them from a distance."

"How's the family at home?"

"Everybody is fine, and they all told me to kiss you from them, but it's not my style."

"In this country, most men shake hands."

"I like that."

"Did you leave any crying girls behind?"

"No one serious. Speaking of girlfriends, I hear you have one."

"Not anymore, but I'll find another one." It surprised Roberto how much it still hurt to think about Julia.

They waited for Antonio's trunk and then carried it between them to the street car.

"I thought you would have an automobile by now," Antonio teased his brother.

"I don't need an automobile here in the city, but I'd like to learn to drive as soon as I can."

The two brothers got off the streetcar and again began to carry the trunk between them.

"Do you live far from here?" Antonio asked.

"No, it's just one block."

"We can use the trunk as a table," Roberto said as they plunked it down in front of the couch.

"And this is where you'll sleep," he said, pointing to the couch. "Tomorrow morning you go to work."

"Will that be where you work?"

"You can have my job. I want to try my luck at being a full-time reporter, and by the way, from now on your name is Anthony."

"Oh, but you haven't changed your name."

"It's too late for me. I'm known as Roberto."

John Whitmore went to the apartment where Roberto was supposed to work. As the president of the company it was not on his schedule, but he felt a need to check on Roberto.

"Who are you?" he asked when his eyes fell on a young man he didn't know.

"I'm Roberto's brother, Anthony. I arrived yesterday, and Roberto has already put me to work."

"I'm Roberto's boss, Mr. Whitmore."

"I thought so," Anthony said as he continued to paint.

Mr. Whitmore looked at the fresh paint applied to the kitchen cabinets.

"Your brother should have talked to me about the switch. You tell him that he cannot come back to me and ask for another job. But you're a good painter, Anthony, so perhaps it will work out for the best."

"I learned the trade in Italy," Anthony said.

"If you're going to do Roberto's work, you'll get paid instead of him, and you'll pay the rent for the apartment."

"That's fine with me, sir. My brother said that he was going to speak to you about my taking over his job."

"Hmm. What's Roberto doing now?"

"He says that he wants to be a reporter."

"I didn't know he could write."

"He has already had an article published in *La Gazzetta.*"

"I see. So that's an Italian-language newspaper?"

"Yes, but he also teaches English to immigrants."

"Oh. How come you two speak English so well?"

"We get a lot of British and American tourists in Genoa."

"I see. Keep up the good work."

"Yes, sir, I mean Mr. Whitmore."

Chapter 9

While Anthony worked, Roberto sat in their apartment and wrote an article about immigrant maids in America. He had interviewed several of his female students. One cute Swedish girl had told him that on her first job, the man of the house had cornered her and tried to kiss her. She left immediately without pay. An Austrian girl had so much trouble understanding English that the mistress put her in the basement to scrub clothes all day long. *How would she learn any English that way?* He wrote about the long hours the girls had to work, and how stressful it was for them when they didn't understand what they were supposed to do.

Roberto took the article to the *Gazzetta* office and asked to talk to the publisher. The publisher referred him to the chief editor, Mr. Parini, who wore cut-off white sleeves on his lower arms to protect his black coat. His eyes darted in all directions while he shuffled papers on his desk.

"What do you want and who are you?" he muttered.

Roberto said his name and mentioned that he had mailed an article to them that was published. "It was about the indoor skating rink," he explained.

"Oh yes, I remember it. It was pretty good. Did we pay you for it?"

"No, not yet."

"Go to the bookkeeper over there and he'll pay you. Anything else?"

"Yes, I have another article here. It's about the way foreign maids are treated."

"And how would you know anything about that?"

"I've interviewed several maids."

"I'll take a look at it, but I wish you would write about something more serious. As for instance what's going on in the textile mills now after the strike last year in Lawrence? You know of that strike, don't you?"

"I don't know much about it," Roberto confessed. "I had other pressing problems on my mind last year."

"Let me know if you can get any interviews with mill workers."

"I'll see what I can do." Roberto thought about the immigrant men in his class. He hadn't talked to them, but now he would. He said goodbye to Mr. Parini and went to the bookkeeper.

"You get paid by the word," the bookkeeper said. Roberto saw him measuring the article, so the word count must not be precise. Next time he sent an article, he would count the words himself.

After his next English class, Roberto spoke with an Italian man, who had been one of the strikers at the textile mill in Lawrence the year before. Little Joe with the dirty finger nails spoke in Italian as he filled Roberto in on what had happened. The American Woolen Company owned the mill and thirty-four other factories in New England. When a new law about a shorter workweek went into effect, the mill owners lowered the workers' wages. Within a week, twenty thousand workers went out on strike. The union, Industrial Workers of the World (IWW), made some gains, but the company fired union activists and hired labor spies. Workers lost their jobs. Many of them were female immigrants. One female worker was killed.

"How long did the strike last?" Roberto asked.

"Two months."

"How did the workers survive?"

"An Italian poet in New York City, Arturo Giovannitti, came to Lawrence to take care of strike relief. He was the editor of the Italian newspaper *Il Proletario*, backed by the Italian Socialist Federation. Each nationality group set up soup kitchens and food distribution. Families received small cash contributions, and doctors volunteered to treat the sick. The mill-owners had not counted on the workers holding out for long. They arrested organizers and held them without trial."

"What were the workers' demands?"

"We wanted fifteen percent increase in wages, a shorter workweek, and double pay for overtime work," Little Joe said.

"Did you get it?"

"The company had to concede."

"Did the conditions in the mill improve after the strike?" Roberto asked.

"They did at first, but then the mills began to lay off people. Now the conditions are no better than before."

"And you're working in a textile mill now?"

"Yes, I am."

"I'd like to interview some more workers and write an article about it."

"You can't use my name," Little Joe said. "The best way to find out is to take a job in a mill."

"I won't mention your name," Roberto promised. "But I may take your advice and work in the mill for a while."

"See you around then."

Roberto went to the *Gazzetta* office and read what the paper had published about the strike. Little Joe had told the truth. Roberto's interest grew. Having taken the notes he needed, he asked the editor if he could see the pressroom.

"Sure, come with me," Mr. Parini said.

The noise and smell of ink hung heavy in the air. The reporters banged on typewriters. The editor pointed to the typesetting machine. "When a page is ready, it's the mirror image of what it will be in print."

The printing press churned out the printed pages, all in one big room. Roberto found it fascinating and inspiring, but it bothered him that he didn't know how to use a typewriter.

"Is it hard to learn to type?" he asked.

"It takes some practice, especially if you're going to use all your fingers," Mr. Parini said. "It's like playing the piano. You have to know where the keys are."

Roberto was hooked enough to want to write a sensational article. He went home and wrote the first part of what had happened in Lawrence the year before. His beard grew and he didn't bother to shave. With a two-day stubble and dressed in work clothes, he went to the mill and asked for a job.

"Do you have any experience?" the man in hiring asked.

"No, but I'm out of work and willing to learn."

"The only opening we have is for a broom pusher."

"I'll take it," Roberto said. It suited him fine. He'd be moving around rather than staying put at a loom. Broom in hand, he walked the floor catching the spills of wool and other scratch. Meanwhile, he noted the plight of the workers and caught a few comments between them. Sometimes he asked questions. After one week, he had enough material to finish his article. When he clocked out, he said that he was quitting and was sent to the bookkeeper to get his pay. The amount was pitiful, but Roberto was glad to get out of the mill. As he headed for the door, a guard stopped him.

"You have to come with me," he said.

"Why?"

"We want to have a word with you. That's all."

The guard had a firm grip on Roberto's arm, and he had no choice but to come along. In a small room, two men confronted him. The husky one said, "When we hired you, you said that you were out of work and needed a job. Why then are you quitting after only a week?"

"I have a prospect of a better job," Roberto said.

"We think that you are a labor spy or a foreign spy. What's your nationality?"

"I'm Italian."

"Do you have any papers?"

"I lost my passport in a robbery."

"So you're a WOP. You have no papers. And you've been asking the workers a lot of questions."

"That's because I was interested in what they're doing."

"We don't think so. Who are you really working for? The IWW?"

"Absolutely not."

"We've a way of finding out. Meanwhile you're in our custody."

Roberto was shocked to be detained in a jail close to the plant. It was his second arrest since he came to America. Before that he had never been arrested.

"I have the right to one phone call," he said.

"Yes, and one only. What's the number?"

Roberto gave Anna's number.

"Is that to a lawyer?"

"No, it's not. It's a private number."

"All right," he said, as he repeated the number to the operator and handed the receiver to Roberto.

"Anna this is Roberto. I'm in jail."

"In jail! What for?" Anna sounded perturbed.

"I'm charged by the textile mill of being a foreign spy."

"And what were you doing in a textile mill, Roberto?"

"I worked there." He looked at the jailer and asked, "What precinct am I in?"

The jailer told him and Roberto related it to Anna.

"I'll tell Mr. Jones. He might be able to get you out. It doesn't sound right," Anna said.

"Thank you, Anna. I knew I could count on you."

Roberto was in jail overnight. He thought of the last time he was jailed. Why did he have so much bad luck? He was just as innocent this time as he had been when he was accused of murdering the homeless man. He wished that he still had his passport. Could it still be in the suitcase, and where was his suitcase?

In the morning, Mr. Jones came and asked him why he had been in the mill.

"I was there because I wanted first-hand experience before writing an article about the conditions in the mill," Roberto whispered. "I'm writing for *La Gazzetta.*"

"Did you tell that to the guards?" the lawyer asked.

"No, I didn't think I should."

"I'll get you out, and I doubt that you'll have to go before a judge."

Roberto was free, but once again he owed Anna for having rescued him. He went home and finished his article while still angry for being arrested. He delivered it to Mr. Parini, who read it standing up.

"We can't put your signature on this one," he said. "We will just call you, 'An Observer,' but you're welcome to write more articles. If you want to, you can come to our office and use our typewriters."

Roberto had his wish, and he had earned the respect of Mr. Parini, although he doubted that John Whitmore would appreciate what he had done. Anna, on the other hand, might sympathize with the workers.

Roberto arrived early for his class and went to the college library to read newspapers. To his surprise, he spotted Julia by the reference desk. His heart began to thump and his knees felt strangely weak. He had to go up and talk to her.

"Hello, Julia," he said, hat in hand.

She twirled around to the sound of his voice.

"You surprised me, Roberto."

"I didn't mean to startle you. How are you?"

"I'm fine. How are you?" Roberto noticed that her face had turned red.

"I'm fine, too. I'm here to teach tonight," Roberto said with pride in his voice.

"I'm here to register for classes that start in the fall," she said. "I thought I should take a look at the text books."

"I see." He admired her pretty face with the rounded cheeks.

"I understand that you are a writer."

"I write for the *Gazzetta*. I don't have to paint anymore."

"Congratulations. That's wonderful."

"I wish we could chat some more, but my class starts in a few minutes. Could I see you after class? If you're still here?"

"I'll be here for a while."

"All right. I'll come back and look for you then. It was good seeing you, Julia."

"I'm glad for all your accomplishments," she said and gave him her hand.

He took it and noticed that it shook. He looked into her hazel eyes, bowed, and kissed her finger tips. With a longing look, he let go of her hand.

"Hope to see you later, Julia."

She was as lovely as he had remembered. No, she was even lovelier.

Roberto had a hard time concentrating on his class that night. He couldn't wait for it to end. Would Julia still be in the library?

When a student stopped him to ask a question after class, he excused himself and said that he didn't have time. "Ask me before our next class," he said. He hurried to the library. Oh, there she was sitting at a table reading.

"Hello again, Julia. Thanks for waiting."

"I wanted to read this," she said, pointing to a magazine.

"Could we go somewhere and have a cup of coffee?"

"All right, I'm getting thirsty, so we could do that."

"I can carry your books," he said.

"Thanks, they are heavy."

He took her books in one hand and Julia's arm with the other. They walked into a café, where Roberto selected a secluded table.

"I've missed you so much, Julia," he said. "I haven't had any fun since you broke up with me."

"I thought you would have found someone else by now."

"I'm afraid that there is no one like you, Julia. Would you see me once in a while this summer?"

"Perhaps. I'm happy for you, Roberto. It sounds like you're doing well. "

"I am. Do you still work at the restaurant?"

"Yes, I do. I saw in the paper that you saved a little girl who had fallen through the ice."

"I was glad to be able to do that," he said.

"My parents read it, too," she added. He could hear the admiration in her voice. Perhaps he had a chance after all.

He ordered two coffees and asked if she wanted something else. She said that she would have a donut, so he ordered two.

As they drank the coffee and ate the donuts, Roberto felt the connection between them. She loved him, no matter how much she tried to deny it.

"When are you working? I'd like to come and have my favorite pizza."

She told him, and he felt happier than he had in a long time.

"I'll see you Saturday then."

He looked into her soft eyes. Oh, how he loved them.

"I look forward to seeing you soon," he said. "How do you get home from here?"

"I take the bus."

When she said that she had to catch the last bus, he walked her to the bus stop and kissed her by the light pole. He pressed her to his chest, and she didn't seem to mind. The bus honked, and she got on. They waved. Roberto knew that Julia was the one for him, but he had the dreadful feeling that he couldn't have her. Why did she have to be so young? He didn't think he could wait four years until she graduated from college.

Roberto was at the restaurant where Julia worked. He ordered his pizza and waited for her to be finished for the day. His eyes followed her as she served other customers. They walked out together. He tried to pull her into dark corners, but she resisted. Out in the open he could kiss her and then she even kissed him back. At the bus stop, he got another chance to kiss her. When someone yelled, "Why don't you two get a room?" Julia reddened. She was embarrassed. "Don't pay attention," Roberto said. "The man is just jealous."

Chapter 10

John Whitmore rewarded Anthony's good work with a pay raise and a larger apartment that he shared with his brother. Roberto paid half the rent. In June, the court approved Lydia's last will, and Mr. Jones transferred the ownership of the beach house on Cape Cod to Roberto. Now, he could really impress Julia. How about a car, too, so he could drive to the Cape? He looked at a used Ford Model T and made a deal with the seller, paying a small amount as a down payment. The rest he would pay in installments. He learned how to drive and drove to the restaurant where Julia worked.

"Would you come with me outside for a minute?" he asked her. "I have something to show you." She just had to see what it was, so she went to the door and stood there as Roberto walked up to his car.

"Would you go for a ride with me? This is my car. I'll use it to drive to my beach house on the Cape."

Her eyes grew larger. "What? You have a car and a beach house!"

"Yes, I do. It's really true."

"You're rich?"

"No, but I have received an inheritance. Now, will you go for a ride with me?"

"I will... after work," she said. "I can't believe this."

Roberto laughed. He had finally impressed her. "I'll be waiting, sweetie," he said.

When Roberto had Julia in his car, he drove to a parking lot and turned off the engine.

"At long last, we're alone," he said.

She sat still and didn't object to his advances. He stroked her arms and legs. He kissed her with passion until she melted in his arms.

"I love you, Julia," he said. "I'll always love you."

"It's wonderful to be loved, Roberto, but my father would kill me if he knew what we're doing."

"I won't hurt you, sweetie. I'll be a gentleman. I promise. I'll only go as far as you want."

"I can say stop?" she asked.

"Yes, you can say stop, and I'll stop."

It took quite a while before she said stop. By then Roberto was fully aroused, but he started the car and drove her home. All he could think of was the goodbye kisses outside her parents' home, and what Mr. Nicolo would say when he found out that Julia's suitor had a car.

Roberto spent the weekdays at the beach house and his weekends in the city so that he could see Julia. He tried to persuade her to come with her to the Cape, but she said that her parents would never allow it.

Anna had left all the furnishings in the beach house. The outside needed a fresh coat of paint, so Roberto painted it in a pink color that shocked the neighbors. He lived a bachelor's dream, doing what he loved, swimming in the ocean every day. The neighbors thought that he was the caretaker, and Roberto let them. They may not have liked that an immigrant from southern Europe owned one of the 'cottages.' With his good looks and considerable charm, he had no trouble making friends. Sometimes, he invited the young crowd he met on the beach to parties at his house. The rich girls flocked to him while their parents were on the mainland. Chaperones and lady's maids had a hard time keeping track of their charges. Roberto soon had offers to captain the rich families' sailboats. That's how he paid the installments on his car.

He read the *Boston Globe* every day, partly because he wanted to keep up on the news, but also because he wanted to check the birth announcements. Anthony had told him that Anna's baby was due any time. One day in July, he found the notice. Anna had given birth to a baby boy. Now, he needed a gift. What does one give a baby born to a couple who has everything? Roberto wanted it to be something special, something that he could make. He knew how to whittle and decided to make a small sailboat with mast and tackle. He carved it to look like one of the boats in the harbor and sanded it smooth before applying the stain and varnish. When he was done, he painted the name "Anna" on its side and carved his initials on the keel. He had already made a stand for it so that it could rock back and forth like it was in the water. Last, he glued on a mast and rigged the 'tackle.'

He called Anna and asked what time would be convenient for his visit. Then he cranked up his Ford and drove to the mainland. It was the first time that Roberto arrived at the Beacon Hill mansion in style. The butler's eyes widened as he opened the automobile door for Roberto.

"Good afternoon, Mr. Cosentino. Mrs. Whitmore is expecting you."

Roberto reached into the back seat and took out the sailboat he had made.

"Do you want me to carry that, sir?" Tom asked.

Roberto noticed the little word, "sir."

"No, thank you. I'll carry it myself."

Tom opened the massive door to the mansion for him and told him to wait. The dog didn't come running as usual. When Tom returned, Roberto asked, "Is Tramp outside?"

"Yes, when the baby is downstairs, Tramp has to be in the back yard," Tom said. "Mrs. Whitmore thinks that he might be too excited seeing the baby. Mrs. Whitmore will see you in the drawing room, sir."

Roberto was pleasantly surprised. The drawing room was an improvement over the library. He was glad that he didn't come empty-handed like last time.

As soon as Anna saw the boat that Roberto carried she broke into a smile. Before she could say anything, Roberto said, "I want to congratulate you and Mr. Whitmore. I made this boat for your son myself, and hope that you approve. See here, it rocks." Roberto demonstrated. "I thought the baby would like that."

"I'm sure he will love looking at it. It's beautiful, Roberto, and it will be a keepsake."

When she saw her name on the boat, she added, "I appreciate that you gave it my name. We'll put it in his room. For now, you can place it on the table."

The baby boy lay in a bassinet beside her, but Roberto hadn't noticed him until now. He looked at the sleeping child, and said, "He's as beautiful as his mama. What's his name?"

"His name is Henry William after his two American grandfathers. We'll baptize him next Sunday at Immanuel Lutheran Church."

"I'm so happy for you, Anna. Your husband must be very proud."

"He is. Please sit down, Roberto, and tell me how you like the beach house."

"I love it. I'm sorry that you lost it though. It wasn't my doing."

"I know. It was Lydia's wish," Anna said.

"I appreciate that you left the furnishings. If you want something back, just say so."

"No, it was nothing special. You can have it."

"I also wanted to thank you for getting me out of jail. It was embarrassing to have to call you."

"Well, I was glad that you hadn't done anything criminal."

"If you hadn't intervened, who knows what they would have done to me. I've learned how harsh the company was to the strikers last year, and now I've learned that the conditions are no better in the mills than before the strike. I wrote an article about it, and it was published in the Italian language newspaper *La Gazzetta*."

"So you're writing for that paper?"

"Yes, I am. As a matter of fact, I will deliver another article to them today. I also wrote a commentary for the *Boston Globe*, but I don't know if they will publish it."

"They probably will. After all, the paper knows that you're a hero. I saw the article about you having saved that little girl who went through the ice."

Roberto didn't say anything, but was glad that Anna had read it. Then John would also know. After what had happened earlier with Danielle, Roberto needed John to trust him again.

"What is the commentary about?" Anna asked.

"It's about the proposed canal between the Cape and the mainland. The canal is supposed to be ready in 1914. We won't be able to drive to the Cape."

"I don't like that canal either," Anna said. "By next summer, John and I should have another beach house on the Cape, and we'll have to ferry over."

"I won't keep you any longer, Anna," Roberto said and stood up.

Anna also rose. "Thank you for the gift. I think it's magnificent," she said motioning to the boat.

"If your husband doesn't like it, you can hide it until Henry gets older."

Anna smiled. "I'm happy things are going well for you, Roberto. I hear that you're not painting any more."

"Well, my brother is a much better painter."

"I saw that you're driving an automobile."

"Yes, with the house on the Cape, I really needed one."

"John has also learned to drive, so we've two vehicles now. Eddy still drives me."

Roberto felt pleased as he said goodbye and drove off to the *Gazzetta* office.

"Where have you been?" Mr. Parini asked. "I haven't seen you for a while."

Roberto told him that he had inherited a beach house on the Cape, and that he would be out there most of the summer.

"Well, well, so you're not a socialist anymore?"

"I've never been a socialist, sir, but I like to stand up for what I think is wrong."

"And so you did. It was a good article. I hope you'll find another cause to write about."

"I will, but the article I have for you today is about the canal between the Cape and the mainland"

"It's timely. I know some wealthy Italians who don't like that it will interrupt both the direct route by automobile and the train between Falmouth and Boston."

"And it will probably be years before bridges are built," Roberto said.

"The ship owners want the canal so they don't have to go around the Cape."

Mr. Parini wanted to talk more about the canal, but Roberto was in a hurry.

"When fall comes and it gets too cold on the Cape, I'll be back to use the typewriters in your office," he said.

"You can take one of our typewriters with you. We've plenty of them."

"That would be good because I need to practice. I never learned to type."

Roberto walked out of the building carrying a typewriter and several issues of *La Gazzetta* that he placed in his car. Then he stopped at the *Boston Globe* and dropped off the English version of his article about the canal that he had written as a letter to the editor.

While Anthony shopped for food, Roberto went to see Julia at the restaurant. Again, he asked her to come to the Cape for a visit. He said that she could take the train and go back home the same day. Anthony would be their chaperone.

She said that it was tempting, but she wouldn't do it unless she had a female chaperone.

Roberto was disappointed, and wondered if she would ever come. He bought wine, typing paper, and carbon paper for his typewriter. The weather was warm and sunny. Roberto looked forward to going to the beach with his brother where they would swim together as they had done at home. But, of course, it would have been much better if Julia had joined them.

Chapter 11

Roberto and Anthony strolled on the beach when they met the two sisters who lived next door. Roberto already knew the girls and introduced them to his brother, "This is Sarah, and this is Jane," he said.

"What are you ladies doing this lovely afternoon?" Anthony asked.

"We're going sailing. You boys want to come along?"

Roberto looked at Anthony. "What do you say, brother?"

"I say, yes."

"We'd love to," Roberto said. He admired the way the girls looked in their bathing suits—their long legs exposed from the knee, their slim bodies sculptured to perfection, their sun-bleached hair blowing in the wind.

Roberto and Anthony helped the girls with the rigging, and Sarah sat down by the tiller. The wind caught the sail, and the bow parted the bluish-green water, leaving it churning behind them.

"This is perfect," Anthony said.

Roberto scanned the sky and saw dark, ominous clouds on the horizon. He'd keep an eye on them. Sarah flirted shamelessly with Anthony, and he flirted back. Roberto wished that Julia could have been with them. Jane seemed shy and she always took a backseat to her older sister, but now and then she cast admiring glances at Roberto. Many other sailboats were out enjoying the good wind, and the occupants of the boats waved to each other as they met or glided by. Roberto recognized the names painted on the boats. He had been the hired captain on some of the bigger yawls that sped past them creating waves. After half an hour of uneventful sailing, Roberto decided that the clouds looked threatening and told Sarah to head back.

A strong gale and rain squall caught her unprepared before she had completed the slow come-about. The sail almost touched the water before Roberto took over the tiller and righted the boat. He fought hard to stay on course. The girls' faces turned white with fear. Sarah found the pail and held on to it while Jane vomited into the ocean. The pounding rain blinded Roberto. Anthony bailed water.

"I think we might have a storm on our hands," Roberto yelled to Anthony.

"You're right. We won't make it all the way home," Anthony shouted back.

Roberto changed course and headed for the nearest cove. The waves splashed over the sides of the boat. Anthony continued to bail.

As the boat leaned heavily to one side, the seasick Jane toppled overboard.

"Oh my God!" Anthony shouted and quickly cast a rope to her. Sarah screamed, "Jane, Jane," as the waves engulfed her sister. Roberto watched Jane, who seemed unable to catch the rope.

"Take over the tiller," he shouted to Anthony and quickly removed his shoes.

"Hold on. I'm coming for you," he hollered to Jane before jumping in. He fought the high waves and lost sight of her. "Where is she?" he shouted to Sarah.

"There, there she is," Sarah yelled back and pointed.

Roberto saw her and dove for her as she went under. He caught her arm and pulled her to the surface. They both gasped for air. Sarah aimed the rope for Roberto and he caught it. Anthony tried to steady the boat while calling to

Sarah to take over the tiller. He had to pull Jane and Roberto aboard. Roberto held on to the rope as Anthony pulled Jane into the boat. He then stretched out a hand to his brother and Roberto climbed aboard. The little sailboat danced on the waves as the rainstorm continued unabated.

"That was close," Roberto panted. "How is Jane?" She rested face down at the bottom of the boat, water running from her mouth. Roberto pushed gently on her back until he was sure that all the seawater that she had swallowed had escaped. Jane coughed and wheezed, but was all right. Anthony had taken over the tiller, and Sarah bailed water.

When they approached the shore, Roberto hauled down the sail and started the small outboard motor that made slow progress in the choppy sea.

The girls looked relieved as the boat glided into the harbor and out of danger. On shaky legs, the girls held on to each other as they stumbled out of the boat, and then waited for the boys to join them.

"Thank you for saving my life, Roberto," Jane said her voice still hoarse.

"I'm glad I got to you in time," Roberto said.

"Our parents will never let us take the boat again, but that's okay as long as Jane is safe," Sarah said.

"We must find a phone and call them," Jane said, but we won't tell them that I nearly drowned."

Drenched and forlorn they all headed for the nearest building, a bait shop, and asked for a phone.

"All the phones are down due to the storm," the shop owner said.

"We don't have any money," Sarah said, "and who knows how long we have to stay here?"

Roberto and Anthony searched their pockets and came up with a few coins.

"This might be enough to buy us chowder," Anthony said.

"I can catch you some fish for dinner as soon as the rain lets up," Roberto offered, stroking his wet, black hair from his forehead.

"I'll give you bait," the shop owner said.

"Thanks, but first I think we'll go to a diner and get us some chowder," Roberto said.

The four of them ate lukewarm chowder by candlelight while staring out the window, waiting for the storm to subside. Their wet clothes clung to their bodies. To cheer the girls, Roberto said, "Why all the gloom? We're safe and we should be thankful for that."

"And that's thanks to you, Roberto. We would never have made it on our own," Sarah said, and Jane agreed.

"But we're all well. It's warm, and our clothes will dry on our way home," Roberto said.

The waiter came to the table and told them that he had listened to his shortwave radio. "The wind is subsiding," he said.

The girls' faces lit up and they cheered.

"Look, the rain has stopped, and the sea is not as choppy," Roberto said. "We can sail for home in a little while."

On their way home, Sarah wondered what their father would say when he saw the boys in the boat. They spotted him from a distance standing by the harbor. Tall and tanned, Bill Drake waved his straw hat to them.

Roberto lay to at the dock, and the girls scrambled ashore into the waiting arms of their father.

"We're so sorry, Dad," they said.

"Thank God you're safe. Your mother and I have been worried sick. We feared that you had capsized. I'm so relieved that you're back safe and sound."

"When the wind increased, we went into harbor," Roberto explained. "The phones were out of order, so we couldn't call you, sir."

"Oh, Dad, Roberto saved my life," Jane said, but her father didn't seem to hear. He had turned to Roberto to thank him for bringing the girls safely home.

"Mr. Drake, I apologize for not bringing your daughters home sooner, but the storm blew up so fast that we couldn't risk heading back," Roberto said.

"I'm Bill to you, Roberto. You did the right thing." To the girls he said, "Now, hurry up to the house. Your mother is beside herself."

"She can relax now," Roberto said.

"Thank you, gentlemen." Bill shook hands with Roberto and Anthony. "The girls would not have made it without you."

After a good night's sleep, Roberto and Anthony were eating breakfast when Bill Drake stopped by and invited them to dinner. "The girls told me everything. I owe you," he said.

"It's all right," Roberto said.

"I have to work tomorrow morning," Anthony reminded Roberto.

"There's an evening train from Falmouth to Boston. I can take you to the station after dinner."

"Then we'll accept the dinner invitation," Anthony said.

Chapter 12

To Roberto's surprise, Julia told him that she would be coming to the Cape next weekend chaperoned by a female cousin. The two women would take the train in the morning and go back home the same day. Roberto suspected that Julia hadn't told her parents that they would see him on the Cape, but he was happy that she was coming.

He stood by the track when the train arrived in Falmouth and was delighted to see that the cousin was a young girl, almost as pretty as Julia. Her name was Jill, and Roberto was sure that Anthony would like her. Roberto gave both girls a welcome kiss on the cheek, but Julia also got a tight hug. With a girl on each arm, he led the way to his car.

Anthony welcomed them at the house and winked his approval to Roberto about Julia and her cousin. While Anthony carried their lunch to the picnic table, Roberto proudly showed the girls his beach house. Julia's eyes beamed up at him and he could tell that she was impressed.

"After lunch, we're going swimming," he said. "We don't have much time if you're going to catch the last train to Boston." He hoped he would get a chance to be alone with Julia.

They changed into bathing suits at the house and ran to the beach. Roberto took Julia's hand and Anthony took Jill's as they plunged into the water. The beach was crowded, and they preferred to be in the water. Julia knew how to swim, but Jill was just learning. While Anthony showed her the strokes, Roberto and Julia swam until they were further out than anyone else. Then he grabbed her and kissed her tenderly.

"I'm so happy that you're here, sweetheart," he said. "I've missed you so much."

"I've missed you, too, Roberto."

"I'll miss you even more when your college classes begin." His voice became husky as he felt her body close to his. "Swim with me, honey, and I'll take you to paradise. I know of a sandbar where the water is warm and shallow."

"This is great," Julia said as she regained her footing on the sandbar. When Roberto moved her legs to encircle his body, she drew closer. She stroked his bronzed, muscular body. The heat between them rose in the warm water. Their kisses became hotter and hotter until they were called back to reality by an approaching swimmer. It was Anthony.

"It's your turn now to teach Jill the strokes," he said. "I want to swim, too."

"Your timing is bad, brother," Roberto said.

"Oh, I see. Maybe I showed up in the nick of time?" He splashed water on Roberto and laughed heartily.

"All right," Julia said. "I'll take over Jill's lessons."

Smiling broadly, she began to swim toward shore while the boys raced away in a fast crawl.

Julia and Jill sat on the beach and talked while waiting for the boys to return.

"You really like Roberto, don't you?" Jill asked.

"I do."

"He's gorgeous, and he has a fantastic place here."

"Don't tell my parents that we visited Roberto," Julia warned. "They'll never let me see him again if they find out."

"No, I won't. Did you kiss out there in the water?"

"Yes," Julia said dreamily.

"How did it feel?"

"Amazing, I can't explain it. Oh, Jill, I'm so attracted to him that it's dangerous."

"You have to be careful then. That's why I'm here, you know…. Anthony is nice, too."

"I'm glad you like him."

They watched as Roberto and Anthony waded through the shallow water and came up to them. Both men had bronzed, muscular bodies, but Julia couldn't take her eyes off Roberto. As soon as she saw him, her strong attraction returned.

"How did the swimming lesson go?" Anthony asked.

"We talked instead," Jill said.

Roberto and Julia locked eyes until Julia blushed.

"How about a walk on the beach with me?" Roberto asked her.

"We'll be right back," Julia said to Jill with a smile.

Anthony plunked himself down beside Jill. "Don't hurry back on our account," he said as he put his arm around Jill.

Roberto and Julia walked hand in hand until they were beyond the beach and hidden by vegetation. As drawn by a magnet, their lips met in a kiss that took their breaths away. Their tongues twisted and danced while their legs and bodies intertwined.

"Where is my chaperone when I need her," Julia moaned.

"Don't worry, darling. We can't go all the way here, but one day, I hope we will. I love you, Julia, and I want to marry you."

"I love you, too, but I can't marry you yet, Roberto. You know that my parents expect me to go to college."

"I know, darling, and you're worth waiting for. Now that I know that you love me, I can wait, but I must see you once in awhile."

"I want to see you, too, Roberto, but, but…."

"But how will we manage our feeling. Is that what you are thinking?"

"Yes."

"I don't know. You tempt me more every time I see you, darling."

"I guess we'd better get back to Jill and Anthony then."

"Julia, thank you for coming. It meant so much to me."

Anthony and Jill had met up with Sarah and Jane on the beach and were engaged in a lively discussion with them when Roberto and Julia returned. Roberto introduced Julia and explained to her who the two sisters were. Julia at once understood that she had competition. If she couldn't keep Roberto interested in her, he could romance these girls who were here all summer. They didn't look like they were older than her, but judging by the way Jane gazed at Roberto, anything could happen. Anthony told Julia that they had been out sailing when a gale blew up and Jane had fallen overboard. "Roberto jumped in and rescued her," he said.

"He saved my life," Jane explained.

Julia had yet another reason to admire Roberto. He, on the other hand, shrugged it off.

When they came back to the house, Roberto made lemonade, and Anthony grilled wieners outside for their dinner. They sat and talked until it was time for Anthony and the girls to take the train back to Boston. Roberto would have liked nothing better than driving them to Boston and be with Julia a little longer, but he knew that it would be best if the girls returned on the train. He said that he needed to practice his typing. "I'll write you a letter, Julia, if you want one?"

"Oh yes, but please send it to the restaurant, so my parents don't see it."

"All right. I'll see you as soon as I'm in town again."

"When will that be?" Julia asked

"I'll come to the restaurant and look for you, sweetie."

Roberto and Julia kissed goodbye in the kitchen before Roberto started up the car and drove his guests to the train station. He stood alone and waved to them as the train pulled away. He felt happier than he had in a long time. He and

Julia had proclaimed their love for each other. His life had turned around, and it was all for the better.

Roberto and Julia met a few more weekends that summer before she began her college classes. When they were alone, which was usually in Roberto's car, he couldn't keep his hands off her. She told him that it wasn't fair to expect her to stop him. He had to stop tempting her. She questioned how she would be able to get through four years of college without giving in to her strong attraction. It would have been easier if she had gone to a college in another city.

When Roberto did not stop tempting her, she saw no other way than breaking up with him—again.

"We can still write to each other," she suggested. "You can still be my boyfriend, but I cannot see you as long as I'm in college."

Would Roberto wait for her? He was older and ready for a serious relationship. She prayed that providence would lead them in the right direction.

Roberto removed his arms from her. What she had said made him feel numb. He couldn't be her boyfriend if she wouldn't let him see her. But then again, he wanted to keep in touch with her.

"I'll give you the address to the college as soon as I can. Then if you want to write to me, you can."

When Roberto didn't answer, she added, "I still love you. It's just that we can't continue like this. I won't be able to study."

"I love you, Julia. That's what makes it so hard to be apart from you." Roberto hugged her hard while struggling to hide his disappointment. Julia hugged him back before pushing him away.

"I know," she said, "but I'd never get through college if I continue to see you."

"All right then. You can write to me, but so much can happen in four years. You might meet someone else."

"And you might meet someone else. It's our big dilemma."

"Good luck with your studies then, Julia." He tipped his hat to her and walked off. When he turned around for a last look, she was still standing there, but quickly turned. Parting was difficult, but he couldn't ask her to skip college. He had to admire her for her determination and could only blame himself for what had happened.

Chapter 13

In the fall, a strong hurricane hit the East Coast. As soon as Roberto heard, he went to the Cape to check on his beach house. His car wouldn't start, so he took the train. Roberto looked in disbelief at the destruction. The roof of his house lay in a pile in the sand and the walls had caved in. Many of the nearby houses also showed damage.

"*Madonna mia,*" he moaned.

The curtains fluttered from a broken window. He walked closer to see if he could save anything. The furniture lay crushed on one side. The waterlogged mattresses rested on the floor. A thought occurred to him. He must find the typewriter that he had borrowed from the *Gazzetta* office. Walking on top of the rubble, he aimed for the place where he had left it. The boards shifted under his weight. In a split second he found himself pinned down by a heavy beam. Unable to move his legs, he used the strength of his arms to lift the beam a few inches. He must be careful not to disturb the rubble again. Sweat dripped from his face as he slowly pulled one leg out. Blood seeped from a vein. Feeling intense pain in his stuck leg, he feared that it was broken. He must call for help, but would anyone hear him? He had seen Bill Drake, and hoped that he would still be close by.

Mustering all his strength, Roberto yelled, "Help, help. I'm stuck. Someone come and help me." While he listened for a response, he sent up a silent prayer to the Madonna.

He yelled louder, "Help, help!" But his voice was not loud enough. He would have to bang on something. Looking around for an item, he saw the alarm clock.

Grazie, Madonna. It's the answer to my prayer. I hope it still works. He set the alarm to ring and waited. It rang! Time and again, he reset the alarm, heard it ring, and waited. In between, he repeated his yells for help. After what seemed like an eternity, he heard footsteps.

"I'm here. I need help," Roberto called out.

"Are you hurt?" Bill Drake asked.

"Yes, I think my leg is broken. I can't pull it out."

"I have to get more help."

"Do you have a phone?"

"Yes, but it's not working."

"Is anyone else around?"

"I see an automobile coming. I'll wave to him."

Roberto hoped that two men could get him out. He heard voices, waited, and continued to pray. Looking up, he saw John Whitmore looking down at him.

"Am I glad to see you, Mr. Whitmore," Roberto said from the rubble.

"We'll have to remove a lot of boards to get to you," John said. "It will take time. Are you bleeding?"

"Yes, I am, but it's not bad. I can't get the other leg out."

John took off his coat and went to work. He handed one board after the other to Bill Drake, who threw it to the side.

"Now, we can see the floor," John said. "I'll try to reach you."

Foot by foot, he inched closer, testing the floor boards before he placed his full weight on them. He tried to lift the beam across Roberto's leg, but it proved to be too much for one man. Bill Drake moved closer. "If we can get some leverage, we can do it," he said.

He used a stud to heave the beam off Roberto's leg. John secured the beam while Bill looked at the leg. "Your leg appears to be broken," he said.

"I know it is," Roberto said, clenching his jaw.

Relieved to be free, Roberto rested on the bare floor with the two men standing over him.

"I'm so sorry to have caused so much trouble," he said. "I was looking for my typewriter."

"The typewriter is sitting right there," John said, and pointed to a spot on the floor.

"You must have uncovered it," Roberto said.

"We can take it with us, but right now it's more important to brace your leg," John said. "I'll see what I have in my automobile."

He came back with a rope and picked up two pieces of board that had split in the middle and then ripped off the curtains that still fluttered in the wind. Bill had ripped the sleeves off his shirt and bandaged Roberto's wound. John wrapped the curtain material around the split boards and placed one on each side of Roberto's broken lower leg. Another curtain ripped into strips secured the brace.

"Now, we need to lift your leg a bit again to get the rope underneath," John said.

"Go ahead," Roberto said, again clenching his jaw tight.

With his leg in the brace, Roberto said, "I think I can stand up if you help me."

Bill came with another piece of wood from the pile.

"This will have to do as a crutch," he said.

"I'll move my Ford closer," John said. Bill supported Roberto as he made his way to the automobile. Together, they managed to get Roberto into the back seat. He leaned against the inside wall of the Ford with his braced leg on top of the seat. The pain was excruciating.

John went to get the typewriter. Bill had gone to his house and came back carrying a bottle with a little whiskey left on the bottom.

"This is to ease your pain," he said.

"Thank you so much, Bill, and thank you for your help in getting me out."

"That's what neighbors are for. You got my girls home in that storm. Good luck!"

John placed the typewriter in the front seat, saying, "You might need this while you are laid up."

"Thank you so much for your help, Mr. Whitmore."

"You can thank Anna. She told me to go and check on the cottage. Even though it's yours now, she was concerned."

"I appreciate that."

"You have saved lives, Roberto. You saved Anna's life, and you saved that little girl on the ice. I was glad to be here to help you."

"I'm glad, too."

"If you don't mind, I'll have the rubble cleared away as soon as the authorities have inspected the damage."

"That would be good. I don't want anyone else to get hurt."

John asked Roberto if he had accident insurance, not expecting that he had. Roberto could only manage a groan, partly because of his pain, partly because he had neglected to take out accident insurance. He worried about what John would say when he found out that he didn't have property insurance either.

"You have two choices," John said. "Either I take you to the City Hospital, where you can become a charity case, or I take you to a private one where you have to pay the bill."

"I'll pay the bill," Roberto said, in a low and shaky voice. His next thought was that he didn't want to tell Julia about what had happened to him or his beach house.

Anna took time from her precious baby to visit Roberto in the hospital. With his leg in a cast stretched out in front of him, he had leaned back in his chair and closed his eyes when he heard her voice.

"Hello, Roberto. How are you?"

"Oh, Anna." Roberto opened his eyes wide. "I'm so glad to see you."

"You visited me in the hospital when I was sick," she said.

"But this is different. I've already caused your husband so much trouble. If he hadn't come, I don't know if I could have gotten out."

"John is a good man," Anna said.

"You are both good people," Roberto said.

"When will you get out of the hospital, do you think?"

"The doctor said in a couple of days. My brother will take care of me."

"But he works during the day."

"Yes, but I can walk on crutches."

"I remember when I walked with a crutch, and you supported me while my ankle healed."

"I remember it well."

"If you need help, don't hesitate to let me know."

"It's very kind of you. How is Baby Henry?"

"He's fine, smiling and cooing now. How's your writing coming along?"

"I wrote an article here in the hospital about the hurricane."

"I heard that you have a typewriter."

"Yeah, your husband brought it here, and I've been trying to type, but it seems easier to write by hand for now. Anthony brought me ink and pens."

"It was unfortunate what happened to the beach house. Did you have the house insured?"

"I thought of it, but I had no policy."

"It wouldn't have covered the hurricane damage anyhow."

"I heard that there might be an emergency fund available from the federal government."

"I read in the paper that there wasn't enough damage on the Cape to declare it a federal emergency area. I don't know about the Commonwealth of Massachusetts yet."

"Well, I won't rebuild in any case. I'd rather take the money if it's offered."

"I'll help you with the application."

"I'd appreciate that. I don't know how to go about it."

"John and I might be interested in buying the lot from you."

"I'll be glad to sell it to you. Then you could rebuild."

"I'd like that," Anna said. She looked at her wristwatch and pulled on her gloves. "I need to get home to the baby."

"Thank you for coming to see me."

"Hurry up and get well," she said.

Roberto had too much time to think in the hospital. He fantasized about Julia, to no avail, of course. He won't win her back now. If he still had the beach house, he might have a chance. The hurricane had blown away that opportunity.

When Roberto was released from the hospital, Anthony came with the Ford to take him home.

"I went by the office to pay, and they told me that the bill had been taken care of. Have you already paid?" he asked.

"No, but Anna might have taken care of it. She was here to visit me."

"She must be a kind and generous person."

"She is. She also offered to buy the beach house lot if I care to sell it."

"Will you sell it?"

"Yes, but first I must wait and see if I get any state emergency aid."

"So you want to be paid twice?"

"Well, the house was worth more than just the lot."

"But who's going to clean up the mess? If you hadn't broken your leg, the two of us could have done it. It's too much for one person."

"Mr. Whitmore offered to have it done."

"So he is as kind and generous as Anna?"

"Well, he probably thinks that he still owes me for saving Anna's life."

"It must be nice to be able to continue to cash in on that act," Anthony said. "I have to work for my money."

"I'm so glad you are here, brother. You are family."

As Anthony drove to their apartment, he said, "I saw in the *Boston Globe* that they have figured out that you were on the Titanic. They had looked in some back issues and read about your heroism."

"I knew I shouldn't have given my real name when I turned in that article about the canal. Now, they will probably find out the rest. I hope they didn't mention Anna's name?"

"No, they did not."

"The worst part of my predicament is that I've lost Julia."

"Oh? A postcard has arrived from her."

"She said that she can't see me while she's in college, but that she would write. Some relationship," Roberto said with a deep sigh as he read the postcard.

Chapter 14

While Roberto's leg healed, he wrote articles for *La Gazzetta* until he ran out of subjects. Being unable to teach or take courses during the fall semester, life seemed a bit dull. He looked again at the postcard from Julia showing Boston College and her address, but decided not to write her. He had nothing to say.

Then one day, he received a letter from the editor of the *Boston Globe*. Mr. Foster wrote that he had published Roberto's piece about the canal, and that it had started a steady flow of letters to the editor about the subject, pro and con. Now, he wanted Roberto to write about his Titanic experience. Feeling flattered, Roberto thought about it. What would he write? He didn't want to mention either Lydia's or Anna's names. He knew that he couldn't make trouble for Anna. He had a better idea for an article. Now that he had recovered enough to walk with a cane, Roberto decided to visit Little Italy.

He stood at the North Street Square at the north end of the downtown area with the seven-story hotel, Roma, in front of him across the street. Beyond stood the tenement buildings—the aging three-or-four story walk-up apartments that he had heard about. Barefoot children speaking Italian played on the narrow sidewalks. Horses pulling loads crowded the streets. The flies buzzed over the fresh horse dung. Spotting a café, Roberto crossed the street with care, side-stepping the manure.

At the café, a few men sat around the tables and talked with empty coffee cups in front of them. Looking up and seeing the stranger, they stopped talking. The group playing cards went back to their game. Children played with the ash trays. Everybody spoke Italian, but in a dialect unfamiliar to Roberto.

"Are you fellows working the late shift?" he asked a swarthy man in Italian, who sat alone at a table.

"Some of us are, but most of us are unemployed. If we ain't hired early in the morning, we come here to talk and play cards."

The man had lost several teeth in his mouth, which made him even more difficult to understand. Roberto offered him a cigarette.

"Thanks. I'm Sonny. Do you have a light?"

"My name is Roberto," he said as he lit Sonny's cigarette and one for himself.

"Are you from Sicily?" Roberto asked.

"Yeah, most of us are. We're so poor that we can't afford cigarettes any more."

"How can you support your families if you don't work?"

Sonny coughed, and he did not cover his mouth until it was too late. "We get day jobs now and then, and our wives are very frugal. But our kids hardly have any clothes."

"So it's not much better than in Sicily?"

The waitress came with the coffee, and Sonny eagerly stirred in cream and sugar.

"In Sicily at least we had our extended families to rely on when things got bad, and we grew our own fruit, grapes, and vegetables," he said.

Roberto looked at the barefoot children in the room and asked, "Shouldn't some of these children be in school?"

"Yes, but if they don't have shoes, they can't come to school. If we have only one pair of shoes for two children, they have to take turns going to school."

Roberto shook his head and pulled on his cigarette.

"Do you feel that the employers discriminate against you?" he asked.

"There is discrimination everywhere, especially here."

"Who are your landlords?"

"The Irish. They weren't liked in the beginning, but they knew English, so they got into politics."

The man coughed again. "The apartments are cold. We have no heat. No hot water and no baths," he said.

Roberto dropped the ashes from his cigarette into an ash tray.

"The worst part is that when we're sick, we don't get any care," the man continued.

"Are you sick?"

"Almost everyone here has consumption."

Roberto had leaned forward, but now he pulled back his chair.

"Ugh. Then you should be in a sanatorium."

"There's no room for us there. We live and we die. And when we die we are buried in the pauper's field." Roberto remembered the pauper's field where the bums had been buried and felt goose bumps on his arms.

He noticed that more people at the café were coughing, even children. What were the children doing here? They just sat around and looked hungry. Perhaps they hoped that they would get something to eat, a stale roll or something.

"What are you doing here, sir?" Sonny asked.

"I'm just traveling through."

"I see that you use a cane. What happened to your leg?"

"I broke it. It's a long story, but I have to leave now," Roberto said.

He had not touched his coffee, and as he turned to leave, he saw the man with the cigarette gulping it down. Roberto paid the waitress and bought a whole tray of rolls. "It's for the children. Give them the rolls," he said, pointing to them.

Outside he took a long breath of fresh air and hoped that he had not been infected with the tuberculin bacteria. He walked behind a woman in tattered clothes with barefoot children in tow. When the woman went into a food store, Roberto followed her. He watched as she bought flour, salt, and lard. It would go a long way. His own mother baked bread and made ravioli and pasta. When the clerk offered the woman a basket of soft tomatoes for a penny, she fished up another coin from her apron pocket and accepted the tomatoes. They would still be good enough for sauce.

The little girl pulled on her mother's hand.

"*Mozzarella, Mama, mozzarella.*"

"Wrap up a pound of mozzarella for the madam, please," Roberto told the clerk.

"*Grazie*, Signor." The woman curtsied when Roberto handed it to her. Her children looked at him like he was God.

After the woman had left, Roberto bought some Italian foods that he had not seen since he lived in Italy. He almost felt like he was exploiting the Sicilians and guessed that's why he had given them food.

Out on the street, Roberto looked for a barber shop. He knew that Italians owned most of the barber shops in Boston. Now, he needed a businessman's view on Little Italy. He didn't have to walk far before he found one.

"I'd like a haircut, please," he said in English.

The barber answered him in English, but Roberto could hear another barber speaking Italian to his customer.

"Don't you need a shave?" the barber asked.

Roberto touched his chin. He had forgotten that he hadn't shaved in a couple of days.

"You're right," he said.

"You're not from here, sir."

"No, I live in another part of Boston, but I'm from Genoa."

"Do you know that the first immigrants settling here in Little Italy were from Genoa? They were merchants."

"No, I didn't know that."

"Then came the Sicilians and it all changed. My own grandparents were from Sicily. They were very poor, but they became fishermen and did quite well."

"I don't suppose that the day laborers can afford to come to you for haircuts?"

"No, the wives cut their hair, I think." The barber shrugged. "Our customers are other businessmen."

"I feel sorry for the children. They look so hungry," Roberto said.

"Yes, some kids look hungry. Each family has up to a dozen children."

"I understand that many are afflicted with tuberculosis."

"That's true. We need a sanatorium just for Little Italy."

When the barber had finished the haircut, he reclined the chair, and Roberto leaned back for the hot-towel treatment and the shave that he could afford only once in a while. When he was ready to leave, he asked for directions to the Sacred Heart Church.

Before the priest could show him to the confession booth, Roberto asked what the church was doing for the poor people in the neighborhood.

"There isn't much we can do," the priest said. "We need a sanatorium and an orphanage, but private funds are needed for that. The Irish politicians are not coming forward with public funds."

"And meanwhile more people die and leave more orphans."

"That's true. We need to pray for them. The Madonna will listen to our prayers."

Roberto left. He believed that more than prayers were needed. He knew how he would write his article.

"Sanatorium and orphanage needed in Little Italy."

His visit to Little Italy had left a bad feeling in his stomach, but now he had enough material for another article. Roberto wrote it first in Italian. Mr. Parini supplied photographs for illustrations. Roberto knew that his appeal needed to reach the general public, and the best way was to get the editor of the *Boston Globe* interested. He translated the article to English, sometimes looking up words in a dictionary.

The next time he was at *La Gazzetta*, he asked for issues from April of 1912. He wanted to see what the paper had reported about the Titanic.

It was more than he thought. There were interviews with Italians and other survivors. Most of the Italians had traveled in what the reporter called steerage, and they didn't know that the Titanic was in trouble until they saw water on the floor. Many had put their lifejackets on backwards. The first to reach the boat deck learned that all the lifeboats were gone. People held hands and jumped into the water from the stern, the only part of the ship that was still above the waterline. Others catapulted into the water. Only the strongest made it. One man said that when he floated from the depths, he hit debris that he had to push aside to get air. He pushed his way among the dead bodies to a collapsible boat that floated upside down. Several men held on to it and strained to get up on the keel. They had to coordinate their movements to be successful. When they were on top of it, they rolled with the waves while pushing away other swimmers. No one wanted to risk his own life to save those of others.

All the survivors had lost one or more family member in the tragedy. When they came aboard the Carpathia they walked around in a daze looking for family members. Some became hysterical. When they reached New York, relatives, who were at the pier searching for loved ones had their worst fears confirmed. They said that they had scanned the lists of victims and couldn't find them there either. They went to all the hospitals that had received injured people and searched. Husbands who had not been on the Titanic searched for their wives and children. Almost all the children in third class had perished. When living relatives could not be found, people began to search for bodies, but became disheartened when they heard that Canadian ships were taking the bodies to Halifax for burial.

Roberto thought that he could translate some of the interviews to English. He asked the editor for permission and went home with a stack of papers. The translations kept him busy for a long time.

When he had one interview polished and ready to show to the *Boston Globe*, he felt both nervous and excited. He no longer needed a cane to support himself as he found his way to the editor's office behind the glass doors with a view of the large press room. The *Globe* was so much bigger than *La Gazzetta* that Roberto felt intimidated. The chief editor, Mr. Foster, was no doubt Anglo-American. He talked on the phone while making notes on a pad. Looking up at Roberto over his reading glasses, he asked, "How can I help you, sir?"

"I'm Roberto Cosentino. Mr. Foster, you were interested in something about the Titanic. I have this interview with a survivor that I have translated from Italian. It was printed in *La Gazzetta*."

"I remember you. You're a hero. I asked if you could write about your own Titanic experience, but I haven't heard from you."

"I felt that it would be too painful to write about my own experience, sir."

Mr. Foster glanced at Roberto's papers and asked if he had permission from *La Gazzetta*.

"Yes, I have."

"This looks interesting. Do you have more?"

"Yes, there are many more, and I'm working on them."

"Well, then we'll start with this one."

"I know that my English is not as good as that of your other reporters, but I hope that it can be corrected," Roberto said.

"We'll take care of it. Don't worry about your English. Our editors always have to correct script, no matter who wrote it. For a story like this, you had an advantage of being able to read Italian."

"I also have a story about Little Italy," Roberto said. "I was up there the other day and talked to some people."

"Bring it next time."

Standing in the *Boston Globe* office a second time, Roberto's confidence evaporated. Why would they accept his articles when they had American-born writers who could write it so much better? Reporting was different than a translation.

Mr. Foster put him at ease when he saw the headline about Little Italy.

"It looks like a compelling story," he said. "How do you know this?" he asked.

"I went to Little Italy and interviewed people, sir."

"Do you take notes, Mr. Cosentino?"

"No, sir, I don't take notes in front of people. Then they won't talk to me."

"It's a good tactic as long as you have a good memory."

Roberto felt better. If the *Globe* published his article, donations might be forthcoming for the people of Little Italy. He also hoped that Julia would read it.

Chapter 15

When Tom, the butler, opened the front door at the mansion one morning, he was surprised to see a basket and a suitcase standing in front of the entrance. He thought he recognized the suitcase as Roberto's. Before touching anything he called on his mistress.

"Mrs. Whitmore, please come and take a look at what's outside the door."

"What is it, Tom?" Anna asked.

"I'm not sure, Mrs. Whitmore. I haven't looked closely." He opened the door for her. When Anna heard a whimpering from the basket, she went up to it and lifted the net that covered it. "There is a baby in the basket," she said. "Where did it come from?"

"I don't know, but someone must have put it here this morning. Doesn't that suitcase look like the one Mr. Cosentino had?"

Anna went up to the suitcase and looked at it. "It does look like Roberto's," she said. "Please open it. It might provide us with a clue about the baby."

Tom opened the case and Anna peaked into it. "These are all clothes for a newborn," she said. *What could Roberto have to do with it? Could he be the father of the baby?*

"What should we do about the baby?" Tom asked.

"We'll take it inside for the time being. Then I want to call my husband."

Once the basket and the suitcase were inside the house, the baby began to cry. "It's probably hungry or wet, or both," Anna said. She took the basket and headed for the kitchen. Tom followed her with the suitcase.

"Will you need me for anything else, Mrs. Whitmore?" Tom asked.

"Not right now," she answered.

"What in the world is this?" Mrs. Anderson, the cook, asked.

"It's a baby. We just found it outside the door."

"I've heard of babies being placed on doorsteps, but I never thought it would happen here," Mrs. Anderson said.

Anna took one of the blankets that the baby was wrapped in, folded it, and placed it on the kitchen table. Then she lifted the crying baby from the basket and rocked it in her arms until it stopped crying.

"Hello, sweetheart," Anna cooed. "Who are you? *Could you be Roberto's child?*

She placed the baby on top of the blanket. Carefully, she removed the wet diaper and discovered that the baby was a girl. She looked plump and healthy. The navel was wrapped.

"It looks like the mother had experience with babies," Anna said to the cook.

"Why would she give up the baby if she already had all these baby things?" Mrs. Anderson said.

"She must have been desperate."

With hands that were used to handle a baby, Anna quickly changed the diaper, wrapped the blanket around the little girl, and put her back in the basket. She then began to go through the suitcase searching for a note from the mother. She found the baby formula first and two bottles with nipples and placed them on the table. She then took out the diapers and shirts and put them on the table, a few items at the time. The clothes were clean and looked like they that had been laundered many times. There was no note from the mother. Anna felt inside the side pockets and pulled out a slip of paper. It had Roberto's name on it and their address. *So it is his suitcase.* She wrinkled her brow and wondered what he had to do with the baby.

"Mrs. Anderson," she said. "Please take the bottles and nipples and sterilize them. Boil them for three minutes and make the formula. While you do that, I'll go and call my husband at the office."

With bouncy steps, Anna walked to the library and lifted the receiver. She was calm but excited as she asked the operator to connect her to her husband's direct number.

"John, you won't believe what I found on our doorstep this morning," she said.

"From the sound of your voice it must have been something special."

"It was… it is, it's a baby girl."

"A baby! What in the world for?"

Anna told him everything she knew. The call ended with John saying, "I'll ask Mr. Jones for advice, and then I'll have a talk with Roberto. He has some explaining to do."

When Anna came back to the kitchen, she took the warm bottle from the cook and tested the temperature of the formula on her arm.

"It's just right," she said as she sat down on a kitchen chair to feed the baby.

"I've heard that people who find babies on their door steps can keep them," Mrs. Anderson said. "The woman who left her baby here probably knew that you would take good care of it."

"I've no idea what she thought, but I feel sorry for her," Anna said.

She had changed and fed the new baby two more times when she heard John's footsteps in the hall. She was still in the kitchen and went to meet him.

"What have you found out?" she asked.

"Come with me to the library and I'll tell you," he said.

When they were seated, he took Anna's hands in his, looked at her, and said, "Honey, Mr. Jones said that we should talk to our pastor. Some churches have their own orphanages and place children in foster care."

"Oh, John, I don't want her to be in an orphanage. I'm so worried that people who are unfit to be parents would get her. They might already have a houseful of children."

"So, so, honey." John put his hand on his wife's shoulder. "There are many childless couples who would love to adopt her. We already have a child, and he's ours."

"I know, and I'm thankful for that. But what did Roberto say?"

"He told me that someone had stolen his suitcase a while back and that he had traced it to a pawnshop in the area where the robbery took place. The proprietor had told him that a blond, pregnant lady had bought it. It's an unlikely story, but I think Roberto is telling the truth."

"So it's not Roberto's child. That's a relief. From the look of the baby, I didn't think so."

"Come and see the girl, honey. She's perfect." Anna took his hand and led him to the kitchen.

"Is she in the kitchen?" John sounded surprised.

"Well for now, but obviously we have to take her upstairs. No one is going to come for her tonight."

Anna took her out of the basket and held her. "She's so tiny," John said. "I suppose that our son was as tiny when he was born."

"Yes, he was. Henry is only three months old, but he has grown so much. Oh, John. I wonder how the mother managed to get the baby here. She couldn't have walked with both the suitcase and the basket."

"I wondered about that, too," John said.

"The mother already had all these baby clothes. Look here," Anna pointed to the suitcase.

John had to admit that the whole thing was strange. "Let's bring her upstairs to the nursery," he said.

"I'll take the baby if you take the basket."

"Tom should take the suitcase outside. It's been in a pawnshop and who knows where else? Everything in the case should be washed."

"You're right, John. I'll see to it. We've plenty of diapers upstairs."

They placed the basket with the new baby beside Henry's crib.

"Tomorrow, I'll have her checked by our pediatrician," Anna said. "Her navel might need attention."

"Whatever you do, don't start to nurse her," John said.

"Of course not." Anna stood and looked at her son sleeping in the crib. She felt so blessed and couldn't imagine giving him away. Their nanny, Josephine, came into the room. She already knew about the new baby.

"She's only here temporarily and she'll be having formula," Anna said. "Tell me when Henry wakes up so I can nurse him."

Anna then left the nursery to go downstairs for dinner. She felt drained but happy.

When the night came, she couldn't sleep. She no longer nursed Henry at night, but she expected the newborn to wake up. She wished that the girl had a name. What would be a good name for her? It might be a temporary one, but she needed a name. She thought of several names, Grace, Olivia, Rachel, Carolyn, Irene. When she heard her tiny cry, she started to get out of bed. But John put his arm around her and held her back.

"Let Josephine take her. You need your sleep." Anna knew that he didn't want her to get attached to the girl.

When she heard Josephine go downstairs to heat the formula, she settled back in bed, but it took her a long time to fall asleep. By then she had decided to call the girl Irene.

The pediatrician, Dr. Clark, came to the house and declared Irene to be a normal, healthy baby. He said that there would be no problem placing her in foster care. Anna wanted to keep her, but what would John say about that? He had told her that in due time, they would have their own baby daughter. Oh, how she wished that would come true.

In the afternoon, she received a phone call from Roberto. He said that Captain Rose at the Salvation Army could verify that the pawnshop had sold the suitcase to a pregnant lady. Anna told him that she had wondered if the baby was his.

"No, I didn't have anything to do with the baby. You have to believe me, Anna."

"I believe you, Roberto. The baby doesn't look anything like you. She has blond hair and blue eyes."

"Lucky for her... and me." Roberto joked. I've enough to worry about without a baby." What Roberto did not tell Anna was that the police had just contacted him about the baby and reminded him of his arrest record.

In the afternoon, Anna called Pastor Lindblade, their pastor at Immanuel Lutheran Church, and explained the unexpected arrival of a new baby at their house. The pastor said that he would be glad to visit and talk about the options available to them through the church. Anna thanked him and said that he would call him back to set a time as soon as she had talked to her husband.

John arrived home at the same time as Pastor Lindblade came walking from the nearby church. They greeted each other and John opened the door for the pastor.

Tom rushed toward them and took their hats. "I'll go and tell Mrs. Whitmore that you're here," he said.

John showed the pastor into the drawing room and asked him to sit down. But as Anna entered the room, he stood up again and greeted her.

"This is the gift from God that was placed on our door-step," Anna said as she showed him the baby.

"It's a precious gift, indeed," Pastor Lindblade said.

He told them that the Lutheran Church had a children's home not too far away, but that it would be difficult to care for a newborn there. The home was already overcrowded. Anna said that she didn't want the baby to go to an orphanage. The pastor also told them that some nondenominational foster care agencies had begun to form, but that he didn't trust them completely.

"In the past, it has been the role of the religious institutions to place orphans in foster care," he said. "It has worked well. Our church takes care of its own. We could find a suitable home for this baby."

"Would that be legal?" John asked.

"We've had no problems with the legality of the procedure in the past."

"What about if the biological mother should come forward and demand the baby back?" John asked.

"I think it would be hard for a mother who has abandoned her newborn to get her back. The mother probably hoped that you would keep the child."

"But we have a baby of our own, and there are many couples who don't have any children," John said.

"I agree. You're already blessed with a child and, God willing, you'll have more. But we have a childless husband and wife, Carl and Sally Hanson, in our church family. They talked to me about adopting a child from our children's home but said that they would prefer a newborn."

"I know Carl and Sally," Anna said excitedly. "Sally is a little older than I, but we went to the same school—and also Sunday school. They would be good parents." She rocked the baby in her arms.

"I can testify to that," Pastor Lindblade said. "If you want me to I could arrange for Mrs. Hanson to come here to see the baby. That is if you, Mrs. Whitmore, are sure that you want to give her up. Forgive me, but it seems to me that you're attached to her already."

"I love her—what's there not to love, but I don't want to be selfish."

"God bless you, Mrs. Whitmore. *Det är saligare att giva än att taga.*" Anna translated for John, "It's more rewarding to give than to take." John smiled. He was happy with the outcome of the discussion.

"Well then, I'll ask Mrs. Hanson to come for a visit. If she feels that the baby is a good fit, then Mr. Hanson can come also."

Anna and John thanked Pastor Lindblade warmly. When they had closed the door behind him, Anna looked at John with tears running down her cheek.

"It will be for the best, honey," John said. "If the child is with Carl and Sally, you can see her grow up."

Chapter 16

Roberto stopped at a store and bought three Christmas cards. He would send one to Anna and her family, one to his family in Italy, and one to Julia. He hadn't written to Julia and felt guilty. The thought of Christmas made him feel lonely. Perhaps he should look up Gretchel again. He liked the friendship he had struck up with her, and she would cheer him up. He thought that his leg would be strong enough to drive, so he cranked up his car, bought a few gallons of gasoline, and then drove to the Dutch restaurant where Gretchel worked. If she wasn't there, he could still enjoy some pancakes. But she was there, and her big smile warmed Roberto's heart.

"So good to see you, Gretchel," he said.

"Good to see you again, Roberto. What can I get for you?"

"I'll have my usual stack of pancakes," Roberto said.

"She wrote it down, and then asked, "How are you? I saw that you're limping."

"Sometimes my leg hurts," Roberto admitted.

"I'm off in a few minutes. I'll get you the pancakes, and then when you're finished I can join you for a cup of coffee."

"I'd like that."

Roberto spread butter on his pancakes and savored them. They satisfied his hunger for food, but he still felt empty inside. When he looked up, he saw Gretchel approaching carrying two cups of coffee on a tray.

"May I join you?" she asked.

"I wish you would."

She placed one cup in front of Roberto and sat down with the other one.

"So what's the matter? Are you homesick?"

"That might be the problem, although I haven't realized it." Roberto could not admit that he was also love sick. He still missed Julia.

"Everyone gets homesick sooner or later," Gretchel said. "The best cure for it is to go back home for a while."

Roberto told her everything that had happened to him except the homeless episode. "I don't have a steady income, and I lost the beach house," he said.

Gretchel looked surprised, but didn't ask why he had lost the house.

"So you feel kind of let down," she said.

"Yes. I lived the good life out there on the Cape among the rich people. I think God is trying to tell me something."

"Like what?" she asked."

"That I've been too greedy, perhaps. I wasn't meant to have that beach house. Easy come, easy go."

"Do you miss it?"

"Yes, I do, but I might receive compensation for the damages, and then I could go home to Italy for a visit."

"It would be good for you, I'm sure," Gretchel said.

"But my passport was stolen, and I don't know how to replace it. My first passport was issued in Italy."

"The Dutch have a consulate office here, and I'm sure the Italians have one also. You could look it up in the phone book. They'll tell you what to bring," she said.

"I appreciate your advice, Gretchel."

The very next day, Roberto called the consulate and found out that he needed a picture of himself and some form of identification. How could he certify his identity without

116

papers? The only person who could do it was Anna. Having called first, he visited her and explained that he needed a new passport and that he would be asked for identification.

"Could you possibly write a paper saying that you knew me in Genoa?" he asked. "I'm not sure what they want at the consulate."

"Of course," Anna said. "I lost my American passport on the Titanic, but I got a replacement. I don't know what the requirements are for other countries, but your records will show that your passport is still valid, so it will be easy to replace. I'll mail the letter to you," Anna said in a cheerful tone.

Roberto was curious about what had happened to the baby that had been found on Anna's doorstep, so he asked.

"Despite John's warnings I had become attached to the little one. It was not only me. Everyone here was fond of Irene—Josephine, Agnes, Mrs. Anderson, Tom, and even John thought that she was delightful. She was such a good baby," Anna said, wiping a tear from her cheek.

"But I knew in my heart that it would be selfish of me to keep her. I already had a baby, and my friends, Sally and Carl, were childless. Our church recommended them as adoptive parents, so I prayed and hoped that they would get the girl. That way I could see her once in a while. Sally came to our house often, and she learned how to care for the baby. Carl makes good money as a machinist, so there was no doubt in my mind that he could provide a home for both his wife and a child. They even liked the name, Irene, I had given her.

"But then two other couples showed up as potential adoptive parents. I didn't know them and I didn't take a liking to them, but I was afraid of letting anyone know except John. I told him that I would not give Irene to any other couple than our friends, Carl and Sally. If they couldn't have her, then we would have to keep her.

"Faced with the possibility that John and I would adopt the girl, the other two prospective parents backed out, and I got my wish. My friends, Sally and Carl, became Irene's parents. My heart ached when they moved her to their house... but I have Henry, and I hope that one day we will have a daughter of our own. Now, I look forward to seeing Irene grow up."

"Did you find out who the mother was?" Roberto asked.

"No, we did not. I still feel sorry for her. It must have been devastating to have to give the child away. It's a mystery how the mother was able to get both the basket and the suitcase here."

Roberto said that he might write a story about it, but that he would send it to Genoa where no one would recognize the facts. Anna said that Roberto could finally get his suitcase back.

As he held the suitcase in his hand, he thought of how much it had been through. Dirty, homeless men had fought and died for it, and after all that, it had held baby clothes.

When Roberto left, he and Anna wished each other Merry Christmas. Roberto didn't think that his Christmas would be 'merry' now that he no longer dated Julia. When he got home, he found that Anna had placed a wrapped Christmas gift with his name on it in the suitcase. Anna was a good person. She always thought of others. The fact that she had given the orphan baby to her friends proved it without a doubt. Before putting the suitcase away, he wiped the outside with a wet rag and gave the handle a forceful rub.

While Roberto waited for Anna's letter, he had his passport picture taken. A few days later, there was a letter from Anna in his mail slot. She had gone to the trouble to have Mr. Jones notarize her signature.

Roberto went straight to the photographer to pick up his picture. If the consulate accepted the letter from Anna, he had what he needed for a new passport. His steps felt lighter. His leg didn't bother him at all. He would be going home to Genoa.

While Roberto waited for his turn at the consulate, he read newspapers that were published in Italy. They were old, but they were the first papers from home that he had read since he came to America. He read about a young socialist by the name of Benito Mussolini. When Italy had declared war with Turkey in 1911, he had been arrested for pacifist propaganda. While he had lived in Milan, he was appointed the editor of the socialist newspaper *Avanti* and had become a forceful labor leader. His goal was to unite the proletariat and seize political power. Roberto brushed it off as impossible. He had heard of the socialist movement in the United States and Eugene Debs, who ran for president in 1912 as a candidate for the Socialist Party, but he doubted that the movement in Italy would go very far.

Having received his passport, which was a replacement for the one he had lost, Roberto again went to the Dutch restaurant. He wanted to tell Gretchel that he now had a valid passport, but he also wanted to ask her if she would go for a ride with him in his Ford.

The offer excited Gretchel. "Oh, would you take me out to the farm country?" she asked. "I haven't seen open fields since I came here."

"Of course, we can drive out in the country. I'd like to see the fields myself. When can you go?"

"I'm free tomorrow."

"All right, I'm a reporter now, so I'm also free," Roberto said.

"You're a reporter! That's fantastic," she said.

They agreed on a time and place to meet the next day. Roberto smiled. With Gretchel there was no pressure. They were just friends, and they had fun together.

There was no snow on the ground, and Roberto was thankful for that. He didn't know how to drive in snow. Ice would be even worse. He drove far enough so that they saw farm houses surrounded by fields.

"Oh, I see cows and horses!" Gretchel exclaimed. "We have so many animals at home. I miss Holland, especially at Christmas. It was so festive. Don't you miss Italy, Roberto?"

"Yes, sometimes I do." Roberto enjoyed listening to Gretchel's chatter, so he didn't say much.

Before they were ready to go back to the city, it started to snow.

"Oh, look at those big flakes, Roberto," Gretchel said. "Aren't they beautiful?"

"Beautiful yes, but I'm worried about getting home if it gets slippery."

"Then we better turn back," she said.

Roberto tried to turn the Ford around, but it slid into the ditch.

"Oh, my goodness, this is not good," Gretchel said. "We have to get out and push."

Knowing the limitations of his leg, Roberto said, "I think I better go for help at that farm."

"I'll go," Gretchel said. "You stay here."

Two tall and lanky fellows came to help. They asked Gretchel if she was Dutch.

"Yes, I am, are you?"

"Yes, we are Dutch."

"I haven't met any Dutch farmers in this country," Gretchel said. She acted as the mishap was a great adventure. The Ford was out of the ditch in two minutes.

"I don't think it would be wise to drive in the snow on those bare tires," one of the fellows said.

"But we need to get back," Gretchel protested.

"The weather report says that the snow will turn into rain this afternoon. You're welcome to wait it out at our house."

"Really?" Gretchel looked surprised. "Do you mean that you're inviting strangers into your house?"

"You aren't a stranger. You're Dutch. You said so yourself."

"And Roberto here's Italian. We're good friends in case you are wondering. He said that he would take me for a ride in the countryside."

"I think we should accept your hospitality," Roberto said to the men. "I'm sorry, but I don't know your names."

"I'm Marius, and he is Jorgen," Marius said, pointing to his brother. The men shook hands.

"Thank you both for rescuing us." Gretchel took off one woolen mitten and stretched out her hand to both boys.

"Come and meet our parents," Marius said.

When the boys' mother found out that Gretchel was born in Holland and spoke Dutch, she welcomed her with open arms and cooked a scrumptious dinner for them. Marius and Gretchel acted like they had fallen in instant love. Roberto spoke to the farmer and asked him questions about his occupation. Perhaps it could be another article. Time went fast, and no one noticed that it had stopped snowing. The snow had turned to rain. It was time for Roberto and Gretchel to leave.

Chapter 17

Just before Christmas 1913, Roberto came down with a bad cold. When Anna's dinner invitation to him and Anthony came, he called her and told her about his cold. He said that he was afraid that little Henry would catch it and politely declined. Anna said that her biological mother and her family would be coming from Stamford to celebrate Christmas with them.

Roberto thought about how the Sicilian at the café in Little Italy had coughed. He worried about having caught more than a cold from him. If he didn't get better soon, he had to see a doctor.

He and Anthony would celebrate Christmas by themselves. Anthony came home with a small Christmas tree and a few decorations. Roberto didn't feel well enough to go to mass, but Anthony did go with a girl who lived in one of the apartments he had painted. It was the first time Roberto had heard that he had a girlfriend.

"What nationality is she?" Roberto asked.

. "She's Italian and her name is Sophia."

"When will I get to meet her?"

"When you are over your cold."

In the afternoon, Anthony surprised Roberto by cooking Mama's Pasta *E Fagioli*. The apartment soon smelled of garlic sautéed in olive oil. Roberto watched his brother adding a can of tomato sauce and a cup of water. After a while he added the can of *fagioli* beans that Roberto had brought home from Little Italy. The *salsiccia* sausage simmered in a pan and the *ditalini* pasta boiled in a big pot. When the pasta was done, Anthony added it to the bean mixture, and flavored it with dried, hot pepper. He said that it would have been nice to have some fresh parsley. Before serving, he sprinkled a generous amount of parmesan cheese on top. Roberto cut the *salsiccia.* They were both hungry and thought that the food tasted delicious.

"Now, where is the dessert?" Roberto teased his brother as he finished the last piece of sausage.

"Sorry, but I don't know how to bake," Anthony said. "Instead I made rice pudding on top of the stove. Perhaps it will satisfy your sweet tooth."

"If it's anything like Mama's rice pudding, it's yummy," Roberto said. Tasting it, he had to admit that Anthony had done an excellent imitation.

"Where did you get the recipe?" he asked.

"I got several recipes from Mama while you were in the hospital. You haven't noticed until now that I can cook? I cooked while you hobbled around on crutches, and now you're laid up again."

"What would I do without you," Roberto said.

The two brothers toasted each other, *Buon Natale* and Merry Christmas! They opened their gifts from home and gave each other one gift—only practical things that they needed. Roberto opened the gift from Anna. It was a nice, warm sweater that he put on at once. Then they sat quietly and looked at their Christmas tree. Roberto looked at the Christmas card he had received from Julia. It didn't say much, but it made him think about last year's Christmas with her and her family.

Anthony broke the silence by saying, "I wonder if we'll ever see our parents again."

"If Mama was here, she would put a mustard plaster on my chest," Roberto said with a laugh.

"Don't laugh. It might work."

"If I get money from the state for the hurricane damage, and if Anna and John buy the beach house lot, I might go home for a visit next summer. I'm a little tired of America. Too many bad things have happened to me."

"I'll probably marry instead," Anthony said.

After the holidays, Roberto still coughed. It prevented him from teaching and taking classes. "I can't go on like this. I have to go and see a doctor," he told Anthony.

"You do that. He can give you medicine."

The doctor asked Roberto to cough while he listened to his lungs. After the examination, he cleared his throat and said, "I'm sorry, but you have contracted tuberculosis. We need to get you to a sanatorium."

The shock of hearing the word tuberculosis was enough to make Roberto's head spin. To learn that he needed to go to a sanatorium made it even worse.

"The disease is very contagious, and you could infect other people. If you're in a sanatorium, you'll get the care you need," the doctor said. "Your disease is not advanced, and with the right care you can get well."

Roberto understood. But how could he afford a sanatorium?

"Aren't those sanatoriums expensive?" he asked.

"We have two here in Boston. One is publicly funded, and you can stay there for free. Then we have a private one, but it charges."

Roberto didn't want to burden Anthony with paying, so he said, "I'll go to the public one."

"I'll arrange it as soon as possible," the doctor said. "If you're a smoker, I strongly recommend that you quit."

"I'm not a regular smoker, so I don't think it would be difficult to quit."

Roberto walked home in a daze. If the disease could spread by coughing, he knew that he had caught it from the

Sicilian in Little Italy. He remembered people in Genoa who had coughed and others had been afraid of them. *Now, I'm a pariah, an outcast. I must try to get well. I have to go to the sanatorium. I'll never win Julia back.*

He needed a cigarette to calm his nerves, but knowing that it was not good for his lungs, he threw his pack in a garbage can.

Telling Anthony was difficult. Roberto knew that it was sad news for his brother.

"You'll get well," Anthony said, but he looked devastated. "You can continue to write in the sanatorium," he said in an encouraging voice.

Roberto sold his Ford and packed some clothes, papers, and pens in his suitcase. He couldn't help thinking about what that suitcase had been through. He had still not written an article about it. He would bring his typewriter and hoped that the *Gazzetta* editor wouldn't mind that the manuscripts came from a sanatorium as long as he got articles. Roberto pictured how he would sit on a balcony with a blanket around his legs and type an article about tuberculosis while living in a sanatorium.

Roberto soon realized that the worst part about being in the sanatorium was seeing people die. Young people, who had come there with the same hope as he, did not get better. Their health deteriorated and they died.

Melinda was on her death bed, and Roberto sat by her side. He asked if she had any relatives who should know about her condition. "I have no one," she replied. "They're all dead."

Roberto wondered who would take care of her funeral, but didn't want to ask. As if reading his mind, Melinda said, "I've told the head nurse that I should be buried with my parents, and I gave the bookkeeper the money that will pay for the funeral." Turning away, she stopped to cough and catch her breath before continuing.

"I've seen you writing on your typewriter, Roberto. Could you please write a funeral notice for me? I've written down all the background information that you'll need. It's in this envelope." Melinda looked at Roberto with begging eyes.

"Yes, I will," Roberto promised.

"The phone number to the funeral home is in this envelope."

Roberto sat by Melinda's bedside. He heard how she stopped breathing briefly, but then took a few more labored breaths before the last gurgling sound ended her life. Roberto crossed himself, prayed for her soul, and cried for her and for himself. Would his life end the same way?

He took the envelope from her drawer and went to tell the head nurse that Melinda had passed away and that someone should call the funeral home.

"Were you with her when she died?" the nurse asked.

"Yes, I was."

"It was good of you to be by her side. Then she didn't have to die alone."

Roberto swallowed a lump in his throat and went back to his ward. He decided to write an article about Melinda and mail it to *Boston Globe* along with the funeral notice.

He was surprised to read about the reaction that his article had created. Dozens of people had showed up at Melinda's burial. The *Globe* had sent a photographer and published pictures of strangers laying down flowers.

Roberto's article also created unexpected benefits to himself. When Anna read it, she had Roberto transferred to the private sanatorium. Again, he was in debt to Anna for her mercy. The patients at the private sanatorium were in better shape. Many got well, and went home. He didn't have to see anyone die. Everyone had private rooms. They could also receive visitors.

Anthony came and gave Roberto two letters that had arrived in the mail. One was from the Commonwealth of Massachusetts. Roberto had been awarded compensation for the hurricane damage that had destroyed his beach house. A check was enclosed.

"What good is money when I can't enjoy it?" Roberto said.

"You'll get well and then you can enjoy it," Anthony said. "I'll deposit it in your savings account."

The other letter was from Anna. She hoped that Roberto was doing well. In closing, she asked if she and John could buy the beach house lot from him.

"You will get rich," Anthony said.

"Not rich, but when I get out, I can afford to go home to Italy. The air is better in Genoa. All the doctors say that it's very important to breathe fresh air. I've been thinking about booking a ticket on the Lusitania instead of the one I didn't use in 1912. You don't know this, Anthony, but Anna bought me a ticket on the Lusitania to get rid of me, but I fooled her and sold it."

"Is that right?" Anthony said. "Why didn't you use it? At least you could have visited us at home."

"I wasn't ready to go back then."

Chapter 18

In the late summer of 1914 war broke out in Europe. Roberto read the newspaper reports. On June 28, 1914, a young Bosnian student had shot Archduke Francis Ferdinand, heir to the throne of Austria-Hungary, and his wife in Sarajevo, and both died. One month later, Austria declared war on Serbia, which was suspected to have had something to do with the murder. Great Britain declared war on Germany on August 4. Austria-Hungary allied itself with Germany and the Ottoman Empire, while Great Britain, France, Russia, Belgium, and Serbia became allies. Italy and the United States were neutral in the conflict, and Roberto hoped that it would stay that way.

He continued to follow the news about the war from the sanatorium. The Germans advanced through Belgium with the goal of taking Paris, but in the beginning of September, the Allies stopped them at Marne. In November, the Allies stopped the German advance toward the English Channel at the first battle of Ypres. An average of two thousand men died daily on the western front, while thousands more were wounded or missing in action. The Germans fought on more than one front and won battles against Russia.

Roberto stayed at the sanatorium over the Christmas and New Year's holidays. His lungs had healed and he would soon be going home. The personnel at the sanatorium put up Christmas trees and decorated all the rooms except the bedrooms. Priests and ministers held worship services. They led the singing of hymns and administered Holy Communion. Roberto partook of it all. He prayed that his sins were forgiven. The holidays were as festive as anyone could expect away from home.

Anthony and Sophia visited him and told him that they would celebrate Christmas with her parents. Sophia was an attractive girl with high cheekbones, wide hips, and a big bosom. Roberto approved of Anthony's choice of a future wife. She would give him many healthy children.

Roberto felt well and had much to be thankful for. He thanked the Madonna for seeing him through the crisis. After New Year's and Epiphany, he was released from the sanatorium.

At home, he had a Christmas card from Gretchel waiting for him. He couldn't expect one from Julia because he hadn't written to her for over a year. He had nothing to offer her. Gretchel had become engaged to Marius and planned a summer wedding. She would move to the farm and enjoy the livestock that she had been so excited about. Roberto was happy for her. As for himself, he still planned to visit Italy in the spring. Anthony and Sophia had become engaged on New Year's Eve, and when they married, they would need the apartment for themselves.

Roberto had enough money to reimburse Anthony for room and board and pay for his trip to Italy. Still, he'd have a nice sum in his savings account. He began to write and send articles to the newspaper in his hometown. One of them was the story about the suitcase murders and the baby adoption. His family would enjoy reading it.

As Anna was ready to board the Lusitania, she saw posters reminding people that Great Britain and Germany were at war, and that the ship could be in danger of being attacked by German submarines. John, who was at her side to see her off, had not been in favor of his wife and son sailing to Europe during war time, but Anna's mother in Sweden was on her death bed, and he understood that Anna wanted to see her one last time. He knew that Germany had started to blockade Great Britain, but he didn't think that they would attack a passenger liner, and if they tried it, the Lusitania could move much faster than the slow subs that he had read about in the papers.

John carried his son when the passengers were told to board. Anna hesitated before stepping onto the gangplank. In the next moment, she fell to the ground. John handed the boy to the nurse, who stood next to him, and leaned over his wife. She had fainted like she did at their wedding. He helped her stand up and supported her. Her face was pale and her eyes hooded.

"I can't board," she said, lifting her eyes to look at John. Fear was stamped on her face.

"Is it because of the Titanic?" John asked.

"Yes and the posters." She lifted her hand to point to them. "I have a horrible feeling that something will happen to this ship."

"It's not likely, but if you're that afraid, you shouldn't go."

He held her until she had calmed down. Then he turned to Agnes, the maid. "You can still go if you want to, Agnes. It's up to you."

"I've promised my parents to come and visit them, and no one else seems to be afraid of boarding," she said while looking at the throng of people walking up the gangplank to the ship."

"All right, you can go. I'll cancel the other tickets," John said.

Josephine still held baby Henry.

"I'm sorry, Josephine, but you need to come home with us," John said.

"I'm glad. I'm scared. I've never been on a ship."

They waved to Agnes as she proceeded to board.

When Anna heard the news about the Lusitania it affected her deeply. The headlines read:

"Lusitania torpedoed. No word on casualties."

John came home at once to comfort his wife. He called the Cunard Line office, but could not get through.

"We have to wait until tomorrow, honey," he said clutching Anna and their son in his arms.

"Did God stop me from entering that ship with Henry?" she sobbed.

"We don't know why things happen the way they do," John said, stroking her hair.

"I'm so worried about Agnes. She wouldn't have been on that ship had it not been for me."

"She had the choice of not going, and she chose to go."

He cradled Anna in his arms and said that as long as they hadn't heard otherwise, they would cling to the hope that Agnes had survived. It's not your fault that she was aboard."

Anna thought about her sister Christina, whose body was never found, and her voice broke. "There is too much bad news. My mother is on her death bed and Agnes...."

"I know, honey. It's sad. But I'm so glad that you and Henry weren't on the Lusitania."

To cheer Anna up, he suggested that they go to the Cape. He wanted to show her the new Victorian house that he had built. It was almost finished.

"Oh, John, let's do that. When can we go?"

"We could go tomorrow. I just have to call the office and say that I'm taking a few days off. We can stay at the hotel in Falmouth."

"I'll tell Josephine to pack for us."

"I think she should come, too," John said.

They left in their Ford with John driving. There was still no bridge over the canal, so they ferried part of the way.

Josephine stayed at the hotel with the napping boy while John took Anna to the new beach house. She had seen drawings of it, but the sight of it overwhelmed her.

"Oh, John, it's so big and beautiful."

"Come inside and look at the interior, but be careful. There're nails on the floor. When the carpenters are done, I'll have Anthony do the painting. You can select the colors, honey."

"I think it should be white on the outside," Anna said.

"I think so, too. We have a view of the sea from all the front rooms."

"It's magnificent, John."

"Here's the living room and next to it the dining room."

Anna walked to one of the large windows and admired the view.

"The view is much grander than from the old cottage."

"That was my intention. The foundation is higher and the windows are larger."

"It's perfect. When will it be ready?"

"I'm aiming for the Fourth of July."

"I'm looking forward to it."

"Here's the kitchen. The carpenters are hanging the cabinets today."

"Oh my. It's as big as our kitchen in town."

"Let's go upstairs and I'll show you the bedrooms. There are five of them."

Anna followed John up the stairs.

"This room is ours," John said, opening the door to the largest room.

"It also has a view of the sea."

"Yes, and this is the children's room."

"We have only one child."

"I know, but I hope that in the future we'll have more."

They looked at each other and smiled. "I do, too," Anna said.

"The adjoining room is Josephine's."

"You have thought of everything, John."

"I showed you the drawings and you approved."

"Yes, but you made them a reality."

"Best of all, look at this splendid bathroom, honey."

"It is splendid, John."

"There are also two rooms for guests."

"Then I can invite Brita and Ole and the girls."

"Yes, it will be fun to have guests here."

"I agree, but now I want to go downstairs and sit on the porch," Anna said.

"We don't have any chairs yet."

"That's all right. I can sit on the steps. Perhaps we could shop for porch furniture."

"Good idea."

"I want you to come with me."

"Of course. I have nothing else to do."

Back at Beacon Hill, Anna read the *New York Times*. The victims of the Lusitania sinking numbered nearly twelve hundred, one hundred thirty-eight of them Americans. Captain Turner had survived and there would be an investigation. The Germans had admitted that their U-20 had fired a torpedo at the liner. Anna thought about the Titanic. That had been an accident, but this was a deliberate murder of innocent people. Would President Wilson declare war on Germany and join the Allies? So far he had insisted on neutrality. Anna wondered what war would mean for them. John might be called up.

Searching for the names of the victims, she found Agnes listed as being buried in Queenstown. It confirmed her worst fears. At least Agnes's parents will derive some comfort from knowing that their daughter had been identified and buried. Anna had goose bumps on her arms. She didn't want to read about the details of the torpedo attack, but her eyes were drawn to it.

One eyewitness reported that he had stood on deck and seen the Irish coast with its trees, rooftops, and church steeples when shrieking seagulls began to circle the ship. About forty-five minutes later, he noticed that the Lusitania turned away from the Irish coast. It had also slowed down. As the eyewitness looked out over the blue water on the starboard side, he saw a white streak coming toward the ship leaving a foamy wake behind. When it came closer, he realized that it was a torpedo. In the next moment, he felt and heard a terrific explosion that made the ship reel. The deck rose under his feet... a geyser of water and steam shot up.... Coal and wood catapulted into the air and began to fall on the people on deck. He recalled the smell of something burning and soot on his hands and clothes. His hat was covered with soot. While running for cover, he heard the hissing sound of steam. But worst of all was the sight of the lifeboat that burst into pieces when hitting the side of the tilting ship... and the shattered bodies floating on the water below. Once he was in a lifeboat, he saw the Lusitania go down, bow first. For a moment, the stern pointed almost straight up before the sea swallowed it up. The Lusitania went down in eighteen minutes. Anna knew it was less than the time it had taken the Titanic to sink. She also knew that her nightmares would return. She sat for a long while with the paper in front of her, praying for the victims and survivors alike. Then she wrote a letter of sympathy to Agnes's parents in Sweden. Her hands shook as she struggled to find the right words, and she had to start over several times.

Chapter 19

Roberto's voyage to Genoa turned out to be uneventful except for the news about the Lusitania sinking that he learned about while the ship took on coal in Liverpool. He swore under his breath when he read the posters and headlines. He scanned the names of the victims and saw the name of Agnes Pearson, a Swedish national. Could it be Anna's maid? He thanked the Holy Mother that he wasn't on that ship himself. The Germans had admitted firing the torpedo from a submarine. Now, the public opinion would surely be against Germany, he thought. Would it prompt the United States to enter the war?

As his ship approached the bustling Genoa harbor, Roberto stood on deck and took in the view of his hometown. It felt good to be home. He lifted his eyes to gaze at the Alps in the distance. The snow-covered tops hid in the clouds.

The town hugged the curve of the port at the Ligurian Sea and extended into the steep hills beyond Genoa's medieval walls that had defended the city through the centuries. The octagonal-shaped bell tower of the Church of San Donato rose above its surroundings. Built in the 11th and

12th centuries, it was a masterpiece of Genoese Romanesque architecture.

A few automobiles waited to take passengers and their luggage to the hotels. Roberto had only his suitcase and decided to walk home.

He passed the warehouses and cranes, the bars, cafés, and cabarets along the harbor, and walked into the medieval town with its ancient buildings. Everything looked smaller than he remembered. The people were all the same race with brown skin. Many looked dirty and unkempt. They reminded him of the poor Sicilians he had seen in Boston. The nuns walked in groups. The heat felt oppressive. He walked past the birthplaces of Christopher Columbus and the famous violinist Nicolo Paganini, who had given his first concert in Genoa at the age of nine. He passed the chapel where John the Baptist's bones were supposed to rest. He saw the marble palaces with their black-and-white striped facades, braided columns, and ornate front doors at a distance. He crossed the widest avenue in town, Via Garibaldi, but bypassed the winding *vicolo* passageways, where weeds grew in the cracks of the stone pavement and only carts could get through. The dense, tall buildings were painted in all sorts of colors. Compared to Boston, this ancient town appeared old and cramped. The odors of decay wafted toward him. The merchants offered their wares on the corners. The gamblers played their numbers games. Horses lumbered beyond the town walls and up the hills to the north.

At last, Roberto reached the dirt incline that led to his home nestled between mulberry and olive trees. Rows of grape vines grew on the terraces beyond. He drew in the aroma of roses, camellia, and orange and lemon trees. He feasted his eyes on the one-story sprawling home where his parents and younger sisters lived. The jacaranda trees that flanked the villa bloomed with flowers as blue as the sky. The dark green cypress trees formed a pleasing background. Roberto stopped for a moment and took in the picture that had stayed in his mind while he was away. The door was unlocked as usual. Opening it, he smelled the aroma of tomato sauce simmering on the stove. It was good to be home.

"Mama, I'm home."

"Roberto. I recognized your voice." His mother welcomed him with open arms. He thought that she was smaller than he remembered.

"Oh, my poor boy," she cooed. "You're home. You've been through so much, shipwreck, and bad lungs. I'll cook your favorite foods and you'll get strong again."

"You look good Mama. Where's Papa?" Roberto asked.

"He's in his workshop."

"I'll go and greet him then."

Papa stood bent over his work bench and didn't hear Roberto come in. Roberto thought that he had aged.

"Papa, it's me. I'm home," he said softly not to startle his father as he approached from behind.

"Oh, Roberto, my son, I'm so glad you're home." Papa Alfonso dropped his plane and hugged his boy.

"Welcome home, son."

"How are you, Papa? You look thin."

"I'm fine."

"How's business?"

"There's only so much one man can do."

"I envy you your skills, Papa."

"If you stay home, I could teach you. You were my apprentice at one time."

Roberto remembered how he had preferred to go swimming rather then helping his father in the shop. Now, he had a valid excuse.

"The doctors say that I should breathe fresh air. Sawdust and paint fumes won't be good for my lungs."

"You're right about that, son."

"Let's go and see what Mama is cooking. I suppose Jolanda and Liliana will be home for dinner?"

"Yes, of course. They're learning to sew at a fine establishment in town."

On his first evening at home, Roberto got reacquainted with his younger sisters, Jolanda and Liliana, both of whom had grown to become attractive young ladies while he was in America.

The next evening, his older sister, Isabella, and her husband, Alberto, and their children came, and so did his older brother, Salvatore, called Salvo for short, and his wife, Laura, and their children. The nephews and nieces had grown and new ones had been born since Roberto left. The adults doted on him, and the children were in awe of him. They all wanted to know about his heroic deeds and adventures and how Antonio was doing. Roberto basked in their love. He had missed his family and was glad to be home.

His mother introduced him to her friends as "My son, the writer." Everyone seemed to know about the articles that he had sent to the local paper. His mother had taken the clippings to church to show to her friends.

When Roberto went to collect his commission from the newspaper, he brought a new article that he had written aboard the Lusitania. The editor told him to continue writing. That was good news. He could use the extra money. He planned to send the same articles to *La Gazzetta* and then perhaps translate them for the *Boston Globe*. That way, he'd be able to collect from three different papers for the same story.

"We'll make a studio for you, Roberto," his mother said, "so you can write in peace and quiet."

His father had started to make a desk for him, but for now Roberto had to write at the dining room table. He sat down to write a letter to Anthony.

Please put the money that comes to me in my savings account, so I can have it when I return to Boston. I hope the war will be over soon and that we will not get involved, but for now, it seems unavoidable. After what happened to the Lusitania, I don't want to cross the ocean again in wartime. I saw the name of Agnes Pearson as one of the victims of the Lusitania sinking and wonder if she was Anna's maid?

A long account followed about the family and how good it was to be home.

Next, Roberto wrote a post card to Julia. He had thought of it for a long time and now it would be all right to let her know that he was in Italy. He could picture her waiting on tables at the restaurant as soon as school was out.

A few days later, on May 23, Italy declared war on Austria-Hungary. The nationalists—cheered on by Mussolini—had whipped the country into a fury, promising that they would liberate Trieste where the Italian nationals were being mistreated by the Austrians. Italy sided with Britain and France. Roberto sided with the neutralist Catholic Party and the prime minister in their opposition to the war. From what he could gather, the country was ill prepared for war.

Within days, the army conscripted Salvo, while Roberto, who was registered as having emigrated, escaped the call to duty. Salvo was a farmer, but had also worked for their uncle, who owned a fishing boat. Uncle Carlo now asked Roberto if he could work on the boat.

"The war will increase the demand for canned and salted fish, and we can deliver. You can pilot the trawler and help with the lighter chores," he said.

Roberto accepted the offer. It was obvious to him that he had to stay in Genoa until the war was over. He loved the sea, so why not. The sea air would be good for him.

Early the next morning when the trawler left the harbor in Genoa, Roberto stood at the wheel, feeling the wind on his face and breathing in the fresh air. His eyes peered through the morning fog. How much better than breathing the paint fumes in Boston apartments. The sun rose on the horizon and the fog dissipated.

When his uncle called out for him to lower the speed, it was time to lay out the nets. Roberto had experienced it all as a boy when he was set to throw back the small fish that nobody wanted, and that's what he would be doing now. The crew worked hard emptying the heavy nets. As soon as one net was pulled up, another went in. The process repeated many times during the early morning hours until the hull was filled with fish, mostly blue-fin tuna. Before noon, they returned to the harbor, where the fish merchants met them and came aboard. The haggling for the best price began. Most of the catch went to the canneries.

Roberto had the rest of the day off and it suited him fine. At home, his mama fixed a hearty meal for him. Then it was time for the best of all, siesta. He stretched out on the hacienda and yawned. If it hadn't been for the war, he would have been perfectly content. Now he worried about being conscripted. He had read the news and seen how ill equipped the Italian soldiers were compared to the enemy troops. Would he ever get back to Boston? Would he ever see Julia again?

As Roberto walked through the city of Genoa, it struck him that the tenement buildings looked like the ones he had seen in Little Italy, Boston. Above him, sheets and towels fluttered in the wind from the clotheslines strung across the narrow street. Barefoot children played on the sidewalks. It warmed his heart to see that they looked healthy and well fed, but would they have enough to eat if the war went on for a long time? The farmers had been the first to be called into service, and now there was a shortage of people to work the land. The factory workers had so far been spared from serving.

Roberto followed the news about the war on various fronts. The Germans had begun to use poison gas in April at the second battle of Ypres, Belgium. The war had spread to Africa and the Ottoman Empire. British troops had landed on the Gallipoli Peninsula, where they fought the Turks. Austrian troops fought the Russians at Galicia. President Wilson had declared, "There is such a thing as a man being too proud to fight." He was sticking to his principles of peace. One million troops of Italy's Second and Third Armies confronted the Austrians with the goal of taking Trieste. The Italian troops in the Alps had secured several peaks at the Plocken Pass, which gave them a good view of the Austrian positions.

One night, Roberto dreamt about the fighting with Austria. Italian soldiers propelled themselves up the steep side of the Alps to get behind the enemy to the north. They didn't have the warm clothes or shoes that they needed. Those who did not obey orders were shot. To enforce discipline, officers shot every tenth soldier in a lineup, disregarding the fact that they were not mutineers. Roberto woke up in a cold sweat. He realized that his dream had recaptured what he had read in the newspapers.

When a letter arrived from Anthony the family gathered to read it.

"What does it say?" Mama Lea asked.

Roberto got the honor of reading it and breaking the news that Anthony had married Sophia in July.

"Oh, my little Antonio is married," Mama said. "Didn't he send a picture? I want to see what Sophia looks like."

"He says that he will send a picture next time, Mama."

Anthony mentioned that the Whitmore's new beach house on the Cape was finished and that the family had moved in for the summer.

I painted the house on the outside and the inside. If Anna gives me a picture of the house, I'll send it to you. The newspapers have reported that the Whitmore maid died in the Lusitania sinking. She's buried in Queenstown. Mrs. Whitmore was booked to go on the Lusitania with her baby, the nanny and Agnes, but backed out in the last moment. Only Agnes went. Something happened with the lifeboat she was in. All the women and children in that lifeboat perished.

Roberto lifted his eyes from the letter to digest the news. He didn't know Agnes well, but he knew Anna and how badly she'd feel about it. Was it the thought of the Titanic that had prevented her from boarding? Whatever it was, he was glad that she was not on the Lusitania with her son. He had considered sailing on the Lusitania, himself, but had changed his mind on account of the war in Europe.

Roberto let out a long sigh and continued to read. Anthony wanted to know how Salvo fared in the war and if Roberto had been called up. The sad truth was that they hadn't heard anything from Salvo.

"I must write a letter right away and congratulate them on their marriage," Roberto said.

"I want to send them a wedding present," Mama said.

"I don't think it's a good idea," Roberto told her. "They might not get it as long as the war is going on."

"That's too bad; then we'll send them a letter for now."

Uncle Carlo stopped by for an unexpected visit. Roberto's father had been sitting quietly at the table as the others talked, but now he rose and gestured with his hands.

"Carlo, you came just in time to give me a hand. Come with me. Lea, too. Roberto, you stay here. I'll have a surprise for you."

Roberto's desk was finished.

"It's beautiful," Lea said. "Where are we going to put it?"

Lea ran her hands over the smooth surface, and her eyes lit up. "We'll move it to the parlor, the best room in the house."

"Do you really want to do that?" her husband asked.

"Yes, I do."

"Then let's move it," Alfonso said. "Carlo, pick up one end, and I'll take the other."

"Ready, Carlo? *Uno, due, tre!*"

Without warning Alfonso dropped his end of the desk.

"What's the matter, Alfonso," Lea yelled.

Alfonso clasped his chest. "Lea... doctor."

Carlo set down his end of the desk and looked with fear at his brother-in-law.

"He needs a doctor," Lea ordered as she bent down over her husband.

Carlo ran to tell Roberto that it looked like Alfonso had suffered a heart attack. Roberto started for the door when he realized that he didn't know who their doctor was anymore.

Turning back, he asked, "Where does he live?"

"He lives where he always lived. It's Doctor Flavio," Carlo said. "Hurry up."

Roberto knew the place and ran while praying that the doctor would be home. It was only at the end of the road.

"It's Papa Alfonso Cosentino. We think he has had a heart attack," Roberto said panting from the run.

"Is he conscious?"

"I think so.

"I'll take the carriage then," the doctor said. "You can go ahead, and I'll be along shortly."

Roberto walked at a slow pace to still his heart, praying that his papa wasn't dying. When he reached the house, he heard the doctor's horse trotting behind him. He waited for Dr. Flavio to arrive and directed him to the workshop.

"Where does it hurt?" the doctor asked Alfonso. Alfonso pointed to his chest.

After a quick examination, the doctor said, "We'll take him to the hospital. I have a stretcher in the carriage."

Carlo helped the doctor lift the patient onto the stretcher and into the carriage. Roberto stayed by his father's side while Mama Lea took a seat beside the doctor.

"Let me know how he's doing," Carlo said. "Sorry, I can't go with you. I have to get up before dawn. I think you should stay with your mother, Roberto. We'll manage without you tomorrow morning."

Chapter 20

While a hospital doctor examined Alfonso, Roberto paced the floor in the waiting room. Mama Lea sat on a chair and fingered her prayer beads, mumbling prayers. When a doctor appeared, she rose to her feet.

"How's my husband?"

"It appears that there is some damage to his heart, but unless something else happens, he should recover."

"*Grazie*, Doctor. May we see him now?"

"He's very tired, but, yes, you can see him for a few minutes."

Roberto and his mother stood by Alfonso's bed while the nurse checked his pulse and heartbeat. Roberto cast an admiring look at the blond nurse as she bent down by the bed. When she stood up, he saw that she was tall, almost as tall as he. She reminded him of Lydia and Anna. She wore the nurse's white cap on her blond hair that was pinned back at the neck.

"What's your name, *Suora*?" he asked.

"I'm *Suora* Tessa," she said. I'll be watching your father tonight. You can go home. He needs to rest."

"Thank you, *Suora* Tessa," Roberto said. "Come Mama, we'll go home. There is nothing we can do here. Papa is in good hands."

Lea was reluctant to leave, but Roberto took her arm and led her out. Quietly, they began the long walk home.

"If he hadn't tried to lift that desk, it wouldn't have happened," Roberto said.

"We don't know that, Roberto," Lea said.

Roberto went to the workshop and looked at his desk. It was beautiful. He wondered what else his father had been working on, but couldn't find a single piece. Had the war affected his business already? Was that why he had time to make the desk?

In the morning Lea wanted to go to the early mass before they went to the hospital.

"Come with me, Roberto, please," she asked. He hadn't been to church since he got home and agreed for his mother's sake.

He could see himself as the altar boy so many years ago. The priest already stood at the altar, singing the Latin liturgy. Roberto gave a monk one lira to light a candle for his father while he said a prayer and crossed himself. His mother said at least ten "Hail Mary's."

"Oh, Alfonso, you're awake," Lea cried as soon as they entered the hospital room. "How're you feeling, today, dear?"

"Much better," he said.

"You'll get well again. We need you. You're the bread-winner."

"The orders are not coming in, Lea."

"Oh, it's the war, it's the war," Lea complained. "When the war is over, you'll get orders again. You can take it easy until then."

Roberto walked the halls when he met Tessa.

"How's your father today, Mr. Cosentino? I just started my shift," she said.

"He's much better, thank you. You must have taken good care of him yesterday."

"Some heart patients recover well and some don't," she said. "He's lucky to have a son at home and not at the front."

"I just arrived from America," Roberto said.

As he looked into Tessa's blue eyes, his heart skipped a beat. She reminded him of Lydia Addison.

"You would have been better off over there, where they're not involved in the war."

"Perhaps."

Tessa rearranged the instruments on her tray. "As a nurse, I might be called to the front also," she said.

It surprised Roberto that women could be called to service, but, of course, they were needed to take care of the injured men.

"I have to go. Hope that your father gets well."

Roberto smiled and bowed to her. He admired her look as she walked down the hall, and wondered if she had a boyfriend.

Roberto made the workshop into a study. His father wouldn't need it for the foreseeable future. Having swept out the wood shavings and sawdust, he sat down by his desk and wrote a letter to Anthony and Sophia, telling them about Papa's heart attack. Then he wrote an article to *La Gazzetta* and one to the *Boston Globe* about the war that Italy fought—how the factory workers had been called to service and that the women had taken their places in the shops, and that they were beginning to experience shortages of certain foods and goods.

He knew that his family was lucky in that they had vegetables from their own garden and could eat as much fresh fish as they wished. Mama kept hens, so they had eggs. His sister-in-law worked hard to run the farm without Salvo. She could still provide them with some meat and flour.

When Mama Lea saw what Roberto had done to the workshop, she sent a servant to scrub the floor clean of the last speck of sawdust. Roberto liked the smell of wet wood and moved his bed into the shop. Now, he had his own place.

"If you're going to sleep in here, Roberto, you need curtains" Mama said. "I'll bring some old ones and you can nail them up." She told him how to do it so that the nails wouldn't show. Roberto had to admit that the curtains made his place look homier.

The next time he visited the hospital, his father's bed was empty. "Where is my father?" he asked the man in the nearest bed.

"They took him to the emergency room," the man said.

Roberto found Tessa and asked her what had happened.

"Your father had another heart attack, and it doesn't look good," she said.

Roberto's mood sank. Was this the end for his father? He had to go back home and get his mother.

He held his mama's arm as they entered the emergency room together. Tessa met them with the bad news. "He's very ill," she said.

Roberto hugged his mother. "Go and get the priest," she said.

The priest got there in time to give Alfonso Cosentino the last rites before he died. Lea made the sign of the cross and moved her beads as she prayed all the prayers she knew.

"I'll arrange for the funeral service," the priest told her.

"You can wear Papa's frock-coat for the funeral," Mama Lea told Roberto as they walked home. Roberto didn't like the idea, but it would save him money.

He walked around the neighborhood putting up posters that announced the death of his father. The posters gave the time and place of the funeral. People began to come to their home to pay respect to the deceased. The casket remained open.

At the funeral, Roberto felt very uncomfortable in his father's frock-coat and high hat. His mama had hired a horse-drawn hearse and carriages for the mourners. She was dressed in black with a long, black veil covering her head and face. Roberto's sisters wore the same attire, but their veils were not as long and heavy. All the relatives, neighbors, and friends of the family came to honor the deceased. The pallbearers carried the casket into the cathedral. When the service was over, they lowered it into the grave at the cemetery. Roberto thought about Lydia's funeral. He felt worse than he had in a long time.

The dinner at the Inn was livelier, but Roberto was relieved when it was all over. He had fielded many questions about his stay in America, his travel on the Titanic, and how he had avoided conscription.

Roberto went back to work at his uncle's fishing boat. In the fall, he helped his sister-in-law in the afternoons with the harvest. Mama had told him that he had to do it. She didn't know how much he hated that kind of work. When he tried to harness the mules, one mule kicked him in the groin.

"Ouch!" Roberto lay on the ground moaning in pain.

"I will not work with the mules," he told Salvo's fourteen-year old son. "Vito, you'll have to do it."

All the other workers in the fields were women, young boys, and older men. After a day's work with the crops, Roberto went to the beach. He sat in the sand and watched a group of young women approaching. Hey, there was Tessa. The others were probably also nurses. He liked the way Tessa looked in her bathing suit. Now, she put a swimming cap on her head to protect her hair. He waited until the girls had gone in the water before he went out on the pier and dove into the deep water. The girls watched him and applauded as he came to the surface. He swam toward them.

"Good evening, Signorina Tessa," he greeted the only girl he knew in the group. He didn't think he should address her as nurse in private.

"Good evening, Mr. Cosentino. That was quite a dive."

"I used to be a lifeguard."

"Then we're all safe here."

"It would be an honor to keep you safe, Signorina," Roberto said with a broad smile. Then he asked her if she wanted to swim with him.

"I'm not as good as you are," she said.

"I'll swim slowly," he promised.

Tessa kept up with him, but only if he floated on his back for long stretches.

"I'd like to get to know you better Signorina," he said. "Could we go for a walk after our swim?" What he really wanted to do was to kiss away the water drops on her face.

"If you call me Tessa? I'm not on duty."

"If you call me Roberto? Being as pretty as you are, I thought you had a boyfriend."

"No, not at the moment. How come you don't have a girlfriend, Roberto?"

"My mama wants to set me up with her friends' daughters, but I'm against it."

"I know what you mean." They both laughed. He hadn't laughed in a long time, and it felt good. He was glad that he had brought a clean shirt and pants to change into after the swim.

When they were both dressed, Roberto asked her, "Can I buy you a drink?" He admired her out-of-uniform looks. Her soft hair was combed in a flattering style without too much restraint. It was the golden color of the wheat he had harvested the same day.

"It sounds like something you would ask an American girl," she said. The memory of Julia flashed back in his mind. But Julia was far away, and he needed female company.

Roberto wasn't dressed to go to the hotel, and Tessa would probably have preferred to wear a hat, so he took her to a casual *restaurante*. He was confident that he had enough money for two glasses of wine, perhaps even a bottle.

The restaurant was empty, and the waiter seemed eager to take Roberto's order. They chose a table at the hacienda, where they had a good view of the setting sun. But Roberto had eyes only for Tessa. "*Salute*," he said and lifted his glass. "*Salute*," she responded. They sipped the wine and looked at each other. Roberto felt like he was drowning in Tessa's dark blue eyes.

"I'm sorry you lost your father," Tessa said.

"It went so fast."

Roberto realized that there weren't many men around to compete for Tessa's heart, but he hoped that she would like him, and only him.

"Next time, we'll eat here," Roberto said. "That is if you want to go out with me again."

"I can't say no to that."

Roberto accompanied her to her gate and kissed her goodnight.

"Such a sweet kiss," he said. "I want another one." He stroked her back.

"Maybe one. Then I have to go inside."

Roberto thought about Julia as he kissed Tessa.

"Thank you for a lovely evening. See you tomorrow, sweet Tessa."

Walking home, he wished that he could fall in love with Tessa.

Chapter 21

Anna and John had moved into their new beach house on the Cape for the summer. Over the Fourth of July holiday, they entertained Anna's birthmother, Brita, her husband, Ole, and their daughters, Ruth and Maria. They were all out sailing when Anna, who was three months pregnant, became dizzy. Brita offered to accompany Anna ashore. The expectant mother rested in the master bedroom when she called on Brita to come to her side.

"I have stomach cramps. Do you think it could be the baby?"

"Does it feel like contractions?"

"Yes, it does."

Brita looked thoughtful. "As a precaution, we should probably call a doctor. There're doctors here on the island, aren't there?"

"There are, but we haven't had to consult anyone yet. I think I should call my doctor in Boston and ask him for advice."

"That's a good idea, Anna. He might also be able to recommend a doctor here."

"I'm glad we had a telephone installed in the bedroom. John insisted on it."

"And it's right here on your night table. Perfect."

Anna asked the operator to connect her. Finally, the doctor's maid answered. She said that the doctor and his wife were out for a ride, but that they would be home at dinner time. The doctor would return the call as soon as he could. Anna gave her phone number and hung up the phone.

"How do you feel, honey?" Brita asked.

"I feel better right now, perhaps it's nothing." Anna sighed and closed her eyes.

Anna's maid, Emily, knocked on the door and asked if everything was all right.

"Mrs. Whitmore isn't feeling well. We're waiting for her doctor to call back. We'll answer when it rings."

"Let me know if you need anything."

"Thank you, Emily," Anna said from her bed.

They both jumped when the phone rang. Anna answered. She told Dr. Wilson what had happened, how she had experienced cramps, but that they had subsided. She just felt queasy. The doctor asked if she had done anything unusual, and she told him that she had been sailing with the family when she became ill. He gave her the name of a doctor in Falmouth and said that she should contact him if the cramps came back. Anna wrote down the name and number of Dr. Richard Cox.

She stood up and said that she had to go to the bathroom. Brita walked behind her and waited outside the bathroom. She heard Anna moan and opened the door. Anna was white in her face. "I hemorrhaged," she said. Brita looked in the bowl and saw blood, but only blood. She pulled the cord. No need to scare anyone else in the house. "Let's get you into bed."

Brita grabbed a couple of towels and helped Anna to her room. Having taken off the bedspread and folded back the covers, she placed the towels on the bottom sheet and eased Anna into bed.

"I'll call the doctor right away," Brita said and reached for the phone.

"I hope I don't lose the baby. I'm hoping for a girl."

Dr. Cox answered the phone himself. When he heard about the hemorrhage, he said, "Dr. Wilson has already called me. It sounds like a miscarriage. I'll call for an ambulance to take Mrs. Whitmore to the hospital. I'll meet her there."

Brita told him that she was Mrs. Whitmore's mother, and that she would be arriving with her daughter. Mr. Whitmore was out sailing, and might not be home in time, she said.

"Anna, Dr. Cox is sending an ambulance. He'll see you at the hospital. Do you have cramps again?"

"Some. This will spoil the weekend for everyone. I'm so sorry."

"Don't think about that, honey. I'll pack you a few things in case you need to stay."

"My lingerie is in my dresser," Anna said and pointed. "What's Henry doing? Is he still napping?"

"I'll check on him as soon as I have packed your things."

She came back saying that Henry was still asleep. Josephine came and asked if there was a problem.

"We'll take Mrs. Whitmore to the hospital," Brita said. "Tell Henry that his mommy will be back as soon as she can."

Neither Brita nor Anna wanted to say the word miscarriage. It was up to the doctor to do that. The ambulance arrived at the same time as the family returned. John came running with fear in his face.

"Who is it? Is it Anna?"

"Yes. She's not well," Brita said.

"I'm coming with her," John said, as he saw Anna being carried out on a stretcher. "You need to stay with your family, Brita."

"All right, but call us as soon as you know something, John."

"I left Ole to secure the boat, but I think he knows what to do," John said.

Brita saw the ambulance drive off. She then walked slowly down to meet her family by the dock.

Everyone felt subdued. Even the children were quiet.

At the house, Henry was awake asking for his mom. Brita held him for awhile before asking the girls to take him upstairs and play with him. The maid asked when she should serve dinner.

"Dinner will have to wait a little longer," Brita said.

She answered the phone when it rang. It was John. He said that they should go ahead and have their dinner. He'd stay in the hospital until Anna was asleep. He would take a cab to the house.

"What did the doctor say?" Brita asked.

"The doctor said that she'll be all right, but she lost the fetus here in the hospital."

"I'm sorry, John. I know that you feel bad, but she can have more children."

"Yes, I hope so," he said.

Over dinner, Brita told the girls to describe their sailing trip. They had had the time of their young lives. Ole said that he had taken the tiller for a while and tied up the boat after the sail.

"I'm almost ready to be a captain," he joked. Then he told them that he remembered sailing with his dad between Kalmar and Öland in Sweden when he was a little boy.

"But sailing here was an amazing experience," he said. "Paul would have loved it," he added.

"Paul is on a big ship, a Navy cruiser. Where is he now, Dad?" Maria asked.

"The last we heard he was in the Caribbean."

"Where is the Caribbean, Dad?"

"It's to the south of the United States, Maria."

"Is it warm there, like here?"

"Yes, it's even warmer."

"Do you think Paul gets to go swimming?"

"Yes, I'm sure he does."

"When is he coming home?"

"Maybe he'll be home for awhile over Christmas."

"I hope he will. Then I'll give him a present."

"If he doesn't come home, we can send him presents. They'll get to him wherever he is."

"That's good. Can we have ice cream now?" Maria asked. "Anna said that we could have ice cream for dessert."

Maria had lifted the spirits of the family. She didn't understand what had happened—just that Anna wasn't feeling well.

"Will Anna get ice cream in the hospital?"

"I don't think so, sweetie. Ice cream is a special treat. After the dessert, I think you should go to bed. You must be very tired after a full day in the sun," Brita said.

"Yes, Mama, I'm tired," Maria said, yawning, but she licked her lips when she saw the big bowl of ice cream in front of her.

When John came home, he asked Ole and Brita if they could stay another day. Brita left it up to Ole as he was the one who worked.

"If John wants us to stay another day, we will," Ole answered. "When do you think Anna will come home?"

"I don't know that yet."

Brita asked if she and Ruth could come along and visit Anna the next day.

"I think that Anna would welcome it. She'll need cheering up. She now fears that she'll never have the daughter she wished for."

Ruth took the opportunity to look around at the hospital. Since they were in the maternity ward, she looked at the newborn babies. In the evening at dinner, she had made up her mind.

"I want to become a nurse," she said.

"I think that's a very good idea," her father said. "You can start nursing school any time."

Chapter 22

With fewer and fewer young men available to date the women, Roberto had a big advantage—unless a warship docked in the harbor and the uniforms attracted the girls. If he were to register for any of the services, it had to be with the Navy.

The American and British tourists who used to stay at the hotels during the winter months would not return. The hotel and restaurant business would suffer as a result. The foreign ships that docked in the harbor were warships, British and French, loading salted fish to take to the African theater. Roberto often saw Italian troop carriers take on soldiers going to the front, and wondered how long he'd be safe.

He still dated Tessa, and they felt closer every time. He had taken her to the hotel for dinner. She had met his mama and younger sisters. Tessa was the main reason he didn't want to enlist.

Then one day everything changed. The recruiting officer contacted Roberto and asked why he wasn't in the service.

"I have had tuberculosis," Roberto said.

"But you look well now. I'll send you to a doctor, and if he says you are fit to serve, you better enlist. Otherwise, we'll conscript you to go to the front."

The doctor said that Roberto would not be strong enough for the Infantry, but that the Navy would be all right for him.

Roberto strolled along the harbor imagining being on one of the ships. When he saw the hospital ship, Italia, with the red crosses painted on its side, he boarded and asked if he could enlist.

"I'm fluent in English. I'm a reporter and translator. I'm an expert swimmer, diver, lifeguard, and sailing instructor," he rambled. Still, he had left out commercial trawler pilot.

The officer smiled. "We need translators. Here's a test for you," he said as he handed Roberto a paragraph written in English.

"Read it and tell me what it means."

Roberto started to read but was interrupted. "Don't read it aloud and don't translate the whole thing. Just tell me what it means."

Roberto complied.

"Good. Your rank will be Petty officer, Third Class. You'll address me as lieutenant. Here is an instruction book. Learn the ranks."

"Aye, aye, lieutenant."

"What's your name and date of birth?"

Roberto answered all the questions and signed the paper.

"You'll get only two weeks of training. Then we sail."

"Aye, aye, lieutenant." Roberto stood up and saluted the officer.

His mother cried, but it couldn't be helped. "It's better that I join the Navy than I should be sent to the Alps," he said.

"I know," his mother cried. "I haven't heard from Salvo. He doesn't even know that Papa died. I don't know where Salvo is."

"He might have gotten our letters even though he hasn't been able to answer."

"I hope so."

"You'll always know which ship I'm on, Mama."

"That's one good thing."

"My sisters will look after you while I'm gone."

"God bless you, son. Write as often as you can."

"I will," Roberto promised. "I'll go and say goodbye to Tessa now, Mama."

Although Tessa had suspected that Roberto would be drafted sooner or later, it was a shock to her that he would leave that soon. It was hard to say goodbye. She admitted that she had grown fond of him. They kissed like they would never see each other again.

"I'll worry about you," she said.

"I'll be all right," Roberto said. "A hospital ship is the safest ship I can be on."

"Will you write to me?"

"Yes, I'll write, and you can always write to me in care of l'Italia. I'll miss you and I promise to answer."

"Don't forget me then when you see other women."

"No, I won't forget you. I won't see any other human beings than men. Most of them will be injured soldiers."

"I wish they would enlist female nurses," Tessa said. "Then I could be on the same ship."

"As far as I know, the Italian Navy has only male nurses or medics, at least on the ships. But that might change."

"When do you think you'll be back?"

"I've no idea, but I hope to be able to come home to my family and my sweetheart once in a while."

"What will you do after the war, Roberto? Will you return to America?"

"I don't even know if I'll have that choice." Roberto knew that it was evasive answer, but it was the best he could give. He thought about his bout with tuberculosis and realized that he should tell her. She was a nurse, and she would understand. He said that he had had a slight case of tuberculosis and that he had been in a private hospital in Boston and received the best of care.

"Then I'd think you're immune to the disease," she said. "It's not a bad thing."

"I passed the health examination for the Navy."

"That's good."

They stood quietly and held each other.

"I think I'm in love with you," he said.

"I'm in love with you, Roberto."

"Wait for me, darling. Don't go and marry anyone else."

"And who would that be? There aren't any men left to marry. I'll wait for you."

"That's a comforting thought. I'm sorry, darling, but I need to go. I report for training early in the morning."

"*Boun viaggio, mio caro.*"

They waved to each other until they were out of sight. He was not the only soldier who left a sweetheart behind.

Petty officer Roberto Cosentino lined up for inspection in his white uniform. This was something new to him, but he fell into his role. As a translator and would-be reporter, he sat in on the officers' briefing. They were headed for the Dardanelles and the Gallipoli Peninsula. The Ottoman Empire had allied itself with the Central Powers. Australian and French troops had been unsuccessful in their efforts to capture the capital of Constantinople. The objective of the Allies had been to open a supply route to Russia because Germany and Austria-Hungary blocked Russia's trade route to Europe. The Ottoman Empire controlled the Black Sea.

"Our mission is to evacuate a portion of the more than twenty thousand sick and wounded British soldiers at Gallipoli and bring them to hospitals in Malta and Egypt. The evacuation has to be carried out in the cover of darkness," the captain announced. "Here is the briefing. Read it carefully. Dismissed."

With the course set on the Aegean Sea, they would pass through the strait between Sicily and the southern tip of Italy and round Greece before they arrived at their destination. Roberto would enjoy the long voyage that left him mostly idle before they took the injured soldiers aboard.

All the doctors, medics, and orderlies had to take a crash course in English. Roberto was selected as one of the teachers. The medical terms that he had to learn were in Latin, so he managed well.

In the evening, Roberto stood on deck and looked at the starlit sky that cast a shimmer on the calm sea. It was beautiful and peaceful. He was at a safe distance from the war, but he knew that German submarines might lurk below the surface.

Roberto thought about his intimate relationship with Lydia on the Titanic. He didn't want Tessa to board a ship. It might be a bad omen.

Chapter 23

The Whitmore family was back in Boston. Anna had recovered from a miscarriage, but still felt sad. The doctor had said that they would have to wait six months to try for another child. She was playing with Henry when Tom came with a yellow letter in his hand that she recognized as a telegram from Western Union. Anna immediately knew what it would say. She prepared herself for the news while she opened it.

"Mama died this morning." That was all it said.

She wished that she could have called Sweden. Now, she had to wait for the letter that she knew would follow. Her father, the florist, would make a wreath that would be from them. It would have broad engraved silk ribbons in the American colors. One ribbon would say, *Vila i Frid.* (Rest in Peace.) The other would have her and John's names inscribed, and "Henry" in smaller script.

Anna felt the sting in her eyes, but she had to remain calm for the sake of Henry.

She would not be at her mother's funeral, but she could picture the grave covered with flowers. That would be the same plot where they had put up a memorial stone for Christina, who perished in the Titanic disaster. Her body was not there, only the marker. It still hurt to think about it. And now her Mama Ellen was gone. It would be so lonesome for her dad. And Erik would miss his mother. But she was glad that her parents had been blessed with two children of their own after they had adopted her. How would Papa and Erik manage without Mama? Anna's only consolation was that her mother's suffering was over.

John came home, and as soon as he saw Anna, he knew that she had received sad news. She sprang into his arms, and then the tears came.

"So, so honey, let me put down my briefcase and we'll talk about it."

Anna felt better after she had cried for a while and shared her feelings with John.

"I've a little news myself," John said.

"What can that be?"

"Anthony told me today that Roberto has joined the Italian Navy."

"That's big news. But Italy is in the war isn't it?"

"Yes, but Roberto is on a hospital ship in the Mediterranean, so he'll probably be safe."

"I hope so," Anna said. "I care about him."

"Of course you do. Another piece of news is that Anthony and Sophia are expecting their first child."

"I'm happy for them," Anna said. Her lip began to quiver. The thought of babies did that to her.

When the letter came from her father, she read it with great interest several times. She learned the details of the funeral and studied the obituary. It was printed within a black frame and had a black cross above her mother's name. Everything was centered, even the date of death and the funeral. After her father's name, it read Anna and John, followed by Henry in smaller print, and then the last survivor, Erik. A hymn was printed in italics. Anna read the familiar hymn aloud several times, and in her mind, she could hear it being played and sung at the funeral service.

Blott en dag, ett ögonblick i sänder (Day by day, a moment at the time.) Her father and brother would be seated in the first pew with the other relatives behind them. In a way, she felt that she was there with them.

When she read the last part of her father's letter, she cried. Her father wrote that he was lonely and that he wanted to return to America after the war. "I think it would be good for Erik," he wrote. About the consequences of the war, he wrote:

The shortages are terrible here now. Everything has gotten so expensive. People living in the countryside can hardly get any kerosene for their lamps and if they can get it, the price is prohibitive for many. I'm glad that we live in the city and have electricity. I know it will be better when the war is over. Still we have to be thankful that we are not fighting the war. It's worse in other countries. I feel for the soldiers on all sides. Half a million men killed for nothing. They just keep killing each other without making any territorial gains. It's difficult to see an end to it. The only way out is probably that the United States tips the scale for the Allies.

Anna thought about that last sentence. If the United States joined the war, John would be called up. So would the other younger men she depended on. Her chauffeur, Eddy, would have to go, and perhaps also Ray, her gardener. Anna knew a few things about gardening, but she didn't know how to drive. Perhaps she should learn. When she suggested it to John, he said, "We'd have to get a self-starting automobile first. I don't want you to strain yourself by hand-cranking as we have to do with the Ford. I've heard that Cadillac has a self-starting car. I'll look into it."

John traded the old Ford Model T for a Cadillac, and Eddy began to teach Anna to drive. She was very excited till she found out how difficult it was to release the clutch at the right time. That beautiful Cadillac bucked like a horse when Anna was at the wheel. "You'll get used to it, Mrs. Whitmore," Eddy said. And she did. In the beginning, Eddy was at her side whenever she drove, but gradually, she began to take the Cadillac out by herself. People stared at her. Why does she have to drive? Doesn't she have a driver? But Anna liked being independent. Besides, it had given her a reason to get out more often. She drove to the church, and she drove to her charity events. Other than that, little Henry took up most of her time.

When she read the *Boston Globe,* she always looked for articles written by Roberto. Sometimes John brought home the *New York Times.* She read that the French forces had defended Verdun on the eastern border to Germany since the beginning of the year without any decisive victory. All they had been able to do was to stop the Germans from capturing the Allied fortifications. It was a senseless back and forth fighting with only one result, hundreds of thousands of dead soldiers on both sides. British troops had been trying to take Constantinople since April, and still hadn't been successful. The Turkish defenders had repelled the attacks time and again. The Italians had fought the Austrians for a long time and lost thousands of men without any lasting gains. The Germans used their dangerous submarines whenever they could. Russia fought Germany on the Eastern front. The war had spread to Africa. Escalation upon escalation. The headlines were all about the war.

Anna looked at the entertainment page. She would like to see one of those new-fangled silent movies with movie stars from Hollywood, but she didn't find anything that interested her.

She decided to call Brita. The fact that Brita had a phone was thanks to Anna. But it wasn't entirely unselfish because Anna wanted to be able to call her.

Anna began by inquiring about the children. Ruth was doing well in nursing school. She lived in a dormitory at the hospital where the students got hands-on training.

"Oh, Brita. I've sad news. Mama Ellen is...." Anna couldn't say the word "dead." "Gone," she finally said.

"I'm so sorry. It must be hard for you."

Anna wiped her tears away with her hand. There was a long pause.

"It's especially difficult because I didn't get to see her as I had planned," she finally said.

"I can understand that. I'm here for you if I can be of help."

"Do you think that you could come for Christmas?"

"I don't know. It depends on how much of a leave Paul will have."

"Of course."

"How about Thanksgiving then?"

"We'll be together with Ole's family then. I'm sorry."

"That's all right. We might invite John's parents."

"Why don't you come here for a visit, Anna? You can take Henry with you on the train, can't you?"

"Yes, I'd love to. I've learned to drive, but I wouldn't drive that far."

"You've learned to drive! You're a modern woman, Anna."

"When can I come, Brita? I'm already looking forward to it. All this news about the war is so depressing."

"You can come anytime you want, honey. Just let me know when."

When Anna had hung up, she thought about the time she had found out that she was adopted and started to look for her birthmother. She had been incredibly lucky to find her. Now, even though her mama in Sweden had passed away, she still had her birthmother.

Anna walked in the garden and chatted with Ray, the master gardener.

"How old are you, Ray?" she asked.

"I'm 35," he said, casting a curious look at her.

"Then you would probably escape military service if we go to war."

"Well, that depends on how long the war lasts."

"What do you mean?"

"They would call up the younger men first, but if more soldiers are needed, I'd have to serve. Are you worried about who would take care of the garden, Mrs. Whitmore?"

"I suppose it's a small worry compared to the war."

"Eddy has been my helper, especially since you learned to drive, Mrs. Whitmore, but he's younger and would probably be called up among the first."

"My father in Sweden wrote that they need the United States to tip the scale in the war for the Allies."

"It's probably true, but President Wilson prefers that our country remains neutral."

The dog came up to her and licked one of her hands. She patted his head.

"I suppose you want to go for a walk, Tramp," she said. "I've been neglecting you." As she said goodbye to Ray, she thanked him for taking care of Tramp while they were at the Cape.

"Any time, Mrs. Whitmore. I like your dog."

Walking Tramp felt like old times. She used to walk him every day. She thought of Roberto, who had also walked the dog. He was already in the war zone on the other side of the Atlantic.

It wasn't often that Anna brought up the subject of war, but now she felt that she needed to talk to John about it.

"Don't you think, John, that our country should prepare for war in case we are attacked?" she asked him.

"I don't think that the Germans will attack us, honey. They're too occupied in Europe."

"But their submarines could start torpedoing our ships, like they did with the Lusitania."

"If they do, then I think that President Wilson would react."

Anna decided to visit Sally and little Irene. It would stop her from thinking about the war for a while.

Chapter 24

The hospital ship Italia sailed into the beautiful Bay of Naples and passed the picturesque Ischia and Capri islands, separated by the deep blue water. Across the bay to the south lay the low hills of southern Italy and the volcanic Mount Vesuvius. When the ship came closer to the harbor, Roberto saw grapes and citrus trees growing on the slopes behind Naples. Church steeples dotted the city. He wished to see more of Naples, but this time they were only to take on coal.

While sailing through the Stretto di Messina that separated Sicily from the mainland, Roberto wondered if the Sicilians here were as poor as the ones he had met in Boston's Little Italy. Allied warships crowded the passage, and ferries crossed the strait. Mt. Etna towered over Sicily's mountainous and hilly landscape. Goats and sheep grazed in the valleys. It struck Roberto that if the world had been at peace, he would not have had the opportunity to see this part of Europe. A whole new world opened up before the crew on the hospital ship.

It surprised Roberto to see two giant liners painted white with red crosses on their sides steaming toward the Greek island of Lemnos. One of them was as big as the Lusitania. He couldn't read the name, but he wondered if it could it be the Mauretania. A passenger liner like that could probably carry three thousand injured soldiers. Behind her came another big liner, also painted as a hospital ship. These giant ships were too large to anchor closer to the mainland.

As l'Italia approached the Dardanelle Strait and Gallipoli, Roberto saw many other large, white-painted hospital ships waiting at a safe distance from the coast.

In the dark of the night, ferries brought the injured soldiers from Suvla Bay to l'Italia. All medical personnel stood ready to receive and care for them. Some troops were no longer alive. They had died on the small boats that took them to the hospital ship. Roberto was there to take notes before they were carried to the hull. The dead soldiers' families had to be notified. Many of the Brits were Australian and New Zealanders and often difficult to understand. Most of the troops were covered with lice and had to be deloused. Orderlies threw the infected clothes overboard. The soldiers were not only injured, they had illnesses ranging from dehydration and dysentery to typhus and tuberculosis. The doctors quickly sorted them according to the care they needed.

The medics assisted in the operating room where doctors cleaned wounds and amputated limbs. All the patients were young, and doctors expected most of them to live. But there were those who succumbed to infections. Roberto wiped sweat from his face. He didn't know if he could stand watching another amputation. An orderly called on him to translate what one patient was trying to say.

"Do you want us to notify relatives?" Roberto asked.

Nodding, the man motioned to Roberto to come closer. When he whispered the name of his father and home town, Roberto wrote them down.

"We'll send a message to your father. What do you want it to say?"

"Tell him I love him and Mother."

"We will relay the message."

Roberto put his hand on the man's chest, and felt his heart stopped beating.

A doctor checked for a pulse. There was none. "He's gone," he said. "He's the second man who has died under my care."

"But you have treated many more, and they are alive."

"Yes, thank God for that."

Roberto was through for the day. He would be back early in the morning, starting over again. It would be the same for several days. A burial at sea took place before they arrived at the British crown colony of Malta.

They docked at Valletta, the British Naval Base, where half of the patients would disembark. Some men were able to walk on crutches, while others were carried ashore in the balmy weather. Roberto took the opportunity to go ashore for a few hours. He heard Italian, English, and the native language, Maltese, spoken as he bought fresh citrus fruit and grapes that had grown on the terraces behind the city. He bought Italian and English newspapers. Scanning the pages, he searched in vain for news about the evacuation of troops from Gallipoli, but concluded that since all the troops had not yet been evacuated, the papers could not write about it. From the English paper he learned that the British passenger liner, the Mauretania, Lusitania's sister ship, had been converted to a hospital ship, as had the Aquitania. Those must have been the huge ships he had seen earlier by the island of Lemnos.

The work aboard eased as they continued to Egypt with the rest of the injured men. No one from l'Italia was allowed to go ashore in Alexandria. That's where the last patients left the ship for transport to a military hospital.

Egypt had belonged to the Ottoman Empire until the start of the war in 1914, but when Turkey sided with Germany, Great Britain had made Egypt into a protectorate. British warships prevented the enemy from using the Suez Canal. Roberto understood that Egypt was a poor country, but an important base for the Allies.

The captain's briefing said that as soon as the injured men had been transferred, the ship would take on provisions and return to Gallipoli. Their mail would be picked up by an

Italian ship anchored beside l'Italia. Roberto hurried to write a letter to Tessa and one to his mother. Then he watched as a crane began to lift big crates from the deck and swing them over to their ship.

They would celebrate Christmas aboard with no injured men to care for. On the day before Christmas Eve, the expectations rose as they all could smell the heavenly aroma of ham and sausages. When all the officers and medical personnel had gathered in the dining room, a priest read a passage from the Bible and wished everyone a blessed *Buon Natale*. The captain invited them to go to the decorated buffet table and help themselves to a variety of smoked meats and cheeses, and that was only the beginning. Warm food and wine followed. When the dessert was carried in, everybody's stomachs were full. They were not going to be filled until Christmas Day as a 24-hour fast always preceded Christ's birthday.

Roberto waited for mail from home. There had been none at Malta, and he was anxious to hear from his family and from Tessa. He talked with the other crew members, and they, too, were lonesome for their families. Roberto had seen mail sacks being hauled aboard and expected that the mail would be handed out the next morning.

Everyone attended a mandatory Christmas morning service aboard, followed by musical entertainment. The old Christmas carols lifted the mood of the crew. Best of all, a man dressed as *Babbo Natale* called out the names of the lucky ones receiving packages or letters. Roberto jumped as his name was called. He got two small gifts and also letters. The first gift was from his mother and siblings. It contained a pen set. His mother had printed a note that said in misspelled Italian, "I know that you love to write, son, so please use these pens to write to us. May God be with you, my dear Roberto, Love, Mama." His siblings had enclosed short messages. The other gift was from Tessa, and it contained stationery with his initials. He tucked the enclosed letter in his pocket to read later when he was alone. Instead he read the letter from his sister-in-law, Laura.

The rationing is now so severe that we can hardly get any sugar. We wanted to make candy and chocolates and send to you and Salvo, but it's impossible. We hope that you have more than we have and that you'll enjoy your Christmas in spite of everything. Most of all, we wish that you'll soon be home and that the war will be over. I got a letter from Salvo. He's alive but ill. When he wrote he was in sick bay. He said that he had not been able to write from the front. Mama Lea is all right, but it's difficult for her to adjust to being a widow. The children and I are well, thank God. We hope that you are, too.

It warmed Roberto's heart to learn that everyone at home was well and that they thought of him. He prayed that Salvo would get well from whatever ailed him.

The spirit of Christmas was broken when the warning sounded. "Mine sighted portside." Crew members quickly disarmed the mine, and they could proceed. It didn't mean that they were in the clear. Italy was at war with Germany. Roberto learned that Austro-Hungarian saboteurs had sunk the Italian battleship Benedetto Brin with four-hundred fifty lives lost.

He sat in the small cubicle assigned to him for his translations and writing when he opened Tessa's letter. She wrote that his absence had made her realize how much she cared for him. She said that she had hoped that he would be home for Christmas. If not, she expected a letter from him. She, too, mentioned the food shortages. She ended the letter with, "I miss you. Write as often as you can. Love, Tessa."

Roberto didn't think that his letter would reach her before Christmas, but it wasn't his fault. He hadn't sent her a Christmas gift either. If they ever got to a port where he could buy something suitable, he would send her a gift.

In early January, 1916, l'Italia was back at Gallipoli to evacuate injured troops from Cape Helles. The British had successfully removed forty thousand troops and the final evacuation of soldiers would take place as soon as the injured men had been moved to hospital ships. This was strictly confidential information. A German submarine, U-11, had captured an Italian hospital ship, King Albert, at San Giovanni di Medua. If Tessa read about that she would be concerned.

Returning to Malta, Roberto read about the successful evacuation of British troops from Gallipoli in the newspapers. A total of eighty thousand troops, five thousand horses and mules, two thousand vehicles, and two hundred guns had been ferried out at night to the waiting ships. To fool the Turks, the British had rigged up self-firing guns that went off at intervals. Lastly, the Brits detonated their ammunitions depots. The generals had estimated that they would lose half of their force, but the evacuation was carried out without a single casualty. Roberto had read dispatches from the captain throughout the journey, but this was the first time he saw the final results of the British evacuation from Gallipoli. The campaign had not come without a price. The British and French had suffered a quarter of a million casualties and the Turks about the same. The Ottoman Empire came out the victor.

Half of l'Italia's injured troops disembarked the ship at Malta while the other half was to continue with them to Genoa, where Roberto presumed that they would be transferred to British ships. Roberto looked forward to a two-week furlough.

He went to surprise his mama first.

"I have missed your cooking, Mama," he said. "You're the best cook I know."

"You're just saying that to flatter me."

"No, I really mean it. May I bring Tessa to dinner?"

"I knew you were up to something. But that's all right. I'm glad you are home, and I'll cook dinner for us and Tessa."

"*Grazie*, Mama."

Roberto went to meet Tessa, who was just as surprised to see him as his Mama had been. They went to a park where they kissed and held each other.

"Mama has invited you to dinner, sweetheart."

"Oh, then I should go home and change. You look so good in your uniform, Roberto."

"You're fine as you are in your uniform."

Roberto compared Tessa to his sisters, Jolanda and Liliana. Their olive skin, dark hair and eyes, contrasted to Tessa's light complexion. The young women talked about their chosen professions. Jolanda and Liliana were still learning to sew.

"It's something that will be useful to them even after they marry," Mama Lea said.

The girls stood ready to help their mother serve dinner.

"In honor of Roberto's homecoming, we're having chicken today," Mama Lea said.

"Poor chicken. He had to lose his life because I came home," Roberto mused.

"Is that basil that I see in the pasta?" Tessa asked.

"Yes. I have lots of basil in my kitchen garden, and soon I'll have fresh asparagus," Mama Lea said. "You have to come back then, Tessa."

"I love asparagus," she said. "You're a good cook, Mrs. Cosentino."

"Anthony is a good cook also," Roberto said. "He's using your recipes, Mama."

"Is he really? I doubted that when I sent them to him. Of course, I don't use recipes myself, so I had to cut them out from a magazine," she said with a hearty laugh.

She looked at Tessa and asked, "Do you know how to cook, child?"

"I'm sorry to say that I don't know much about the culinary art."

"If Anthony can learn to cook, so can you, my dear."

Tessa asked Roberto's sisters if they could cook, and they said that since their mother was a fantastic cook, they didn't get much of a chance to practice.

After dinner, he took Tessa to the workshop and showed her the desk that his father had made for him.

"It's beautiful, Roberto. Are you planning to do any writing while you're home?"

"Yes. I'll write a couple of articles about the war and life on the hospital ship and send to the newspapers in Boston."

"Is this your bed?"

"Yes. Do you want to sit on it? It's the only comfortable place here."

"No, I better not. It won't be proper."

"I want to hold you close. I've missed you much." Roberto tried to kiss her, but she was on her guard.

"Don't you love me anymore?"

"I do"

"Then what's the matter?"

"We shouldn't be alone in here."

In the morning, Roberto went down to the fishing pier and looked up his uncle's trawler.

"Hi there, Uncle Carlo! How's it going?"

"Roberto? Good to see you. How are you?"

"I'm fine. Came home yesterday."

"How was your stint in the Navy?"

"Better than I thought. I'm going out again. How's the fishing? Do you have enough hands?"

"No. I don't. Most of the young men are in the service. I have some older men, but I do a lot myself, like sorting fish," he said grimacing.

"But business should be good. There're many ships in the harbor that need fish."

"Business is good. The military is a good customer."

Carlo threw more fish before asking, "Did you see any fighting on your tour?"

"No, we didn't see any fighting, but we transported injured troops from Gallipoli. It's awful what war can do to a human being."

"I can imagine." Carlo heaved more fish before he straightened up and asked, "So what was your role?"

"I acted as a translator between the injured British soldiers and the doctors and medics. I also had to learn the codes that were used in dispatches from the British and translate it to Italian."

"So your English skills came to good use."

"Yes, I have more talents than I thought," Roberto said with a grin. "See you later."

Roberto went home and sat down by his desk. He stroked the smooth surface and pictured his father sanding and polishing it. He pulled out the middle drawer and took out lined writing paper. Wish I had a typewriter, he said to himself. Where would he start? He had so much to write about. When Tessa came in the evening, he still worked on his stories.

"I'll finish this, and then I'll join you for dinner."

After dinner, Roberto and Tessa went for a walk. The hospital ship was getting a thorough cleaning, inside and out. They stopped to admire the sunset to the west.

"I wonder what it's like on the western front," Roberto said. "The battle of Verdun is still raging. More people will die and neither side is winning."

Tessa was more open about her feelings when they were outside.

"I've missed you," she said.

"I've missed you. But now we're together, and we should make the most of it."

"We can't."

"But each time I see you I want more of you."

They practiced French kissing, but Roberto could not get enough of Tessa.

The next day, he mailed his stories to the *Boston Globe* and *La Gazzetta*. He hoped that they would arrive safely.

The thought struck him that they might go through the censure process and be confiscated.

Chapter 25

John accompanied Anna to the train and installed her in a first-class compartment. He didn't like that she would be traveling alone with Henry.

"Are you sure that Brita will meet you at the train?" he asked.

"Yes, she promised."

As an extra precaution John asked the conductor to see that Anna and the boy got safely off the train and that her relatives were there to meet them. John reached into a pocket indicating that a tip was forthcoming.

"Yes, sir, will do," the conductor said, and John slipped him a dollar for the trouble.

Anna read stories for Henry until he fell asleep. She then put him down on the seat and covered him with a blanket. Having brought a book to occupy herself, she settled down to read.

"Stamford next." The conductor opened the door to her compartment and said that he would help her off the train.

"The boy is asleep," she said. "I have to wake him up."

"No need to do that. I can carry him in his blanket."

When the conductor picked him up, Henry woke and protested, and wanted his mama to carry him."

"I'll take him," Anna said, "if you take my bag."

177

"All right then."

The conductor held on to her elbow as they came to the steps that descended to the platform.

"Watch your step, ma'am," he said, and walked down one step ahead of her. Anna thanked him.

"Now, where are your relatives, ma'am?"

"Anna, Anna, here, I am," she heard Brita calling.

"That's my relative," she told the conductor. "Thanks for your help, sir."

He bowed and waited until Brita came up to them.

"Have a nice stay in Stamford, ma'am," the conductor said.

"Oh, Anna, I'm so glad you are here," Brita greeted her. Anna put Henry down to hug Brita. She thought he was right by her side, but when she looked for him, he was gone.

"Henry," Anna screamed. "Where are you?"

She heard him cry, "Mommy." In the same moment she saw a man carrying him off.

"Help, help!" she screamed. "A man took my boy."

The conductor came running. "Where did he go?"

"That way," Anna pointed. She started to run, but tripped on someone's luggage.

"Police, police," the conductor called out on top of his lungs. "A child has been kidnapped."

Ole had been late arriving from work, but saw what had happened and took up the chase after the man.

Anna sobbed in Brita's arms. "John didn't want me to travel without Josephine," she cried. "It's my fault. Dear God, I hope that Ole will catch up with the man."

Ole came back panting. "He got on another train, just as it left. He won't get far before he's caught. I talked to a policeman."

"Why would he take my boy?" Anna cried.

"Money. You'll probably get a ransom note," Ole said. "Once you pay, you'll get Henry back."

"He must be so frightened." Anna's legs were so weak that Ole had to support her.

"Do you have any checked luggage?" he asked.

"I do, but let's not worry about that now."

"We'll go to the police station and make sure that they act fast," Ole said. "Then we need to call John."

Oh, poor John, Anna thought. *What dreadful news he would get so far away. He was right when he said I should have brought Josephine.*

"Did you get a good look at the man, Ole?" Brita asked.

"Only from the back, but I noticed his build and what clothes he wore. A man carrying a crying child shouldn't be hard to spot."

"You'll get him back, Anna," Ole said, patting her shoulder.

At the police station, Ole phoned John and told him what had happened.

"I'll pay anything to get my son back," John said. "How's Anna holding up?"

"As well as can be expected."

"Will you be at the station for a while?"

"Yes, until we hear something."

They sat at the police station and waited and waited. After a while, an officer asked Ole, "Do you have a telephone at home?"

"Yes, we do."

"Then I advise you to go home and wait for a telephone call."

"I'll get your luggage and a cab," Ole said. "You both wait here."

"We'll provide the transportation to take you home. We want you to be safe, Mrs. Whitmore. An officer will stay with you in case you get a ransom call."

The phone rang at the station. An officer answered.

"And you saw the man getting off a bus in Bridgeport?" he said.

The officer covered the mouth piece and said to Anna, "They're tracking him in Bridgeport."

"Bridgeport. I have relatives there," Anna said.

"Just a minute, so I can notify the police in Bridgeport."

When the officer had done so, he asked Anna who her relatives in Bridgeport were.

"Mr. and Mrs. Fredrick Graham."

"Do they have a phone?"

"Yes." Anna gave the officer the number, and he asked the operator to connect him. Anna could hear that a man answered.

"Are you Mr. Graham?" the officer asked.

When the answer was yes, the officer said, "Someone here wants to talk to you. Mrs. John Whitmore."

Anna reached for the phone.

"Oh, Fred, something awful has happened. My son was kidnapped at the train station in Stamford. A detective has tracked the kidnapper to Bridgeport, where he got off a bus."

"That's awful. Do you know what the man looked like?"

"Yes, he was a Caucasian, tall and slim. He wore work clothes and a cap." Her voice rose, "He has my son, Fred."

"I'll put a detective on it at once, Anna. Someone must have seen him. We have to find witnesses."

"John says that he'll pay anything to get our son back."

"If you get a ransom note, we someone can meet up with the kidnapper. Will you be at the Petersons?"

"Yes, in a little while." Anna gave Fred the number. "I appreciate anything that you can do."

"The man won't harm your son, Anna. All he wants is money."

Anna felt a sliver of hope as she sat down in the squad car. *If only I had heeded John's advice to take Josephine with me. If only I had left Henry at home. If only I hadn't put him down to hug Brita.* Her guilt weighed on her shoulders. She wondered if the man had been following her. Had she seen anyone suspicious? She couldn't recall. The shock of it all overwhelmed her.

Brita and Ole also had qualms. Brita wished she had taken Henry from Anna's arms. Ole regretted being late coming to the station.

Their arrival at Ole's and Brita's was not the happy occasion that they had anticipated. The officer followed them into the house. When the phone rang, he picked it up. It was John, and the officer informed him about the latest development. Again, John repeated that he would pay anything to get his son back. The officer explained that they had other ways of recovering the child. They would pretend that they would deliver the money to the man in exchange for the boy. The man would have to bring the boy, and then they would take it from there.

"Don't risk my son's life," John warned.

"No, Mr. Whitmore, we won't."

"I'll be on the first train to Stamford and I'll bring money," John said.

"Don't bring much. Here is what you should do. Place a one-hundred dollar bill on top of a stack of one-dollar bills."

"Will do."

"Is my husband coming?" Anna asked. "May I have a word with him?"

"Oh, John. I'm so glad you're coming. Fred has hired a detective to trace the man in Bridgeport"

"We need a detective in Stamford also," John said.

"The police station has already provided one."

"I've hired a private detective for you, and a policeman waits in my office in case we'll get a ransom call. But I'll be leaving as soon as I can. You can probably put off an encounter until I arrive. Keep your chin up, honey. We'll get our son back. We're doing everything we can."

"But I'm so worried about Henry. He must be so frightened."

"I know, but the man won't harm him and we'll get him back."

Brita made coffee to keep her hands occupied. Ole took off for the train station.

"The kidnapper might try to come back to Stamford. I'll ask a neighbor to drive me," he said.

The telephone rang. It was Fred, asking for Anna.

"Someone has seen the kidnapper with the boy downtown in Bridgeport," he said. "Policemen are patrolling the area on foot and in squad cars. I don't think he'll be able to get away undetected. I'm not good on foot, so I'll watch out for him at the bus station. I've told the people in the ticket booths to keep an eye out for a man carrying a three-year-old boy."

"Thank you, Fred. Ole has left for the station here in Stamford, and John is coming on the next train."

When John arrived at the train station in Stamford, he heard the police sirens go off. He rushed forward as he saw a policeman stopping a man, who had a boy in his arms.

"It's not Henry," John yelled as he approached them.

"Who are you?" the officer asked.

"I'm John Whitmore, Henry's father, but this boy is not Henry."

"I'm so sorry," the officer said. "I just saw that the boy was blond and reacted."

The man and the boy looked frightened, but when a policeman came forward and explained that they were looking for a man who had kidnapped a boy, he understood.

"You'll get police escort to your train, sir," the officer told the innocent man.

"I'm meeting my wife," he said.

"Then we'll wait with you."

"No harm done. Hope you'll find your son, sir," the man said to John.

Ole came running. He had also seen the man with the boy. John introduced Ole to the officer.

"I will take you home to your wives then," the officer said. "The radio stations are broadcasting the kidnapping. We're asking the citizens for help."

Anna ran into John's arms. "Oh, John, I'm broken-hearted, but I'm so relieved that you're here."

"Go and rest for a while, honey. I'll take it from here, and I'll let you know what happens."

Brita led her daughter to the guest bedroom. She held Anna close.

"Lie down and close your eyes," she said.

"May I call you Mother?"

"Yes, of course."

"You're the only mother I have now, and I need one." Anna said.

"I feel honored."

Somehow, Anna felt that Henry was all right, and she trusted that John would get him home safe and sound. Before she drifted off to sleep, she thought of Roberto and how he had lost Lydia and been robbed of all his belongings. She understood him better now. Being rich meant that the stakes were higher. She had never thought of herself as rich, but now she realized that it made her and John vulnerable. She would gladly give it all up in exchange for her son. Poor Henry, he must be so scared. Dear God, let this nightmare end.

Brita made sandwiches and more coffee. She thought that they might be up all night.

Fred called and said that he had spotted a man with a child getting on a bus in Bridgeport.

"I've notified police in Stamford, but you might get there faster," Fred said to the officer.

"Come with us, Mr. Whitmore. This time, we better make sure that we have the right man and child," the officer said. The detective checked his gun and followed along.

They stood on the platform as the bus rolled in. Policemen hid behind benches and pillars while other officers pushed the crowd back.

"Don't shoot," John warned. "My son might get hurt."

"I'll trip the man, and you take the child if he is yours," the detective said to John.

"Daddy, Daddy," John heard his son shout. That warned the man who was holding him, and he turned around and ran the other way. John ran after him, and so did the policemen, and the detective.

"Daddy, Daddy," Henry stretched his arms over the man's shoulder toward John and cried. The detective came up from the side and tripped the man. Henry fell out of his arms, and John caught the boy.

The man stopped and pointed a gun at them. "Don't come closer or I'll shoot." The detective knocked the gun from the man's hand and wrenched his arms behind him until the policeman came and handcuffed him.

"You're coming with us. You'll face kidnapping charges," the officer said.

John clutched his son in his arms and cried with happiness.

"Don't cry Daddy. Where's Mommy? The man said that we would meet Mommy here."

"Mommy is with Mo-mo. She'll be very glad to see you."

Anna dreamt about her miscarriage, the baby that was placed on her doorstep, and about Henry being gone. She had no children left. But then she heard Henry's babble. She thought that she was still dreaming, but she was awake. It really was Henry's laugh that she heard. She ran into the living room, picked up her son, and danced around with him.

"Mommy, Mommy, I'm getting dizzy."

"Thank God, you're safe, my child. I'm so sorry I lost you at the station."

"The man gave me candy," Henry said.

"He was still a bad man for taking you from me."

"Bad man, bad man," Henry repeated. "But Daddy came and got me."

"Yes, thank you, Daddy," Anna said.

John embraced them both. Brita and Ole stretched out their arms and encircled them. "It's wonderful to have all of you here," Brita said.

That night Anna and John slept in Paul's bed with their child between them.

Chapter 26

Roberto had been away from home for six months when l'Italia received new orders. The captain said that rather than being on furlough the crew would get extra pay. It was time to come to the rescue of fellow Italian injured troops. They would sail around Italy's coast into the Adriatic Sea, but the place where they would evacuate the injured countrymen could not be disclosed.

Roberto didn't have much to do. The captain had asked him to assist in the ship's office. He used a typewriter to write messages that came in on the wireless. If they were in English, he translated them to Italian. But most of all, Roberto would like to learn to use the wireless himself.

"Is it hard to learn the Morse code?" he asked the wireless operator.

"It's like learning a new way of spelling that consists of dots and dashes. There is a combination of marks for each letter in the alphabet."

"Do you have a chart that shows those marks?"

"Yes, I got it somewhere," the man said and looked for it in a drawer.

"Here it is. You can practice by tapping on the table. Start with the numbers. Good luck."

Roberto practiced every day and soon learned to tap out and recognize the numbers. He then went on to tap out the letters of the alphabet. He enjoyed it and thought about it all the time even at night after he had gone to bed. He couldn't get the codes out of his head. It was like a snappy tune that lingered in the back of his mind. He knew that he wouldn't get to use it on board, but it could be useful at other times.

An alarm went off and got Roberto on his feet. He ran up on deck, saluted an officer, and asked what had happened.

"A British warship has been torpedoed and is sinking. We'll try to rescue the crew from the water."

Roberto watched the torpedoed ship going down and l'Italia's lifelines being thrown out to the men in the water. As soon as one had caught a line, he was hauled in, but Roberto also saw several men clinging to the same line. Rope ladders were lowered along the side of the ship. As the men came aboard, doctors and medics met them. Roberto was there to translate.

"We have medical staff but no patients, so you'll be well taken care of. If you can't walk, you'll be carried on stretchers," he said in English.

"Aye, aye, sir," a British officer who had just been hauled aboard said, "That's terrific. But I wish everyone could have been saved. Many, I'm afraid, went down with the ship or were blown to pieces in the explosion."

Roberto noticed that some of the men in the water were too weak to hang on to the line. Without thinking, he jumped overboard.

"Man overboard!" Someone yelled.

"Don't worry! It's Petty Officer Cosentino. He's an expert swimmer and former lifeguard," the captain said.

Roberto took hold of a man in the water, grasped a lifeline and let them both be hauled to the ship. He helped the man into the cradle that lifted him aboard. Then he saved four more men who would otherwise have drowned.

"Bravo, Officer Cosentino!" the captain said as he helped him aboard. "We now have saved fifty men, and you alone have saved five."

Roberto was tired but satisfied. He recognized the feeling from the time he was a lifeguard. It always felt good to have saved a life, and now he had saved five.

"If you're not too exhausted, they might need you as a translator in sickbay, but change clothes first."

"Aye, aye, Captain."

The next day, Roberto was called to the captain's quarters.

"At ease, Cosentino. It was a heroic thing you did yesterday. I'll recommend you for a medal."

"I couldn't let the men drown, sir."

"If you hadn't been such a good swimmer, it would have been a foolhardy act."

"I swam every day while I was on furlough, and knew I could do it, sir."

"And I commend you for it. You are now Petty Officer, Second Class. You are advancing fast. Anything I can do for you, *sergente*?"

"Yes, Captain. I've learned the Morse code by tapping on any surface available. Would it be possible to practice on the wireless keys?"

"You really surprise me, Cosentino. I'll speak to the operator in charge and he might let you do easy transmissions. But you also need to be available in sickbay and do any necessary translations."

"Of course, sir." Roberto saluted and turned on his heel.

He had always wished for recognition, but now that he had it within reach, it didn't mean that much to him. It was more important to stay alive so that he could come back to Tessa. It was also more important that his brother Salvo was alive and could return to his family. He wondered why saving a life in uniform meant that much more than saving a life in civilian life? It wasn't fair, he thought, although what he had received from Anna was better than any medal. She had given him a new start in life. Without Anna, he might still be a poor immigrant in Boston.

They sailed along Italy's east coast and saw the ruins in the port of Ancona caused by Austrian artillery bombardment from the sea. Roberto guessed that l'Italia was on the way to the Gulf of Venice. His brother Salvo would either be in the mountains or on the plains.

They passed Venice and arrived at Lesolo, where the river Di Piave had its outlet. In the cover of darkness, the Italian wounded men came in small boats by the hundreds and were taken aboard. After fierce fighting and severe injuries, they had floated down the river in small boats, hoping for rescue. Roberto looked for his brother among them. Would he recognize Salvo? There was no need for Roberto to translate here. They were all Italians. He stood like a man transfixed, staring at the soaked, long-haired men in tattered clothes, some of them with limbs in bloody rags.

The healthier among them said, "We need food. We're hungry."

Roberto directed them to first-aid stations or the dining halls.

"Roberto," one of the men said. "What the hell are you doing here?"

Roberto looked in the direction of the voice that sounded familiar.

"Is that you, Salvo?"

"No, I'm Dezi, your next door neighbor and school-mate."

"Holy Christ, I'm glad to see you, Dezi," Roberto said. "But I hoped that you would be Salvo. Do you know anything about him?"

"Yes, he's still at the front. He was all right when I saw him last."

"That's good news. Why is everybody soaking wet? Did you fall in?"

"Yes, but it actually felt good. The water was quite warm." Dezi walked with the help of a crutch.

"You're only skin and bone," Roberto said, looking down at Dezi's bandaged foot.

"My foot is mangled."

"I'll make sure that you get the best of care. A medic will have a look at you. Are you hungry?"

"I'm starved."

"I'll get you a sandwich."

"Have you seen my family lately?" Dezi asked.

"They were all healthy when I saw them in the beginning of the year."

"I'm so glad to hear that."

"They'll be happy to have you home, I'm sure."

"Only, I won't be able to do much work," Dezi said with a sigh.

"It could have been worse. You could have lost a leg."

When Roberto brought the sandwich, Dezi was already dressed in deckhand clothes. Clean bandages covered his foot. He was clean-shaven and had a close-crop haircut.

"Do you feel better now?" Roberto asked.

"It's good to look like a human being again. I got to keep my foot, at least for now. It hurts like hell though. They gave me medication that will numb the pain."

He grabbed the sandwich, nibbled at it and said, "I can't eat too much too fast. My stomach has shrunk to almost nothing."

Roberto told him that Papa Alfonso had died and that he had met Tessa at the hospital.

When Dezi had finished his sandwich, he was too sleepy to talk.

"I'll take you to the ward," Roberto said. "We can talk more tomorrow."

Dezi told Roberto about life at the front. He talked in fragmented sentences, punctuated with swear words. Roberto cleaned it up when he wrote the statements down in his notebook.

The Austrians attacked us with four hundred thousand men and two thousand guns in May of last year. They knew the terrain. *We were swept away by their artillery. The mountainside provided no shelter. We could not entrench, but were forced to withdraw from the territory we had won earlier. When we ran out of ammunition on both sides, we hurled rocks at each other. Refugees from the villages fled down the slopes with their belongings and cattle. The damn Huns had taken their wine, which was their only protection against malaria.*

We were forced farther south to the open country, and there we made a stand. This summer, the fighting became fierce, and that's when I injured my foot. I was taken to a field hospital, where they patched me up the best they could. It was not the first time I was in sickbay. I had malaria bad at one time. My only consolation is that we inflicted much damage on the Austrians. I hope that the tide has turned and we are winning the war.

Thousands were killed in avalanches on both sides. The river flooded after the snow melted in the mountains. We are twice as many as the Austrians and still we can't beat them. It doesn't matter how many divisions the generals bring in. We were close to winning in the fifth battle of the Isonzo, but the enemy gained the upper hand.

Chapter 27

Many of the patients disembarked l'Italia in Venice to recuperate at hospitals before returning to their villages. They were mountain men, who had fought fiercely against the Austrians in Alpine terrain. While the ship took on coal and provisions, Roberto enjoyed a gondola ride on the canals and got off at Saint Mark Square, where he read a plaque outlining the city's history. Venice had once been independent and had fought several wars with Genoa, and defeated it in the 1300s to gain control over the Mediterranean Sea. At one time, Venice had included Crete and parts of northeastern Italy. When Christopher Columbus discovered America and Vasco Da Gama discovered the sea route to India, the trade routes shifted to the Atlantic Ocean, and Venice lost its naval prominence. After the Napoleonic wars, Venice came under Austrian rule. In 1866, it became a part of the Kingdom of Italy.

Admiring the architecture that surrounded the square and some of the famous art created by Venetian masters, Roberto entered the Cathedral of Saint Mark and offered prayers of thanks for the good news about Salvo. He knew that things could change by the hour, but as far as he knew, his brother was okay.

While l'Italia docked in Naples to take aboard new Army uniforms for the men they had rescued, the captain allowed the crew to go ashore for a few hours. It was enough time for some of the men to make quick visits to houses of ill repute. Roberto would not risk getting venereal disease. He had always preferred to romance girls before bedding them. The hunt played a big part in his satisfaction when seducing women. He must have changed, he thought, because he had no desire to romance any woman except Tessa. He couldn't wait to see her again, and now he had a chance to buy her a gift before sailing for home.

The patients waited on deck as the ship anchored in the Genoa harbor. An orchestra played the Italian national anthem, *Fratelli d'Italia, l'Italia s'è desta* (Italian Brothers, Italy has Arisen). Dezi saluted the flag with tears streaming down his face. It looked like the entire population of Genoa had assembled on the pier to welcome them. People carried welcome signs with their heroes' names in bold letters. They waved handkerchiefs and flags.

The men on deck shaded their eyes searching for their loved ones. How could they find them in this sea of humanity? The patients disembarked first, some walking, others stumbling on crutches, or sitting in wheelchairs, all dressed in new Infantry or Cavalry uniforms with hats that covered their shaved heads. Military officers stood in line to bid them goodbye. A colonel gave a speech thanking the veterans for their service and for having put Italy on the road to victory. He saluted each one and read their names as they disembarked. Dezi saluted and hobbled ashore into the welcoming embrace of his family. Roberto thought that all the men who had fought the Austrians deserved a medal. Many of them had risked their own lives to save those of others. His eyes searched for Tessa. Would she be there?

Then he heard her voice, "Roberto, Roberto, here I am." She waved him in her direction.

Roberto sprinted the last few yards, embraced her, and showered her with kisses.

"Oh, Tessa, it's good to see you and have my arms around you again," he said. "It's been too long."

Then he remembered the gift he had bought for her.

"I have something for you, sweetheart," he said as he pulled a small gift-wrapped box out of his uniform pocket. "It's a late Christmas gift that I bought in Naples."

"*Grazie*, Roberto. I'm glad you thought of me." She opened it and found the small golden cherub attached to a chain.

"Oh, Roberto, it will be my guardian angel," she said. "Would you help me put it on?"

"I'll be glad to." Roberto welcomed the opportunity to touch the back of her neck. When he had closed the clasp, he kissed her neck with an intensity that made their feelings soar. She thanked him again for the necklace and nibbled on his ear before kissing him on the lips. She had forgotten about the people around them.

All the family members gathered at Mama Lea's house. The women had scraped together their meager rationings and baked and cooked for days to prepare for the feast. Roberto gave a speech. He raised his glass, and said, "*Grazie* everyone for making this homecoming so special. *Salute!*"

He told them that Dezi had seen Salvo at the front and asked if the family had heard from Anthony in Boston.

"Yes, we'd a letter from him," Mama Lea said. "He got the option of returning to Italy or registering with the American military. He chose to register with the National Guard."

"He did the right thing," Roberto said. "He has a family over there now. Being in the National Guard might keep him from going overseas if America joins the war."

"He wrote that his boss's son had been kidnapped," Lea said.

"No! Not little Henry?" Roberto gasped.

"Yes, the boy's name is Henry, but he was found safe and sound."

"Thank heavens for that," Roberto said. Anna must have been in shock. Rich people don't always have it as easy as one might think.

After the party, he walked Tessa home. They had their arms wrapped around each other and stopped often to kiss.

"I want to see you every day while I'm home," he said.

"I'll be at the hospital during the day, so I can only see you in the evening," she said. She was eager to please him, but there was only so much she could do with a good conscience.

Roberto wrote and mailed more reports to the newspapers in Boston. He knew that Anna read the *Boston Globe*, and hoped that she would see his story. He also wished that Julia would read it, but since he had met Tessa, Julia had faded more and more from his memory.

Next, he wrote to Anthony and asked for more information about the kidnapping and also about Anna. He wrote about Tessa and Italy's war with the Austrians. He wrote about Dezi and that he had met Salvo. He mentioned that the Russians had helped them by attacking Austria from the north. He described the wonderful feast that the family had enjoyed the night before. He asked if Anthony had to go in for training in the Reserve; how Sophia and Collette were doing, and what the general opinion was about the war. At the end of the paper, he wrote, "I'm on furlough for two weeks, then I go out again. Write soon, dear brother. The letters take a long time to cross."

After he had mailed the letters, he went for a long swim with his younger sisters. Jolanda and Liliana. They glided like dolphins in the water.

"I'm proud of your skills," he said.

"You taught us, Roberto, and you're the best."

For now he was happy, but he wondered how long the war would go on and what he would do after that. Should he try to take over his father's trade? He thought that his lungs would be strong enough, but he would have to hire a skillful woodworker and buy more efficient machinery.

Roberto walked around the workshop and inspected the saws, the planes, the carpenter bench, the stain and varnish cans, and the brushes. Everything was clean and orderly. Then he looked at the stacked lumber that was ready to be used. Here's a fortune in lumber, he thought. Mama could rent out the business and sell the lumber.

What was he going to do with his life? Was Tessa the woman for him? Would her parents approve of him? They had probably heard stories about him being a gigolo when he went after the rich Lydia Addison. Roberto was not sure at all that Tessa's father would accept him as his son-in-law. The family was what was referred to as "White Italians," and the same could not be said about Roberto. Was it discrimination that prevented Tessa from inviting him to her parents' home?

He thought of Julia in Boston and how her father had actually admired him. Would he have a chance of becoming a reporter here in Genoa? It wouldn't pay as much as in Boston. Those were the thoughts that occupied his mind. In a way, he longed for Boston and its many opportunities. Tessa wouldn't go with him to Boston. She was anchored here. He couldn't propose to her because he didn't have anything to offer her. He didn't even know if he would live through the war. If he did, could he then make a career in the Navy? It would be difficult to have a wife and children if he were away at sea.

Chapter 28

It was November 21, 1916, and Roberto was on another tour in the Mediterranean. Off the Greek Island of Kea, the wireless operator received a distress signal from the HMHS Britannic, Titanic's sister ship, that had been converted from a war ship to a hospital ship. More than one ship sped to her rescue, among them l'Italia. Roberto had seen the Britannic in Naples a few days earlier when both ships had waited out a storm before heading north to the Dardanelle Strait.

He peered into his binoculars and saw two lifeboats being lowered while Britannic's giant propellers still churned. The lifeboats were sucked into the propellers and cut to pieces. It was a horrible scene to watch. When the ship cut the engines, the Britannic's bow dipped lower. The machinery from the deck spilled into the sea. About thirty minutes later, the giant ship plunged with her stern rearing into the air just like the Titanic and the Lusitania had done. Roberto held his breath as it disappeared below the surface. Other ships that were closer began to take on survivors. A British cruiser, HMS Heroic, was the first on the scene.

Roberto volunteered to go out in a lifeboat to rescue survivors in the water. A chill went up his spine as he thought of the Titanic disaster. But *Grazie, Madonna,* now he was not among those who needed rescuing. It was time to give back.

The lifeboat that Roberto was in took on the last survivors. He reached out a hand and hauled them aboard. Speaking English, they told Roberto about the horrifying moments they had just been through. One man said that five watertight compartments had flooded first. The sixth one flooded because the door to it hadn't closed all the way. Even so, the ship could have stayed afloat had it not been for the fact that many of the windows and portholes were open. A surviving nurse said that they had been airing out the wards.

Roberto helped them aboard l'Italia and translated what he had been told. There was no doubt in his mind that the Germans had sunk the Britannic despite its markings as a hospital ship. Those bastards! They had no conscience whatsoever. Would any hospital ship be safe? He hadn't thought of the dangers until now. The enemy could still be lurking somewhere in the waters below them.

The survivors of the Britannic debarked at Malta. While in port, Roberto learned that thirty people had perished. The ship had been hit by an underwater mine and sank in thirty-five minutes. The wireless operator had wired the White Star Line about the tragedy. The sinking of the great liner shook Roberto to the core. It brought back the bad memories of the Titanic that he had tried to forget.

With shaky hands, he sat down to type a report for the Boston newspapers and asked them to provide the background information on the Britannic. He had been an eye witness, and was certain that his articles would be published.

The captain had received orders to proceed to the Greek island of Lemnos, where the hospitals overflowed with injured and sick soldiers. The Britannic would not get there to relieve the situation. Once again, Roberto received an accolade from the captain for helping in the rescue of survivors from the Britannic.

"You'll receive a promotion and new shoulder insignia when we get to Naples. I'll also recommend you for another decoration," he said.

Among the patients that they picked up at Moudros on the island of Lemnos were the first shell-shocked soldiers that Roberto had seen. He had read that there were thousands of soldiers with bizarre symptoms on the western front. Some shook uncontrollably. Others appeared to be in a trancelike state, maintaining rigid postures as if frozen in place and unable to use their senses. The Army categorized them as either hysterical or depressed. Those who were unable to talk endured electric shock treatments until they screamed. The objective was to get the men back into action, not to find the underlying causes. One in six victims was a junior officer. Their horrible experiences included having to shoot their own soldiers when they refused to advance in the lines.

Roberto was awakened in the middle of the night. There was fighting in the wards between an injured man and a shell-shocked man. When he got there, the man with the physical injury admitted that he had accused the speechless man of being a coward by pretending to be shell-shocked to avoid the fighting.

"He hit me. I'm injured and I can't defend myself," he said.

"We need to separate these two men," Roberto said. "They should not be in the same ward. I think that all the shell-shocked men should be in a separate ward."

"We don't have a separate ward to put them in," the orderly said.

"Well, at least put this shell-shocked man in another ward," Roberto said.

While speaking with the doctors aboard, Roberto learned that an English psychiatrist had determined that the victims were neither cowards nor crazy. Rather it was the soldiers' natural defense system against inhuman conditions in trench warfare. If the victims felt safe and not threatened with harsh treatments, they recovered.

During the stop in Naples, the captain made good on his promise to Roberto and issued a new white dress uniform for him with the shoulder insignia Petty Officer, First Class.

He was back in Genoa before Christmas. Again, Roberto's family made it a happy homecoming for Roberto, but Mama Lea complained that they had not picked all the grapes.

"Papa always made the wine, and I'm not a wine-maker," she said. "I made grape juice and the girls sold grapes at the market place. It gave us some cash, but there are more grapes on the vine."

"I'll pick them for you, Mama." Roberto knew how to make wine, but it was a long process that required constant monitoring, and he wouldn't be home to do that. All he could think of for the moment was that he wanted to see Tessa again.

"You look thin, darling," he said as they met, "Aren't you well?"

"The work is very demanding," she said with a whimper.

"Do you get enough to eat?" She lowered her head and said something that Roberto could not hear.

"I can't hear you, darling."

"There isn't much to eat," she said barely audible.

"Honey, I'll find food for you."

"The Army takes all the cheese and meat."

"I'll go to Salvo's farm and get some."

He talked to his mother about it and asked why Tessa looked starved.

"I think she gives her rationing coupons to her parents, and then she eats at the hospital, where the food is poor."

Roberto was at Salvo's place and talked to Laura. First he'd gone to Uncle Carlo and picked up two large fishes. He'd given one to his mother, and now he gave Laura the other one.

"*Grazie,* Roberto, I'm glad to get fresh fish. Thank Uncle Carlo from me," Laura said.

"I need something in return, Laura, but I'm willing to pay for it. We need milk, flour, and meat if you have any to spare," he said. "I think that Tessa needs milk even though she's a grown woman. She looks like she's starving."

"I have an idea," Laura said. "You can borrow one of our goats."

"A goat! How would we feed it?"

"Mama Lea has a big enough yard to support a goat. It will eat almost anything."

"But do you think that Tessa will drink goat's milk?"

"If she's hungry, she will. I think it's a good idea. Your mother knows how to milk a goat."

They went out to the meadow, where Laura put a rope around the neck of a ewe with a big udder. "You just lead her home," she said and gave Roberto the end of the rope.

Roberto pulled, but the goat didn't budge. When he pulled harder, the ewe put the brakes on by planting her front legs stretched out in front of her. Then without warning, she charged for Roberto's behind.

"Ouch!" Roberto landed on his face. Laura and her son, Vito, laughed. "That was funny," Vito said, but Roberto fumed.

"I think it's best that Vito leads the goat," Laura said. "You, Roberto, can go behind it with a stick. Use it if she doesn't mind."

"I'm not good with animals," Roberto admitted, feeling a little ashamed.

As they walked back to the house, Laura said, "I'll send along some flour. I know it's difficult to find any. We can't get the Russian wheat anymore."

"Do you have any meat?"

"Come with me and I'll give you both flour and cured ham."

"I want to pay for it," Roberto said.

"Money's always welcome. The children need new clothes and shoes."

Laura brought out a ham and cut a generous piece. She gave him a pouch to carry it in. Then she gave him a small sack of flour. Roberto took up his wallet and gave Laura some of his cash.

Walking behind the goat with a stick in his hand and carrying a sack of flour on his back, Roberto felt foolish, but he did it for Tessa. Vito carried the meat.

Once they were home, Roberto couldn't have been more proud if he had brought home a new automobile.

"A goat!" Mama Lea said. "I thought you were going to get milk."

"This is milk. It's like a milk wagon that will deliver milk every day."

"Can we keep it?"

"Yes, Laura said we can keep it as long as we want."

"That's wonderful. Now I can make goat cheese."

Mama Lea took the flour and began to make bread. It wasn't long before Roberto smelled the aroma of it baking in the oven.

"I want to ask Tessa to come and have some of the fresh bread," Roberto told his mother.

"Go ahead. It'll be ready in a little while."

They ate the fresh bread with sliced ham, cheese, and wine, and for the first time in a long time, Tessa said that she had eaten her fill.

"Will you try to drink some goat's milk, honey?" Roberto said. "You need it."

"I have to milk the goat first," Mama said.

"I could take some milk home with me this evening. My mama knows how to use it in cooking," Tessa said.

Roberto carried a can of milk as he walked Tessa home.

"You need to go and get milk from my mother every day," he reminded her.

"I will. I appreciate what you're doing for me, Roberto."

"You must eat to keep up your strength."

"I promise," she said.

Having taken a tender goodbye of her, he walked back home. It had become harder and harder for them to part. He felt the need to take care of her.

Roberto had received a letter from Anthony and a Christmas card from Anna and John. He read Anna's card first. She wrote that Henry enjoyed the sailboat Roberto had made for him. He pushed on it so that it rocked. He was now three and one-half years of age. They had read Roberto's articles in the *Globe*. Anna wished him and his family a Merry Christmas and a happier New Year with an end to the war.

Roberto then eagerly read the letter from Anthony. It was in Italian.

"Money has arrived for you from the newspapers in Boston, and I've deposited the funds in your savings account," he wrote. That was good, but Roberto wondered if he would ever get to use the money.

The factories are going full steam in preparation for war. We're sending war material with every ship that goes abroad. I work in a factory that manufactures guns, and I make much more money than working for Mr. Whitmore. I'm paying rent for the apartment, but I'm still ahead. Americans want to go to war, but the president is holding out. I'm training in the National Guard.

On the last page, he wrote:

I hear that Italian homes are short of food, and it makes me feel bad. Wish I could send you some, but I fear that it would be confiscated along the way. Sophia says that we should send you coffee and she might do that. We have enough of everything, but people have started to hoard sugar and coffee, and there have been food riots in some parts of the country. Collette is growing and thriving.

Roberto sat down by his desk to write a response to Anthony's letter. It was impossible to paint a rosy picture.

The war was going badly for everyone involved. There were no winners. Millions of men had been killed for no purpose at all. He had seen what battle could do to the soldiers. He continued:

I'm lucky not to be involved in trench warfare. Don't believe the Germans when they talk about peace. It's just to keep the Americans out of the war. The Russians and Austrians are weakening. Romania has surrendered. The major powers are France and Great Britain against Germany. Germany cannot be allowed to win. We continue to fight in the Trentino region, and Salvo is still stationed there. The last we heard, he was okay. Our troops have fought nine battles at the Isonzo River and have now been pushed back to the Piave River. There won't be much fighting over the winter. This Christmas our money will go toward necessities. We're lucky to have produce from our garden and orchard.

Chapter 29

The United States Congress voted to declare war on Imperial Germany, and President Wilson signed it. What had made the president change his mind? John read that in part it was due to Germany's declaration of unrestricted submarine warfare, but the president had also found out that Germany had made a secret deal with Mexico. In exchange for an alliance with that country, Germany had promised to help Mexico recover land lost to the United States after the Mexican War.

President Wilson declared, "The world must be made safe for democracy." The country mobilized for war and required all men between twenty-one and thirty to register for the draft.

John stood in line to register before driving home from work. He was glad that almost all his employees were above the age of thirty. Addison Enterprises would manage without him as president. He listed his college degree and title and hoped for the best. The recruiting officer put John's registration aside and said that he would receive a letter from them in a few days.

When John heard, "Next," he stepped aside. The men who gathered outside complained that they all had been assigned to the Infantry on the spot.

Anna met her husband at the door. They were so happy to be expecting a child in another month, and now John had to leave her. Quietly, she put her arms around his neck.

"Have you registered?" she asked.

"Yes. I had to, darling."

"I know. Do you know where you'll be going?"

"No, not yet."

They sat by the radio and listened. The country had about eighty thousand men in the National Guard, most of them deployed at the Mexican border. The rest of the enlisted men amounted to less than one hundred twenty-two thousand and about five thousand seven hundred officers. All the newly inducted men had to be trained and equipped. It would take time before the United States could ship troops to Europe. "This is only the beginning," John said.

Anna waited anxiously for John's assignment. She felt enormous relief when the word came that he would serve at the War Department in Washington, D.C. The drawback was that he didn't need any military training for his post and had to leave immediately.

'I'll be all right, darling, and so will you." We can correspond, and I'll call you as often as I can. Try to spend as much time as possible with Sally and Carl. Carl will probably have a deferment due to his job."

The butler announced that Eddy was at the door.

"Show him in," John said.

"I just want to say goodbye," Eddy said. "I'm shipping out in the morning."

"What's your assignment, Eddy?"

"The Navy. I got my wish. There're six destroyers anchored in Boston harbor, and I'll be on one of them heading for Ireland."

"I'm glad you got your wish, Eddy. "I'm going to Washington D.C. tomorrow morning."

"We'll have to do our duty," Eddy said. "I thought I should tell you that I've moved my belongings to my parents' house."

"I wish you God's speed, Eddy. This war will be over before we know it."

The two men shook hands. They were no longer the employer and the employee, but two men ready to go and serve their country.

John read a story to Henry and tucked him in.

"Daddy has to go away for a while. I'll be at our nation's capital, where the president lives."

"Does he live in a castle?"

"No, he lives in the White House. We don't have any castles in America."

"And no king and princesses?"

"No, Henry, we don't. We aren't supposed to."

"Oh."

"I'll be thinking about you every day. I'll come back as soon as I can."

"I'll miss you, Daddy."

"I'll miss you, too. I love you very much."

"I love you, Daddy."

John had tears in his eyes as he kissed his son on the forehead and stroked his hair.

Anna could not sleep at all during the night. She thought of Brita's son, Paul, who would do war service in the Navy, about Sophia, who would be alone with a small child when Anthony left; about Roberto, who was on a hospital ship, about Eddy's parents and John's parents who didn't get a chance to say goodbye to their sons. Thousands and thousands of nameless women lay sleepless this very night, worrying about their men and the future, wondering how they would make a living and praying that their men would survive.

John turned to Anna and said, "I know that you love to drive, but with the baby coming, you should hire a chauffeur. You can't do everything yourself. If you want to go to the

Cape for instance, it would be too far for you to drive, especially with children in the car."

"I'm sure you're right, John. Do you know anyone?"

"You could ask Tom if he knows someone suitable."

"I will."

Before John left in the morning, he had one more instruction for Anna.

"You may be called to attend a company board meeting, honey."

"Oh, I don't know if I can do that, not in my condition."

"Don't worry, darling. It's just a matter of formality. Mr. Wright will take care of all matters of importance."

"If you say so, John."

"Take care of yourself, honey. It's not likely that I'll be here when the baby comes, but I'll be with you in spirit. Keep your chin up!"

"I'll do my best."

"My cab is waiting. I'll be riding the train all day before I get to Washington."

There was one last hug and kiss, and one last "I love you" before John was in the cab that pulled away from the driveway. They waved. Anna stood outside the door long after the cab had disappeared.

Then she fled to Henry's room, where she stood and looked at her sleeping child. He had John's features, but her blond hair. "Dear God," she prayed. "Keep Henry and John safe."

She thought of how lonely her evenings would be without John. Henry went to sleep early, and there would be no one to talk to other than the servants. Would she be alone at the dinner table? She longed for the birth of her baby. He or she would keep her occupied. She thought about Sally, Carl, and Irene. She thought about Brita's parents, who were her maternal grandparents. They lived in Boston, but she hadn't seen them for a long time. She could mail them an invitation to dinner. Or she could deliver it herself? She decided to take a drive and visit them all.

Eddy had filled up the Cadillac with gasoline and washed it. She had never done that. She realized that she needed a chauffeur after all. But would there be any gasoline for private cars? The newspapers were full of dire predictions of rationing. People were already asked to conserve fuel.

Anna went to see Sally first. The two women enjoyed talking about their children. Little Irene was doing well. The blond, curly-haired girl ran back and forth showing her aunt one doll after the other. Anna tried to lift her to her knee, but with her protruding stomach, she didn't have much room for her, and Irene had no time to sit and slid down right away. When Anna said goodbye, she told Sally that she would visit her grandparents next.

Anna parked her Cadillac outside the modest home where Brita's parents lived. Her grandfather watered flowers that grew by the fence. She waved to him.

"Mr. Erickson. Your flowers are beautiful," she said. At first he didn't recognize her.

"It's me, Anna Whitmore, Brita's daughter."

"Anna, what a nice surprise. How are you?"

"I'm fine. How are you and Mrs. Erickson?"

"We're doing all right. Just getting a little slower."

His wife came out on the porch to see who had come to visit them.

"It's Anna Whitmore. She's driving herself."

"How nice of you to come and visit us. Please come up on the porch and we'll have a chat."

The three of them sat down on the screened-in porch, and Anna told her grandparents that John had left and that she felt lonely.

"We can understand that. Lots of women are in the same predicament. I see that you're expecting, and that makes it harder," Mrs. Erickson said.

"Yes, in another month."

Anna noticed that Mrs. Erickson spoke with a slight Swedish accent and recalled that Brita had said that her mother was born in Sweden.

"We've a lot in common. I lived in Sweden until I was eighteen years old," Mrs. Erickson said.

"I didn't know that," Anna said. "I lived there from the time I was twelve until I was eighteen."

"My original name was Elsa, but here everyone calls me Elsie. I was born in Karlstad, and I have been back twice, once on my own before I was married and the second time with my husband after our children were grown. I still have brothers and sisters over there."

"*Det visste jag inte.*" I didn't know that.

"*Vi hade roligt.*" We had fun. "I haven't used the Swedish language for so long."

"You're doing fine. So I have a Swedish grandmother right here in Boston," Anna said.

"Of course, I married a Swede also, but Walter was born here."

"I'm proud of my Swedish heritage," Mr. Erickson said. "We visited the place my parents came from, outside Skara, and met my cousins."

"*Fantastiskt,*" Anna said. She felt elated about her visit. "I'm so glad I decided to come to see you," she said. "I'd like to have you over for dinner. I can pick you up."

"We have a car," Mr. Erickson said.

"Oh, you do." They agreed on a date, and Anna rose to leave.

"Won't you stay for a cup of coffee or lemonade?" Mrs. Erickson asked.

"If it's not too much trouble, I'll have a glass of lemonade."

"It's not very often we get company," Mr. Erickson said as his wife stood up to go to the kitchen.

They talked about Brita, their other children, and the war until Mrs. Erickson returned with a tray. Putting it down, she said, "It doesn't seem right that you call us Mr. and Mrs. Erickson when we call you by your first name. If you want to, you can call us Grandma and Grandpa?"

"I'd love to," Anna said. "I don't have any other relatives here in Boston."

Before she left, she went up and kissed both of her grandparents. She felt much better as she pulled her bulky body into the Cadillac and drove off, waving to her grandparents standing by the gate. As she passed her church, she saw a crowd outside and decided to stop to see what was going on.

In the sanctuary, there was a prayer service for all the American soldiers going to war. Anna found that meaningful and decided to attend. The pastor said that after the service, the ladies would gather for a meeting in Fellowship Hall to determine what they could do to help the war effort. Anna wanted to do what she could.

The chairwoman of the sewing circle said that they could roll bandages or knit men's socks. Anna offered to roll bandages. She knew how to knit, but she wasn't sure that she could knit men's socks. Now, she had two things to do, plan a dinner and roll bandages.

When her grandparents came, Anna had arranged for a social hour with Henry before his bedtime. The boy made them feel at ease. Anna had been afraid that her big home with the butler and maid would intimidate them, but they seemed comfortable. As a younger man, her grandfather had worked as a chauffeur for the Addison Senior family and was well acquainted with big homes. He also knew Tom from that time.

"Later, I started a cab company," Grandpa said. "For several years, I had two cabs and drove one myself until I'd put away a nest egg so I could retire. A chauffeur drove the other cab until I sold it a couple of years ago."

"You had a cab company, Grandpa? I didn't know that. Brita never told me."

"Well, once you retire, you're just plain old dad, who isn't doing anything."

"I wish you had something to do," his wife said. "I think you're getting a bit restless."

Anna saw her chance. "I need an occasional chauffeur. Would you be interested, Grandpa?"

"Well, I'd love to drive that Cadillac of yours."

"What do you think, Mother?" he asked his wife.

"I don't mind. I think it would be good for you to get out more," she said.

"You're someone I can trust," Anna said, "That's important to both John and me."

"I suppose this would be mostly when your baby is born and after that?"

"Yes, as long as we can get gasoline. I'd like to go to the Cape in the summer. We've a beach house there, and it can't stand empty all summer. You could come along, Grandma."

"I'd like that, especially being with Henry. You've a nanny, of course, but she needs time off."

"Well, then that's settled. We'll reimburse you for your work, Grandpa."

"No, I don't want to be paid. It would be an honor to drive you, Anna. It won't be a full-time job, would it?"

"No, only once in a while. I can always get a cab if need be. Do you have a phone so I can reach you?"

"Yes, we've a phone. It was necessary when I had the cab company, you know."

Anna couldn't have been happier about the arrangement.

Chapter 30

Anna waited every day for a letter from John. When it finally came it was stamped "Censured" on the outside of the envelope. Is that why it had taken so long? She opened it and saw that some of John's sentences had been blacked out. He wrote that he served at the Food Administration. It didn't sound to her like it had to be a military secret. Best of all, he was all right. Now she had an address to write to. When the baby was born, she had a way of letting him know.

She sat down to answer the letter, telling John that her own grandfather, Brita's father, would be her driver. She continued:

Henry asks about you every evening and kisses your picture. After he's gone to sleep, I rip up old sheets and roll bandages that I take to our church. Sally is doing the same. Grandma is knitting socks for the soldiers. I made friends with some of the women in the sewing circle. I'm getting heavier with each day and tire easily. The baby kicks at night, so it's difficult to sleep. It won't be long now. You'll get a telegram if the censure allows. Henry and I love you and miss you. Write soon. Stay safe. With all my love, Anna. Henry will now draw a picture for you.

Anna addressed the letter to 2nd Ltd. John W. Whitmore, the way he had written it in the return address. Then she was tired and wished to lie down. Walking back to her room, she felt a contraction. Was she in labor already? She had not expected it for another two weeks.

It was two o'clock in the afternoon when she went to lie down. Ten minutes later she felt another contraction. She rose to call her doctor. Of course, he was not available, and Anna had to wait for him to call her back. Meanwhile, she had another contraction, more intensive than before. When Dr. Wilson finally called, he advised her to come to the hospital.

"With the second child, it could go much faster than with the first," he said.

Anna was almost ready to call for a cab when she thought of her grandfather. It would be more personal to have him drive her. Perhaps Grandma could come along.

She called on Emily to pack a few things, and then asked the operator to connect her with the number to her grandparents. Her grandmother answered.

"It's me, Anna. It's time for me to go the hospital."

"We'll be there as soon as we can," Grandma said. "Is it all right if I come along?"

"I wish you would, Grandma. We can take the Cadillac to the hospital."

Anna went to Henry's room. He no longer took naps, but enjoyed listening to stories that his nanny read.

"Henry, sweetheart," Anna said, "Mommy has to go away for a few days. When I come back, I'll bring you a little sister or brother."

"Goody, but don't stay away long, Mommy. I don't want you to be away as long as Daddy."

"No, I won't, honey."

Henry put his arm around her neck and clung to her. She gave him a squeeze before darting out of the room to lean down for another pain.

"Your suitcase is packed, ma'am," Emily said. "Is there a cab coming for you?"

"My grandparents are coming any minute. Mr. Erickson will drive me."

They walked downstairs to wait.

"There's a letter in my study to Mr. Whitmore, ready to be mailed. Please go and get it. I want to take it along, so that we have the address handy. My grandfather can send my husband a telegram after the baby is born."

The grandparents arrived just as Anna had another pain. There wasn't time to get the Cadillac out of the garage. Emily helped Anna into the backseat of the Ford and gave Mr. Erickson the bag that she had packed.

"Do you want me to sit by your side, Anna?" Grandma asked.

"Yes, please," Anna moaned.

"Which hospital?" Grandpa asked.

"The Presbyterian."

"I've been there many times, and know exactly where it is," Grandpa assured her. "We'll be there in ten minutes."

The road was far from smooth and every bump increased Anna's pains. She estimated that the contractions came five minutes apart.

"I have a letter to John ready to be mailed. You don't need a stamp," she said as she reached into her purse for the letter and handed it to her grandmother. "Please send a wire to the same address after the baby is born."

"You can count on us, Anna. We'll wait at the hospital until we have the good news," Grandpa said from the driver's seat.

"I'm glad you're coming with me," Anna said. "With John gone, I have no other relatives."

Grandpa drove up in front of the hospital. He left the Ford idling and went to get a wheelchair.

Anna braced herself for another pain as she sank down in the chair.

At the admission desk, Mrs. Erickson said, "This is Mrs. John Whitmore. She's in labor."

"Dr. Wilson knows that I'm coming in," Anna said, panting.

"Did your water break, Mrs. Whitmore?" the nurse asked.

"No, but the pains are coming five minutes apart."

"We'll take you to the maternity ward right away."

"I'm her grandmother. May I come along?" Mrs. Erickson asked.

"Yes, you can come and wait in the waiting room."

Everything happened so fast. Grandpa Erickson squeezed into the elevator just before the door closed. Both grandparents wished Anna good luck, and she waved to them as she was wheeled away.

A nurse examined Anna, and then said, "I'll go and get Dr. Wilson."

Anna waited. She sweated through another pain before she heard Dr. Wilson's voice.

"The nurse tells me that your baby is breeched," he said.

"It sounds bad."

He listened to the baby's heartbeat and smiled.

"The little heart is pumping well, but the baby is not in the right position yet. If it doesn't turn by itself, we'll help. Don't worry. We'll do the work. You won't feel anything."

"I'm in your hands, Dr. Wilson," Anna stammered while a new pain began.

"Is your husband here?"

"No, he is in the service. My grandparents Erickson are in the waiting room."

"We'll wheel you into the operating room now."

Anna counted to seven or eight before she was out. When she came to, she heard doctors and nurses talking.

"She's blue." Then she heard a faint cry. She wanted to ask if it came from her baby, but she couldn't talk. The floating image of a nurse appeared above her. She was holding a crinkly baby.

"Congratulations," she said. "It's a seven-pound girl."

Everything seemed unreal to Anna. She had no recollection of the birth. The image of Dr. Wilson floated above her next. "The baby is fine, Mrs. Whitmore," he said. "Now the nurses will take care of you and wheel you back to your room."

Anna managed to whisper a weak, "Thank you, doctor."

She drifted in and out of sleep. The nurses wet her dry lips. They wrapped her up in clean linen from top to bottom. Ceilings and walls whirled by as they moved her.

The next time she opened her eyes, she saw her grandmother standing by her bed with a bouquet of flowers in her hand.

"How are you dear? Congratulations are in order," she said. "You have a beautiful baby girl."

"Is she all right?"

"She looks fine to me."

"Thank you for waiting and thank you for the flowers. They're lovely."

"I'll place them here in the window, dear, so you can see them."

Anna's eyes followed her grandmother's movements until she came back to her bed.

"Someone said that my baby was blue," Anna said in a worrisome voice.

"She was rosy pink when we saw her through the glass wall."

"Rosy pink. That sounds good. Is Grandpa here?"

"Yes, I am. Congratulations, Anna," Grandpa said as he rose from a chair.

"Would you please send a wire to John, Grandpa?"

"I did so two hours ago, and I mailed your letter to him also."

"Have I slept that long?"

"You're drowsy from the anesthesia, dear," Grandma said. "You need to sleep it off."

"But I want to see my baby," Anna said.

"Now that you're awake, they'll bring her to you. We'll go home and call Brita and Ole about the good news."

"Please tell Henry that he has a little sister."

"Yes, of course. Do you have a name for her?"

"Yes, Kristina—in memory of my sister. We'll spell it with a K."

"I like it. We'll be back tomorrow."

Anna pressed the call button for the nurse. When she came, Anna asked, "May I see my daughter now?"

"Yes, Mrs. Whitmore, I'll bring her to you."

Anna lifted her head from the pillow when the nurse came carrying the baby wrapped in a pink blanket. The little girl was asleep.

Anna looked at her and was relieved to see that she was rosy pink like Grandma had said.

"She's beautiful," Anna said.

"You have nursed before, Mrs. Whitmore, so I don't have to teach you."

What a wonderful feeling it is to have a new baby, Anna thought. If only John could be here.

"Hello, Kristina. I'm your mommy," she said. "Do you want to practice eating?"

Kristina opened one eye and when she felt the nipple in her mouth she began to suckle.

"From the looks of it, she'll do fine," the nurse said. "You can have her for a little while, but don't go to sleep."

"No, I won't. I don't want to miss a minute of this."

Finally, she had the daughter she had wished for. She thought of the newborn, who had been placed on her doorstep and who was now Sally's daughter. *She was the last baby I held in my arms until now. I now have my very own daughter. I'm so blessed.* She thought of the birth announcements she would write. One would go to her father in Sweden, one would go to her cousin Ethel in Worcester, and another one would go to Roberto in Italy. She mustn't forget Sally and Carl.

Chapter 31

The patients aboard l'Italia had been transferred to a British ship anchored in Genoa, and Roberto walked ashore. There were no welcoming ceremonies. Tessa was not there to meet him. She was at work and didn't know he was coming. He walked straight to his home.

"Mama, I'm home," he announced from the doorway.

"Roberto, my son, welcome home." Mama Lea wiped her hands on her apron and came and stretched to kiss both of his cheeks.

"How's the grape harvest this year, Mama?"

"I sold my grapes to a winemaker, but I haven't been paid yet."

"We've got to see to that."

"Carlo wrote the contract and he'll collect."

"That's good. You'll need the money, Mama. How's Tessa?"

"Tessa is still very thin. I don't think she's well, Roberto. She has had a cold for a long time and she still coughs. She always worries about her parents, and I think she's helping them with money. Everything has become so expensive, and they seem to have a harder time than most."

"They shouldn't lean on her."

"But you look well, Roberto."

"I'm well. How's the rest of the family?"

"Isabella's children have the measles. There's a measles epidemic in town."

"Is the goat still giving milk?"

"Oh, yes. I'm happy about the goat."

"Has Laura heard from Salvo?"

"No, not for a long time. This war is going on too long, Roberto."

"I know, but now that the Americans are coming, it won't be long before we have peace. Anthony might already be in Europe. The Russians have stopped fighting because of their revolution, and the British will be coming to our aid in northern Italy. If the Germans would stop assisting the Austrians, it would be much easier for our troops."

"You know so much, Roberto. Anthony will fight on our side, won't he?"

"Yes, Mama. He'll be on the Allied side, but probably on the western front."

"I'll go and make dinner. It will be a meatless meal of pasta and vegetables. Meat has become a luxury. I suppose most of it goes to the military."

"I'm sure it does," Roberto said. "The fighting men need meat. I hear that the German soldiers hardly get any meat, and that they have to wear paper underwear because they can't get any cotton."

"Paper underwear." Mama Lea laughed. "That sounds awful."

"At least they don't have to be washed."

"You're right about that." His mother laughed again.

"May I invite Tessa for dinner?"

"Of course."

"Then I'll go and get her."

Roberto knew what time she was coming home from work, so he planned to surprise her. When he saw her coming toward him with her head down, he called her name. She looked up when she heard his voice.

"Roberto, you're home. What a nice surprise." They both ran to cover the distance between them. Roberto put his hands around Tessa's face and kissed her. Her lips were no longer plump. When he put his arms around her, he felt what he had already seen. She was even thinner than the last time he saw her, and she had dark circles under her eyes.

"How're you feeling, sweetheart?" he asked

"I'll be fine now that you're home, Roberto."

"I hope so. But you don't look well to me. Have you consulted a doctor?"

"No, I haven't. The doctors are always busy treating veterans."

She coughed, and Roberto recognized that cough. He had heard it every day at the sanatorium.

"Tomorrow, you're coming with me to see Dr. Flavio. Nurses can get sick, too, you know."

"I know Roberto, but it's just a cold."

"What kind of wounds or illnesses do the soldiers in your ward suffer from?"

"Some have tuberculosis in addition to their injuries. They should be in a sanatorium and not in the hospital."

"I agree."

Roberto had reason to be concerned.

While placing a stethoscope on Tessa's back and chest, Doctor Flavio asked her to cough. Then he inquired about her work and said, "You need to take time off from the hospital and rest."

"But there's so much to do at the hospital," Tessa said. "We don't have enough nurses."

"If you don't take care of yourself, they will have one less," Dr. Flavio said.

"It sounds serious. I'll do what you say, Doctor. But I'll need a statement from you that I have to stay home."

"Yes, I'll write one," Dr. Flavio said.

While Tessa dressed, Roberto talked to Dr. Flavio.

"I hope she hasn't become afflicted with tuberculosis," he said.

"Not yet, but her lungs are weak. She doesn't breathe the way she should. She needs fresh air and should not be among patients with tuberculosis. I know that there're some at the hospital."

"I go back on duty in a couple of weeks, but until then, I'll take her for walks on the beach every day," Roberto said. "She can have dinner with Mama and me every night. My mama is a good cook."

"It will be good for Tessa. She should come back to my office in three months, and by then I'm sure that she will be much improved. I'll write a statement for her."

Roberto felt enormous relief that all that Tessa needed was rest. He didn't have to fear anything else.

"Do you want to come with me to the beach?" he asked her as they walked home.

"Yes, I'd like to go with you, Roberto. Going to the beach is such a luxury for me."

"After that we'll go home to Mama and have dinner."

"It sounds wonderful. You two are spoiling me."

With their arms around each other, they walked back and forth on the beach, looking at the ever-present shrieking gulls catching fish in the water.

Tessa filled her lungs with the fresh breeze from the sea and felt invigorated. They talked about the upcoming Christmas and all the restrictions that were in place.

"I want you to celebrate Christmas with my family," Roberto said.

"I like that, Roberto, but I'll to go to church with my parents."

"Yes, of course."

"When you get better, I think it would be good if you would not work at the hospital anymore."

Tessa was quiet while she thought about it. Nursing was all she knew.

At dinner, Roberto fussed over Tessa. "Please eat some more, sweetheart. You haven't had enough."

"This is much more than I usually eat," she said. "I feel full."

"Then you should eat more often, honey. How about some goat's milk in between meals and some cheese?"

"If you insist."
"I do. I want you to get well."

Chapter 32

Mama Lea came inside with a letter in her hand. "It's from Antonio," she said.

"Please, give it to me, Mama, and I'll read it to you," Roberto said. It was mailed from the United States.

The New England National Guard has formed a division, and we're shipping out to Europe as soon as we can get ships for transport. I believe we're going to France. I hope to get an opportunity to come home for a visit. Until you hear from me again, you can write to me at the return address listed on the envelope. Mail will be forwarded to me wherever I am. Live well, Anthony.

"I hope that he can come and visit us," Mama Lea said. "That's a short letter."

"We'll hear from him again once he arrives in France," Roberto assured his mother.

"Roberto, I need money to pay bills and go shopping," Lea said.

He reached for his wallet and took out some lire. "Is this enough for now?" he asked. "I can go to the newspapers and pick up my pay for some articles I wrote."

"It's enough for now, Roberto. But I want you to come with me to the store and help me carry what I buy. Then you'll see how expensive everything has become."

"Certainly. I haven't thought about the money situation. Didn't Papa leave you anything?"

"We had some cash when he died, but he hadn't worked much since the war started, and I don't think that his customers had paid their bills either."

"Do you know if he kept records?"

"Yes, he had a ledger. I'll show it to you. Perhaps you can make sense of it."

"Let's go to the store first, Mama, and then I'll look at it."

Mama was right. Roberto couldn't believe how expensive everything was, and how little they could buy with their rationing coupons. He wondered if his small salary from the Navy would go far enough. He noticed that the other customers didn't pay when they left. The clerk entered all their purchases in a book.

"Mama, do you owe the grocer money?" Roberto asked.

"Yes, I owe him for the last few times I was here."

"Let's find out how much it is."

Roberto reached for his wallet again and paid up. His Mama already had lire to pay for the day's purchases, but Roberto knew that she needed more until he came back home on another furlough.

He sat down to study his father's ledger. Papa had paid for his own purchases of lumber, but had not collected on the last bills he had written. Roberto would write new bills and deliver them himself, and hoped that the customers would pay. He was glad to find a savings book with a nice sum posted to the account. Mama would have to come with him to the bank to withdraw money.

Roberto again looked at the huge inventory of lumber and had a thought, but it would have to be the last resort. They could sell some of the lumber. But would they get what it was worth? His siblings should also have a say in the matter.

He wrote new invoices and told Mama that he was going out to try to collect. No one paid in full, but he received small, partial payments that he deducted from the bills. He realized that everyone was hard up for cash. When his father had passed away, their obligations to him had been postponed.

That evening, he had a talk with his mother.

"Did Papa have a written will?" he asked.

"No, it's only the upper-class people that bother with such things."

"Didn't you have to have some kind of settlement after Papa died?"

"No. With the war coming, no one has reminded us about that."

"I found this savings account in Papa's name. I'll go to the bank and talk to the banker about what we should do according to the law. You should come with me, Mama."

"Yes, I will, Roberto, but not today. I need to take care of the meat we bought before it spoils."

Roberto thought about Lydia's will and how he had inherited the beach house. He still had some money in the United States, but he had no way of getting it now that Anthony was in the service.

He decided that he needed to write for the local paper to get more cash. But what would he write about? He had already written about the rescue missions to the Dardanelles and northern Italy. Could he write about the measles epidemic, or had someone else already done that? Or should he write about Little Italy in Boston? Would anyone here be interested in that? He decided to seek out the local editor and ask him what he wanted.

The editor thought about it and said, "Both subjects would be good, but write about the measles epidemic first. Make it a personal story about a few families that have been affected and how they coped with it. You don't have to mention names, but find out as much as you can. Many children have died." While Roberto was at the newspaper, he got paid for articles that he had already submitted.

Instead of taking a siesta, Roberto sat down to write. He knew some of the bereaved families. For the others, he would visit their neighbors and find out as much as he could.

Dezi sat on the veranda with his injured leg up on a chair and his foot in fresh bandages. Roberto greeted him with, "How're you, old buddy?"

"Good of you to stop by, Roberto. The front of my foot has been amputated."

"That's too bad. How much?"

"All my toes. It will be difficult to walk, at least in the beginning."

"Are you getting any compensation from the military?"

"Very little. If it wasn't for the fact that I could live with my parents, I don't know if I could make it."

"Do you know of any other veterans who are in the same situation?"

"Yes, I met some at the hospital. By the way, I didn't see Tessa there. Isn't she working as a nurse anymore?"

"She had to take some time off."

"Do you know that our neighbors lost their youngest?"

"Yes, Mama told me. How well do you know them?"

Dezi went on to tell Roberto about the family. They had three more children who were sick. Roberto made mental notes. Then Dezi told him about another family where the father was an injured veteran. He had shot himself when his son died. "Now, his family is impoverished. Since it was a suicide, I don't know if they will get a military pension."

"So much misery. Do you know of any other hardship cases?"

"Yes, I know of several from my stay in the hospital. They all have hardship stories to tell, and now they have the measles epidemic to cope with."

"Anyone I know?"

Dezi asked if Roberto knew so and so, and told him what had happened to their mutual friends and classmates, who were now more or less maimed.

"Are there any local organizations that can help these veterans?"

"Not that I know of."

Roberto had material for two articles, but first he went to see his sister, Isabella, who according to Mama had all her children down with the measles.

Isabella met Roberto on the hacienda. She said that her youngest was very ill. The older children had almost gotten over it, but measles was much more serious for infants and toddlers.

"Little Fonso is burning up with fever. The doctors are too busy to come by. I don't know what to do."

"I could ask Tessa," Roberto said. "She's a nurse."

"Would you? Please let me know what she says. I'm so worried."

"Then I better go right away."

"There won't be any Christmas celebration at our house," Isabella said. "We aren't going anywhere, and we'll not have any company."

"I understand. Hope your little one recovers."

Tessa told Roberto that Isabella should take off the baby's clothes and bathe him in tepid water until he cools down. She should also try to get liquid into him to prevent dehydration. Roberto took the message to Isabella at once.

Isabella didn't answer the door. Roberto went to the back of the house and banged on the kitchen door. After a while, Isabella came to the door. Her face was drenched in tears.

"It's too late, Roberto, my little Fonso just died. We named him after Papa Alfonso, and now he, too, is gone."

"I'm so sorry. Is Alberto at home?"

"No, he's at work."

"I'll go and get him."

"Bless you, brother."

Chapter 33

Mama Lea went to Mass the next morning to pray for little Fonso's soul. Then she went to Isabella' house to comfort the family.

After Fonso's funeral, she went with Roberto to the bank. Dressed in her black clothes and veil, she sat by his side. The banker looked at the papers in front of him and turned to Roberto.

"In the absence of a will, I believe it would be best to leave everything the way it is," he said.

"That's good," Mrs. Cosentino said, her voice coming from behind the black veil. "I don't want to sell my house."

"You don't have to, but now that your husband is deceased, Signora Cosentino, you'll need someone to watch out for your interests. Do you have anyone in mind?"

"My brother, Carlo."

"Does he live here?"

"Yes, he's a fisherman."

"Very well. Please ask him to come and see me. You can withdraw money from your savings account for general expenses, signora, and your brother can do it for you, as soon as he has signed the papers."

"*Grazie*, signor."

"My younger sisters are under-aged. They'll need a guardian," Roberto said.

"I'm glad you mentioned it."

"Mrs. Cosentino, would you like to have your brother be the guardian for your under-aged daughters as well?"

"Yes."

"Very well. How are your other children, signora? What are they doing now?"

"Salvo is at the front. Antonio is on his way from America to France, and Isabella's children have all had the measles. Her youngest died and was buried yesterday."

"I'm sorry to hear it."

Roberto went to take Tessa for a walk and tell her about Fonso's death.

"I'm so sorry," she said. "It could have been prevented."

As they walked along the harbor, he looked at all the ships anchored there. There were ships carrying the flags of all the Allied countries, except the United States. He wondered if American ships would ever come as far as Genoa.

He worried about the risks that Anthony would face while fighting in Europe. He thought of Anna. Her husband might have been conscripted. How would she manage alone? He knew that she had few relatives for support. Would Salvo survive all the battles in Northern Italy? Would Italy ever win, or would the casualties keep mounting?

Roberto and Tessa walked over to l'Italia as it prepared for another mission to save lives. Every time the ship was in the home harbor, she was scrubbed down and sterilized. Dock workers loaded new supplies, and when she sailed again, Roberto would be on board.

As they walked home, they heard the church bells peal for another funeral and the hoofs of horses pounding against the pavement as they pulled another hearse to the cemetery.

Jolanda and Liliana said that they would like to apply for work at the fish cannery.

"So many men have been called up that they need to hire women at the cannery," Jolanda said. "Would you go with us, Roberto?"

"I don't like it," Mama said. "It's not suitable for women."

"But Mama, we'll be paid for our work rather than just learning to sew."

"But learning to sew will give you a chance to make money from your skill later on."

"Sewing is better suited for women than factory work," Roberto said.

"We want to take a look at the cannery and make up our own minds," Jolanda said.

"In that case, Roberto should go with you, so that you're not taken advantage of because of your young age," Mama Lea said. She turned to Roberto.

"Show them the stinking place so they change their minds."

"I'll go with them," he said, "but I agree with Mama that it doesn't sound like a good place for women to work."

The smell of fish permeated the air as they approached the cannery. Jolanda and Liliana were only seventeen and sixteen years old, and Roberto didn't think that they understood what it would be like to stand by a table and clean fish all day.

"You two are old enough to get married," he reminded them.

"Married. There aren't any boys left to marry. They're all in the military," Jolanda, the oldest said.

"Yeah, we'll be two old maids before the war is over," Liliana chimed in. "It's just as well. Mama will never be able to pay for our weddings, or give us a dowry."

"That's probably true," Roberto said. "I've just gone over her finances, and she'll need her money for every day expenses."

"We could help her with money if we worked at the cannery," Jolanda said.

"I've been told that women make only half of what the men make doing the same work," Roberto said.

"That's not fair," Jolanda said.

"No, it isn't," Roberto admitted. "But that's the way it is. Do you still want to work there?"

"Yes, we still want to work there," they both said.

"How're you going to get to work? It's too far to walk here every day."

"We'll ride bicycles," Liliana said.

"Or we could rent a room in one of the apartments here. This one says that there are rooms available," Jolanda said, pointing to one building.

"I don't think that Mama would like that," Roberto said. "She wants you to live at home, I'm sure."

"You're right, Roberto. The job is only temporary anyway. After the war, we'll go back to sewing," Jolanda said.

"Let's take a look at the gutting place and see if you think you can work there."

"Gutting place." Jolanda backed off. "I don't want to gut fish."

"There might not be any other openings," Roberto said.

"I'll gut fish, if I have to," Liliana said.

Roberto took the girls to the gutting place. The girls turned and ran out the door, holding their noses.

"Well, then. Do you think you can stand the smell and the heat in the cookery? It won't be much better."

"Isn't there some other work we can do?" Jolanda asked.

"Perhaps you could pack the fish into cans?"

"Yes, that sounds better."

Roberto signed them up to begin work in the packing plant the following week.

"Now, we've some explaining to do to Mama," he said.

"Would you fix up two old bikes for us?" Liliana asked him.

"Yes, I'll do my best."

Mama Lea disliked that her girls were going to work at the cannery, but she accepted it.

Roberto sat by the kitchen table and had breakfast with his mother.

"I think you'll need to rent out the workshop and sell the lumber," he said.

"I suppose I could, but you should discuss it with your siblings."

"I can write to Anthony about it."

Roberto sat down to answer Anthony's letter. He wrote about the circumstances at home, including their nephew's tragic death, and went on to tell him about the war.

They're fighting mostly in Mesopotamia and Africa now, and it looks like it will be up to the American forces to drive the Germans out of Verdun, France. Us Italians with the help of French troops failed in an attack on German and Bulgarian forces at Salonika, Greece. Two Austrian destroyers attacked an Italian convoy of three merchant ships and one destroyer in the Straits of Otranto, sinking the destroyer and one merchant ship. They continued their barrage until British and French destroyers came to their assistance. Then the Austrians managed to escape. I read that President Wilson is enlarging the American Army and that General Pershing will be the commander of the U.S. forces in Europe. We're eagerly waiting for his arrival in London and Paris.

At the end of the letter, Roberto asked Anthony what he thought about the idea of renting out Papa's work shop.

Before boarding the ship, Roberto bought the local newspaper and saw that the two articles he'd written were published with big headlines and his name as the feature writer. He showed it to Tessa, and asked her to buy two copies for the family.

"We're so fortunate compared to the people I write about," he said as he kissed her goodbye.

Chapter 34

In November of 1917, Roberto read a newspaper article about the conditions on the Western front. The life expectancy of the pilots who flew the small planes was three weeks. Yet they preferred the flying to fighting on the ground. Life in the trenches was horrible. The rats were as big as cats from eating the dead. The soldiers shot the rats if they had enough ammunition, but ammunition shipped from the United States was sabotaged on the ships, and it arrived more or less useless. Many ships carrying military supplies were torpedoed by the Germans. From what Roberto could gather, no ships with American soldiers had been sunk.

Both sides used poisonous gas and tanks on the front lines. If the soldiers happened to turn back rather than attack, they were shot by their own sergeants. It was the generals' war, and they often made bad decisions, resulting in the needless slaughter of millions of men and mutiny among the troops. The French General Nivelle had been replaced by General Foch, who seemed to be liked and in control. The first American soldiers had begun to fight in France. The young, fresh troops referred to as the "dough boys," marched gaily into battle, not knowing that tens of thousands of them would die in their first offense. The dead and wounded were quickly replaced by fresh troops. They were Europe's hope of winning the war against Germany.

Roberto knew that the conditions on the so-called Southern front where his countrymen fought the Austrians were no better. He thought of his brother Salvo, who had been one of the first Italian men to be called up. The Italian General Cadorna had failed in most of his offensives, and he'd lost big in his defense of Caporetto. The Austrians, who no longer had to fight the Russians, applied stronger pressure on the Italians. The Caporetto attack alone had cost the Italian army ten thousand dead and thirty thousand wounded. Roberto was relieved to see that General Diaz had replaced General Cadorna. He was also pleased to read that British and French soldiers had been dispatched to assist Italy. Another hopeful sign was that three German divisions had been recalled to the Western Front. Now, Roberto thought that his country had a chance of winning decisive victories.

Before Christmas, l'Italia would make another trip to the Gulf of Venice and evacuate wounded soldiers. Roberto always felt anxious about going to that region. Would he get to see his brother this time?

Once again, l'Italia anchored at Lesolo where the river, Di Piave, had its outlet. Roberto stood on deck with his binoculars peering through the mist for ferries that would carry the injured troops. He reported to the captain that none were in sight. The captain said that they would wait until morning.

In the morning, when still no ferries or boats had arrived, the captain asked for volunteers to board lifeboats and go up the river to find out what delayed the rescue operation. Roberto volunteered. Doing something was better than waiting. The fog closed in on the men as they rowed up the river. Their guns rested on the gunwale. It was quiet. The cold numbed the hands of the rowers. A lieutenant stood in the front of the first boat with his binoculars raised, but they fogged up and he couldn't see anything.

A shot rang through the air and swished by the lieutenant's head. He ducked and called out, "medical rescue, medical rescue" in Italian. Another shot hit the stern of the boat. The shots had come from the left bank of the river.

"If they don't identify themselves, they are the enemy," the lieutenant said. "Steer to the right shore," he commanded. "We don't want to be sitting ducks."

The men rowed toward the right bank and hid the boat among the vegetation. When the shots continued to hit the water around them, the lieutenant ordered all the men into the woods. They thought they were safe until they encountered fire from the woods. One bullet hit Roberto in his thigh. With medics at his side, he got first aid, but the wound hurt like hell. He heard the lieutenant's order to fire back. After a while, the shooting stopped.

They lay low and listened for any sound, raising their heads when they heard a ferry approach from the north. The lieutenant and a few of the men ran toward the river. Two men came back and said that the ferry had white crosses painted on the side and that it was Italian.

"We're to carry our wounded to our lifeboat and board the ferry," a medic said.

"We've only one man wounded badly enough to be carried," a man said. "It's Cosentino."

"Make a stretcher," the medic said.

"It takes too long," Roberto said. "I'll walk with the help of a crutch."

"No, you will not. It's better that two men support you," the medic said.

He was exhausted when they reached the shoreline. Strong arms lifted him into the lifeboat and onto the ferry, and later he swung in a cradle up the side of l'Italia.

He waited for a doctor to remove the bullet in his leg, but with the injured evacuees arriving in a steady stream, he had to wait a long time. A male nurse gave him a morphine shot and he drifted off. When he awoke, a doctor stood over him, saying that the enemy bullet had been removed, and that he would be on sick leave.

There were many injured British and French soldiers aboard. Roberto heard a Brit saying, "We held our lines. Now, we have a chance to win. It might not be until next year, but we'll win."

Roberto strained his ears to listen for an Italian voice that sounded like Salvo's. He asked the Italians around him if they had seen Salvo Cosentino. No one had. He told himself that his brother could be on another hospital ship. There was a chance that he still fought, but how could he hold on for so long without being injured? He could also be dead, or captured, or he could be one of the four hundred thousand deserters hiding somewhere and risking being shot by military police. Not knowing was the worst of all.

So far, l'Italia had not had any female nurses aboard, but Roberto knew that there was a serious shortage of male nurses on the ship. The orderlies had to change his bandages.

While l'Italia made a stop in Naples, Roberto asked for a newspaper. He read that the Turks had evacuated Jerusalem after four hundred years of rule over the Holy City. German and Russian negotiators had signed an armistice. British fighter planes had bombed Mannheim and Ludwigshafen from thirteen thousand feet. President Wilson had issued a proclamation giving the federal government control of the nation's railroads. Roberto guessed it would make it easier for military transports to proceed by rail.

When l'Italia had anchored in Genoa, Roberto was carried ashore on a stretcher and transported to the hospital by ambulance. He had an infection in his wound and it had to be cleaned. A nurse was supposed to give him morphine before the procedure.

"Roberto, you're my patient."

He opened his eyes and looked into Tessa's.

"Are you here, sweetheart?" I thought you were still on sick leave."

"No, I'm fine. Dr. Flavio said that I could go back to work."

"I'm glad that you're here. How bad is my injury?"

"I'll know in a little while. How could you get shot on a hospital ship?"

"I wasn't on the ship when I got hit. I was on land. I'll explain later. Now, please give me that injection."

When Roberto woke up, Tessa stood over him and smiled at him.

"You're doing all right, *mio caro*," she whispered.

Roberto's mouth was too dry to speak. Tessa swabbed his lips with a ball of cotton drenched in water. He motioned to her for a drink of water.

"Not yet." She stuck a thermometer in his mouth and waited.

"You're running a fever, but it's not bad," she said. "Go to sleep, and I'll be back later." She gave his arm a tender pat.

Roberto slept. When he awoke, he rang for the nurse. But it wasn't Tessa.

"Tessa," he said.

"No, Tessa is not here at the moment. She has been sitting by your bed for hours, but she needed a break. "

"Water," he begged.

"You can have a sip of water."

The nurse gave him a paper straw in a glass, and he sucked up the little water there was.

"More."

"No, not yet." He knew why, but he was so thirsty.

"Next time you wake up, you can have more to drink."

With that thought in mind and knowing that Tessa would be back, Roberto went to sleep.

In the coming days when he felt better, he stayed awake until Tessa was off duty. She then came to his ward and pulled the curtain around his bed so they could embrace and kiss in private. Roberto wanted her to climb into bed with him, but she refused.

"It wouldn't be proper," she said.

"But you're the one making me well," he said. "I can feel my strength coming from you."

"Good, then you can soon go home,"

"Will you visit me at home?"
"Of course, I will."

Chapter 35

After a week in the hospital Roberto was fever free. A doctor told him that he could go home the next day. He'd rather have stayed under Tessa's care at the hospital, but the hospital was short of beds because so many patients had come in from l'Italia. Roberto talked with some of them. His sisters had visited him, but not his mother. In her younger days, the distance would not have prevented her from walking to the hospital. He hoped that she was all right.

"How am I going to get home?" Roberto asked Tessa as she gave him his clothes to get dressed.

"Dezi will take you in his cab. Your mother arranged it."

"How's Mama? She hasn't been here to visit me."

"She's had a cold and didn't want to give it to you and the other patients. But she's better now."

Tessa wheeled him in a wheelchair to Dezi's cab. She gave him his crutch and said that they couldn't kiss outside the hospital.

Dezi chatted with Roberto about the war. He said that the so-called Spanish Influenza had claimed many lives on the western front. Roberto wanted a newspaper, and Dezi stopped to buy one for him before helping him into the Cosentino home.

Mama Lea had prepared a room for Roberto beside the kitchen. She wanted to have him close.

"I'm all right now, Mama, and I'll be up walking around."

"I'm glad to hear it."

"Do you still have the goat, Mama?"

"No, Vito came and got it. She was ready to mate."

"Are there any letters for me?"

"Yes, there is a letter from Anthony mailed from France. We've already read it. There's also a card from Sophia, and she sent us coffee. You need to write and thank her for that. There's also a card from your friend Anna in Boston. I put them all on your night table."

Roberto read the one from Anthony first. He wrote that after training under the French, he was among the first American troops to occupy the line in the Sommerville sector. The letter had taken a long time to arrive. So there was no recent news from Anthony.

He read the card from Sophia, who wrote that she and Collette missed Anthony and that she felt lonesome. Anna wrote that she had given birth to a daughter, that John served in Washington, D.C., and that Tom, the butler, had died of a stroke.

Roberto felt tired and lay down on his bed. After a while, he would start writing the article about the rescue mission when he was injured.

In the evening, Tessa came to visit him, and that perked him up more than anything else. After their evening meal in the kitchen, Roberto coaxed her into his room.

"I'm lonesome without you," he said, and asked her to sit beside him on his bed.

"I've longed for you, too, Roberto, but I have something important to tell you."

She paused and looked at him.

"Tell me what it is then."

"I've been called to service as a nurse on l'Italia."

"No, I don't want you to be on a ship. It can be dangerous."

"Roberto, you told me yourself that hospital ships are safe."

"They're relatively safe, but I won't be there to protect you. You mean so much to me, and I couldn't stand it if something happened to you."

"Now you know what I've been feeling while you were gone."

"It's not fair that you'll be at sea while I'm home."

"It's ironic, to say the least," Tessa admitted.

"I'll get well soon, and then I'll be back on duty," Roberto said stroking her hair. "Then we can have a shipboard romance."

"My tour is only for three months."

"Perhaps it will be extended."

"No one seems to know. Several other nurses from our hospital are going."

"Until then, we've only two weeks together."

"I'm training in the evenings."

"You've had enough practice caring for me."

"It's not the same as being on a hospital ship. What's it like?"

"We had only male nurses, and their hands are rough compared to yours." Roberto took her hand and stroked his face with it. They kissed and hugged until Roberto was too exhausted to do anything.

"*Buona notte, mio caro*," Tessa said as she covered him with a blanket. Her big, brave man slept like a baby.

When Roberto felt better, he asked Dezi to drive him to Salvo's for a visit with Laura.

"How are you, Roberto? So sorry you were injured," Laura said when she saw him hobbling on his crutches.

"It was only a bullet wound to my thigh. I'll be on sick leave for three months though."

"I had a letter from Salvo. He sent it with one of the evacuated injured troops."

"Really? I asked almost all of them if they had met Salvo."

"Here it is," Laura said, handing it to Roberto. "You can read it if you want."

Salvo had written the letter in pencil because they didn't have any ink. He said that the British had arrived and some Americans. He hoped the war would be over soon so that he could come home. He wondered what his brothers were doing. The rest was personal to his wife and children.

"I'm so glad he's safe," Roberto said.

"I am too, but it can change fast."

"It won't be long now before the war is over. The Americans will make a big difference. They have shipped over one million soldiers, and more are coming."

"God bless the United States."

"Brother, Antonio, serves in the American Army."

"Where is he?"

"He's in France, not far from Switzerland."

"Just think if he could come and visit us."

"Perhaps after the war."

Roberto told Laura how the goat's milk had restored Tessa to health and that she had been called to serve as a nurse on l'Italia.

"Are they recruiting women? It's unbelievable."

"Only as nurses, but we didn't think it would come to that."

They talked about the measles epidemic and how tragic it was that Isabella's little boy had died. "I'm going to visit Isabella next. Dezi is waiting outside, so I have to go."

"Do you need flour? I have some."

"I'm sure that Mama would appreciate it. And it would be easy to take it home in the car."

"I'll go with you outside then and give you a small sack."

Roberto watched his sister-in-law scooping flour from a bin into a sack and closing it up with a string.

"*Grazie mille*. It will make lots of bread and pancakes."

"I deliver flour to the military, and I'm hoping that it might benefit Salvo," she said.

"It might." Roberto called on Dezi to come and carry the sack to the cab.

"How're you, Dezi? I heard that you were injured earlier in the war," Laura said.

"Yes, but I'm all right now. I can't do any heavy work, but I can drive a cab."

"Do you get enough gasoline?"

"Having a cab is the best way to get gasoline."

Isabella and Alberto were home and were surprised to see Roberto coming in a cab. The crutches told them why. Dezi and Isabella knew each other well from the time they were neighbors. The children gathered in a corner to watch and listen. There was much talk about the war, about Roberto's and Dezi's injuries, about shortages, and the measles epidemic that had now subsided.

"*Grazie, Madonna,*" Isabella said and crossed herself. "But not before it took our son. It was God's will. Now little Fonso is an angel in heaven. We've four healthy children left, and we're thankful for that."

Roberto asked Alberto about his work.

"I still work at the ammunition factory, and I'm making good money. They're not drafting men my age, and I hope it won't come to that," Alberto said.

"They're drafting the ones that are turning seventeen," Roberto said. "They are also accepting nurses. Tessa is serving right now on the hospital ship."

Isabella and Alberto were as surprised as Laura had been. Roberto then asked them whether they thought that Mama should rent out Papa's workshop, and they said it would be a good idea if she could get someone honest and skilled.

Chapter 36

Roberto went to see Dr. Flavio. The wound in his thigh had healed but after nearly three months, it still hurt to walk.

"The bullet could have hit a nerve," Dr. Flavio said. "I'm sorry to say that it might take a long time for that pain to go away. I'll give you three more months to recover."

He could still swim, and now that the weather was warm, he swam every day. It was good for his leg and general condition. He thought about his life in Boston. He had enjoyed the days at Cape Cod and he had enjoyed writing the articles. But he could do the same in Genoa. He could start sailing also, and he could pilot Uncle Carlo's fishing trawler. No one looked down on him. He was not a foreigner as he had been in Boston. He hadn't heard from Tessa yet and wondered how she coped. She must have been seasick in the beginning. The sea swells could be difficult, not to mention the storms.

Roberto read in the newspapers that German shells had fallen on Paris from 'Big Bertha' seventy-five miles away. If the Allies still had to defend Paris, it didn't seem that they had made any progress at all. Marshall Foch had been named commander for the combined Allied forces. The British had created the Royal Naval Air Force with more than half of their planes being fighter planes. Most of the German and French planes were used for reconnaissance. The first American troops had been in the Ansauville sector for three months while training with the French army. Roberto knew that Anthony was stationed there. The troops had suffered casualties while repelling German raids and gas shells. He prayed that Anthony was safe.

In May, he received a letter from Anthony saying that the First Division 28th Regiment, with the help of the French, had captured all Germans in the town of Cantigny, but lost more than one thousand men. The Germans lost more, he said. Anthony had been in his first battle and seemed proud of it.

In June, Roberto read about the awful battle at Di Piave. The Italians had pushed the last Austrians across the river, but it had cost them eighty-five thousand men. The Austrians lost almost as many, but they also lost men due to desertion.

Dezi came to see how Roberto was doing.

"I saw that your ship is in, so I suppose you'll be leaving in a few days." he said.

"I didn't know that l'Italia had come in," Roberto said with surprise in his voice. "Tessa hasn't been here to see me. I hope she's all right."

"Maybe she's trying to find her land legs," Dezi joked.

"Well, I'm ready to go out. I've been laid up long enough."

"You must have gotten a lot of writing done."

"Yes, I did."

They talked about the war, and both hoped that it would be over soon.

"What will you do after the war?" Dezi asked.

"I haven't decided," Roberto said. He didn't want to say anything about staying until he knew what Tessa was up to.

"Well, I wish you a good tour. Perhaps it's the last one."

"Thank you, Dezi."

Roberto walked down to the harbor to find out how long l'Italia had been in and when it was leaving. He was surprised to learn that it had been in for a week already and was leaving as soon as it had been reloaded with medical supplies.

Why hadn't Tessa come to see him? Was she ill? He began to worry about her, but he had never been inside her parents' apartment and didn't want to go there now. He went back home to get ready to ship out. His last newspaper articles would have to be either delivered to the local newspaper or mailed to Boston.

He read the newspaper when Mama came and said that Tessa was at the front door, but that she couldn't come in. Roberto put his paper down and hurried to meet her.

"I've been waiting for you," he said. "Are you all right?"

"I'm all right. How are you?"

He asked her to come in, and she did, but kept standing by the door. He sensed something different about her and did not kiss her.

"I'm declared ready to ship out. Welcome back, Tessa. Please sit down," he said motioning to a chair, but she just stood there, casting nervous glances toward the front yard.

"I can't stay," she said.

He wanted to ask why, but instead he said, "How was your tour?"

"When I got over my seasickness, it was all right."

Why were they having this conversation when they should be hugging and kissing?

"So you got seasick. Did the other nurses get sick also?"

"Not all of them. But I haven't been to sea before."

"Where did you go?"

"To Di Piave."

"That's where I got injured."

"I thought about that, Roberto."

"You didn't see Salvo this time either?"

"No. I'm sorry." It seemed to Roberto that they kept on talking to fill the void between them.

"How difficult was it to treat the evacuees?"

"It was hard, but the orderlies did most of the dirty work. They took off the soldiers' clothes. Sometimes they had to cut the clothes open to get them off."

"Yes, I know. And then they put the clothes in sacks with weights and heaved them overboard."

"Yes. If the patients didn't need immediate surgery, the orderlies washed their entire bodies, and cut their hair and beards. Most of the injured had lice."

"And they were starved."

"Yes, they said that the only food they got at the front was cabbage soup, potatoes, and stale bread. Oftentimes, they didn't get bread at all."

Roberto started to feel uncomfortable. They were just talking about work. Tessa averted her eyes too much.

"Is there a problem?" he asked.

"I'm not going out again. There have been too many complaints about romancing between crewmen and nurses. The Navy has recruited nuns as nurses for the next tour. I'm back at the hospital, and I hardly get any time off."

"That's too bad. I was looking forward to having you on the ship with me."

"Well, I'm kind of glad I don't have to go out again."

"I want to walk you home." There must be a way he could get through to her.

"I didn't come alone. A nun is waiting for me outside. Goodbye, Roberto."

"What? I don't even get a kiss?"

She turned and walked out. Roberto was dumbfounded. Was this the end of their courtship? Had she met someone else on the ship? Could her parents be behind her strange behavior? It wasn't that long ago that she had promised to wait for him until the war was over. Had she changed her mind? Why the nun? Could Tessa be thinking of becoming a nun?

Chapter 37

The captain welcomed Roberto back to duty.

"You volunteered for a dangerous mission and you were injured in action, so this time, it might be a gold medal. Congratulations."

"Thank you, sir, but my brother Salvo deserves it more." Roberto snapped a smart salute.

"I'm sure that he'll get one as well. I trust that your wounds have healed?"

"Yes, sir. It's good to be back. Where are we headed now, Captain? "

"Back to Di Piave."

"Aye, aye, sir."

The first evening, Roberto stood at the railing and looked at the setting sun. The sea was calm. It was so beautiful. He wished that the people in the war zones could enjoy calm and beauty like this. He appreciated his promotion, but what was the matter with Tessa? Had she found someone else? As for Anthony, he still sounded enthusiastic about the war, but Salvo had been at the front for so long that he must be sick of the fighting. It must be difficult to keep warm. Where he was it could snow and it could be cold and windy. What was Tessa doing now? Was she with another man? She hadn't come to see him off. Perhaps she worked and couldn't get away, but what about if she had stayed away deliberately?

One day he overheard some comments between the doctors suggesting that they missed the pretty nurses aboard, "especially the beautiful Tessa." It didn't have to mean anything. Roberto knew that he wasn't the only man who had found Tessa attractive and beautiful, but he still wondered if there was something more to the men's remarks.

Once again, l'Italia anchored at the mouth of the river, Di Piave. This time, several ferries loaded with evacuees waited for the hospital ship and the boarding began. Roberto stood ready to translate when needed. Many American soldiers had arrived from training camps in France to assist the Italians.

He could hardly believe it when he saw Anthony walking toward him dressed in an American uniform and pushing a wheelchair.

"Brother! Am I glad to see you, but what the hell are you doing here?" Roberto said.

"Some reunion! Look who's sitting in the wheelchair."

"Is that you, Salvo?"

"Yes, don't you recognize me?"

"I've been looking for you with every evacuation."

Roberto thumped Anthony's shoulders, but hesitated to do it to Salvo, who looked like he was in great pain. Instead, he touched him on his head.

"What's the problem, Salvo? Where are you hurt?"

"I have a shotgun wound to my stomach. It's bad."

"Let's get you to First Aid right away."

Roberto showed Anthony the way, and he motioned to a doctor he knew that he had a bad case. "It's my brother," he said. "Please take good care of him. He needs help fast. He has a shotgun wound to his stomach."

"I'll do my best. I'm a surgeon."

Roberto knew that the surgeon was a captain with much experience, so he could leave Salvo with him in confidence. He then turned to Anthony.

"Have you been fighting at Piave also?"

"No, I had just arrived there when the officers found out that I could speak Italian, so they told me to translate between the English-speaking troops and the Italians. When an American doctor looked at Salvo, he waved me over, and I recognized Salvo. The doc told me to take him to the rescue ship and stay with him until he was aboard, but I have to go back or else they will think I'm deserting."

"I understand. Take care of yourself, dear brother."

"So long Roberto. Hope I'll see you again. Will you be back on this ship?"

"As long as the war lasts. There seems to be no end to injured soldiers."

"Take care of Salvo and greet everyone at home for me."

"I hate to see you go, but be safe. If you're a translator, you stand a good chance of surviving."

"The Austrians are on the run. I'll be fine."

And with those words, Anthony climbed down the rope ladder.

Roberto felt numb. He didn't know which way to turn. But he got himself together and walked toward the doctor who was taking care of Salvo. He saw a nun nurse assisting the doctor.

"You look like you've seen a ghost," the nun said to Roberto."

"Not a ghost but my brother, Anthony. He joined the American Army and just came aboard with my other brother, your patient. Anthony is in Italy working as a translator, just like I am. He had to go back. We saw each other for only a few minutes."

Salvo was in surgery. The doctors worked on him for two hours and then sewed him up.

"He's in God's hands now," the nun said. "We've done what we can."

Orderlies wheeled Salvo to a ward. Roberto sat down by his side and prayed. If anyone deserved to live it was Salvo. He had been fighting since the beginning of the war, and he had a family at home waiting for him.

The nun came at midnight and touched Roberto's shoulder. "You need to go and lay down. I'll sit with him."

"What's your name, Sister?" Roberto asked.

"My name is Marta."

"*Grazie*, Sister Marta, but let me know if he wakes up. Pray for him."

"I will."

In the morning, Roberto returned unshaven and sleepy-eyed.

"Any change?" he asked Sister Marta.

"No, he's still sleeping. It's good for him."

"Go to bed, I'll take over."

"Shouldn't you clean up first?"

"Does it matter? Salvo has a longer beard than I."

"Wet his lips now and then."

"Yes, I know."

Roberto thought of the time he had wet Anna's lips in the hospital in New York. And he had received the same treatment from Tessa when he was injured. So many memories danced in his head. Had he lost Tessa like he had lost Julia? He didn't seem to have any luck with girlfriends. He shrugged and turned his attention to Salvo. Now everything depended on his survival. Roberto didn't care that he had taken time off from his other duties. No one had asked for him, and he thought that the captain would understand. He didn't know how long he had been sitting there when Salvo stirred and moaned.

"Salvo, it's me, Roberto. You're on a hospital ship. We're going home."

Salvo muttered like he didn't understand. "Home?"

"Yes, home to Genoa. You're injured, but you'll get well."

"Good." That was all he said. Then he closed his eyes again. Roberto wet his brother's lips.

In the morning when Sister Marta came to the ward, she brought a thermometer and stuck it in Salvo's armpit. She looked at Roberto and said. "Now, it's your turn to rest."

The nun wrote down the temperature on her pad and said that it was high. "It's to be expected," she said. "I'll start to wash his face and neck with cold water. It will cool him down, and he'll feel better when he wakes up. If it doesn't help, we'll bathe his chest and arms with cold water."

"It's good that we're in a cold climate right now," Roberto said.

Salvo hovered between life and death for two days. Roberto and Sister Marta took turns watching over him. Then one morning, Marta smiled. "His fever broke," she said. "That's a good sign."

"*Grazie, Madonna*," Roberto said. Exhausted, he went to bed and slept the whole night.

The rest of the injured men were Italians and they would continue to Naples or Genoa. Salvo was awake and talking. An orderly had shaved off his beard and hair, washed his body, and changed his sheets.

"Are you feeling better now, Salvo?" Roberto asked.

"Much better. How's my family?"

"Your family is fine. I see Laura every time I'm on leave, but she worries about you."

"Is there any way we can send a message to her?"

"I could try to send a wire. I know how to tap out messages."

"You really amaze me, Roberto."

"You're getting the best care in the entire ward. It's like you were a first-class passenger."

"I suppose it's thanks to you."

"The doctors and Sister Marta have done more."

"I'm thankful to be alive. Many of my fighting buddies are dead. But we're winning now."

"I think we're winning on the western front as well, thanks to the Americans."

"Where's Anthony?"

"He had to go back to Di Piave."

Salvo nodded.

"I'll go and send that wire now. Take a rest."

Roberto found the captain and asked if he could send a personal wire.

"My brother who was badly injured is recovering here on the ship," he explained. "He's fought in the Trentino region since the war started. I'd like to send a wire to his wife."

"By all means, Officer Cosentino."

"*Grazie*, Captain."

The wireless operator, Lorenzo, vacated his chair for Roberto.

"Who do you want to send the wire to?"

"Laura Cosentino, Genoa."

"And what do you want it to say?"

"Met Salvo and Anthony. All OK. R." Roberto had written it down on a slip of paper.

"All right. I'll check so that you get it right."

Roberto began to tap in the message. Feeling nervous, he made a mistake, and started over.

"All right, now you can send it," Lorenzo said.

As soon as he was done, a message came in. Roberto picked up a pen and wrote it out.

"The Austrians have surrendered. General Diaz." The date said October 29, 1918.

"We've won the war!" Roberto yelled.

"Correct. That's fantastic," Lorenzo roared. "Take the message to the captain. I've got to stay here in case there're follow-up wires."

Roberto was more than happy to be the messenger of the good news.

"Captain, this is of utmost importance," he said as he handed the captain the message. The captain glanced at the paper and said, "It's a cause for celebration. I need the musicians and lots of champagne."

"Aye, aye, Captain."

Roberto scooted around from one place to the other shouting, "We've peace with the Austrians. We've peace with the Austrians. The captain wants to celebrate."

He didn't forget the wards. Sister Marta was there, and he grabbed her and danced around with her. The look on her face was utter disbelief. "We have peace. We've won the war with the Austrians," Roberto shouted.

Roberto put Salvo in a wheelchair and wheeled him to the narrow stairs. Then he carried him upstairs and put him down on a regular chair. Salvo kept on repeating, "We did it. We did it. After all this time, we finally won."

The musicians played, and the captain gave a short speech announcing the peace with the Austrians. "But let's not forget that the Germans have yet to surrender. *Salute* to General Diaz, his brave soldiers and to our flag."

"*Salute*," the crew roared. The bottles went from one mouth to another. "Hooray for General Diaz. Hooray for peace." Officers doused each other with champagne.

"I hope that the armistice will be complete when we get home to Genoa," Roberto said to Salvo.

"Roberto, I want to stand up and salute," Salvo said.

Roberto helped him to an upright position, and Salvo, holding on to his chair, saluted the green, white, and red Italian flag.

"That's wonderful, brother. We're going home."

"We're going home," Salvo repeated with tears streaming down his face.

Chapter 38

Thousands of people had gathered to welcome the injured soldiers and the crew on l'Italia. "Armistice, Armistice," the crowd shouted. The orchestra played and the crowd sang, "*Il Piave mormorava... non passa lo straniero*" (The Piave whispered... the foreigner shall not pass.)

The entire Cosentino family was in place to welcome their own hero. Salvo walked off the ship as straight as he possibly could. The wound in his stomach still bothered him, but he didn't have to walk for long.

Laura received him with open arms. The children clung to him.

Dezi was there welcoming his old war buddy. He offered Salvo and his family a ride in his cab. Vito told them to get into the cab then rode on the side step waving a flag. He and Dezi had decorated the cab with flowers, banners, and flags. A sign in the back said, "Welcome home, Salvo."

Roberto, Mama Lea, Jolanda, Liliana, Isabella and Alberto, and their children, all walked behind the slow-moving cab as it made its way through the crowd. There was a huge party in the town square. The mayor gave a speech, welcoming all the veterans and especially *Sergente* Salvatore Cosentino, who had served the longest. The crowd applauded. The mayor said that he was sure that a medal would be forthcoming.

He then announced that armistice had gone into effect at 11:00 a.m. and that the guns were falling silent. The Germans would probably be required to evacuate all the areas they had occupied in France, Belgium, Luxembourg, and Alsace-Lorraine. The Allies would then occupy these areas as the Germans left. The people would be free. "Hooray for freedom" The crowd echoed "Hooray for Freedom."

The town orchestra played the Italian National Anthem, *Il canto degli Italiani*, which began with the words, *Fratelli d'Italia* (Brothers of Italy). The crowd sang it with bravura. Never had it meant so much to Salvo as now. He was overcome with emotions.

Roberto searched for Tessa. Could she be working at a time like this? He asked Mama.

"I don't know," Mama said "You've a letter from her waiting at home."

"A letter. Why?"

"I don't know, Roberto."

The party continued at Mama Lea's place. Tables had been set up outside. Lanterns swung from the trees. Family members, neighbors, and friends had carried food and wine all day to Mama Lea's place. Uncle Carlo and his family had brought fish that they cooked outside.

Carlo thumped Roberto on the shoulders and said, "I've found a man who wants to rent Alfonso's shop and pay for the inventory."

"That's good. I'm glad. It takes a load off my shoulders," Roberto said. "Have you told Mama?"

"Yes, she knows."

While Salvo was the center of attention, Roberto headed for the house to look for Tessa's letter. It was sitting on his night table. Full of anxiety, he opened it and read the word that blurred his eyes.

"I have met someone else, a doctor, and he has asked my father for my hand in marriage. I'm sorry, Roberto."

He didn't have to read the rest. The doctor had gone to her father and received his blessings. He, Roberto, had not done so. He had never been inside Tessa's home. Now, he knew why. He wasn't welcome there because he wasn't good enough. But the doctor, of course, was more than good enough. It sounded like an arranged marriage. Or could she have met him aboard l'Italia? The more he thought about it, the more likely it seemed. That's why she had acted so strangely after her tour. Roberto sat down on his bed and took a long breath. He felt rejected and it hurt. It was over. He had to face it and go outside and join the celebration.

After they had eaten, Roberto gave a speech, saying that it was Anthony who had brought Salvo aboard the hospital ship at Di Piave, and that Anthony was one of the American soldiers who had been dispatched from France to assist the Italians in their offensive. He had also been the one who had brought Salvo on board the hospital ship.

"This feast is to welcome brother Salvo home, safe and sound. Welcome brother. May you live many years and thrive on your farm. *Salute* to Salvo and his family"

Everyone joined in the salute. "I also want to salute Anthony for being with the American forces that saved us. *Salute* to Anthony. God bless America."

The guests roared with approval.

The glasses clinked together, "*Salute*, Salvatore! *Salute*, Antonio, *Salute* America!"

Salvo thanked them all for the rousing welcome. "Now, if you'll excuse me, I'm very tired and wish to go home to my farm and sleep in my own bed with my dear wife." Everyone applauded as Laura walked with him to Dezi's cab and they drove away with their children.

Roberto retreated to his room and reflected on his life.

When I left Genoa in 1912, I didn't think much of my life here. I looked for adventure and fortune with Lydia. But when I had to make it on my own as a housepainter in Boston, I found it hard to cope. I was robbed, homeless, and penniless. I relied on Anna and her husband. I fell in love with Julia and liked her family. She should be through with college by now. Perhaps she's married. Now that I don't have Tessa anymore, it feels like it would be best to go back to Boston. Planning for it might fill the emptiness in my heart. I know that I was careless, selfish, and immature in my younger days. God punished me with tuberculosis. Yet, it was a blessing because it brought me back to my roots. I love my family, but the family will be all right without me. Now, that the war is over, my sisters can stop working at the cannery and go back to sewing.

Roberto wrote a letter to Mr. Parini at *La Gazzetta* and asked if he had a job for him. He enclosed two articles about the war. As he sealed the envelope, he heard a man's voice in the front yard. It sounded like Anthony's. He put down the letter to see if it was really him.

"Oh, Brother! I'm so happy you came."

"I'm happy, too," Mama said. The little woman hugged her tall son around his waist like she would never let him go.

"Is that an American uniform you're wearing?" she asked.

"Yes, Mama."

"Mama, it's my turn now to welcome Anthony," Roberto said.

The two brothers hugged and thumped each other on the shoulders.

"Where did you come from?" Roberto asked.

"From France."

"How long can you stay?"

"A few days."

"How's Salvo?" Anthony asked.

"He's doing much better. For a while there, he couldn't stand up straight."

"I'd like to go and see him."

"Of course. We can both go tomorrow."

"You must be hungry, son, having come all the way from France." Mama Lea said.

259

"I can't wait to have a good Italian meal," Anthony said, rubbing his stomach.

"Let's go to the workshop," Roberto said. "I want to show you the desk that Papa made for me."

They entered the shop, which was so familiar to Anthony. It was hard for him to believe that his papa wasn't there any more.

"It's a beautiful desk," Anthony said.

"Here are some clippings of articles that I wrote," Roberto said.

Anthony looked at them and said, "It's impressive. I'll read them later."

"I think I'll take the desk with me to Boston," Roberto said.

"Are you going back? I thought you had a girlfriend here." Anthony sounded surprised.

"Tessa is going to marry a doctor. I just found out."

"Sorry, about that brother. Did you tell Mama that you're leaving?"

"Yes, she knows. It's probably for the best. Now, I don't have a reason to stay here. Carlo has found a man who wants to rent Papa's shop and buy the inventory."

Anthony looked around. "It should be valuable," he said. "Mama's future will be secure."

"Yes, and I'm glad. She deserves it."

"You've money in Boston to give you a new start."

"That's what I'm counting on. But I also wrote to *La Gazzetta's* editor, asking if he has a job for me. I want to continue writing."

"You can stay with me and Sophia until you have a place of your own."

"I appreciate that, but as soon as I have a job, I'll be on my own. Now, let's go and have lunch with Mama."

Anthony reached into his wallet for pictures of his wife and daughter. "I hope to be home with them for Christmas," he said, handing the snapshots to Mama.

"Finally, I get to see pictures of your family," she said.

"You can keep them. I'm going home."

"*Grazie mille.* They're beautiful, son." She went to the window to look at them in better light.

"I have a wedding gift for you that I've been working on since I first heard of your marriage. I'll go and get it," she said.

She left the room and came back with a beautifully embroidered linen tablecloth and held it up for her sons to see.

"Do you think Sophia will like it?" she asked Anthony.

"I'm sure she will. We'll both treasure it. Thank you very much, Mama." Anthony kissed her on both cheeks to show his appreciation. "You'll have to wrap it so it's protected in my bag. It's too beautiful to be soiled."

"I'll wrap it up for you, son."

In the afternoon, the two brothers visited their sister, Isabella, and her family. Their brother-in-law, Alberto, brought out the wine to celebrate the happy reunion.

In the evening, the two sisters came home from their last day of work at the cannery. First, they had been to the bathhouse and washed off all the fish smell and changed their clothes. Anthony said that it was a good thing. Or else, he wouldn't have hugged them.

"Are you going back to sewing now?" he asked.

"Yes, thank heavens for that. We'll open a dressmaker studio," Jolanda said. "Now that the war is over, fine fabrics will be available again, and we've saved enough money to buy sewing machines."

"You can have your studio here," Mama Lea said. "Or you could clean out the cottage in the back and work there."

"Oh, Mama, the cottage would be perfect," Liliana said.

"Until we can earn enough money to have a studio in the center of town," Jolanda said.

The next day, Anthony and Roberto went to visit Salvo and Laura on the farm. Salvo was already busy supervising the work. "I can't do much myself yet," he said. But he was strong enough to greet Anthony with a hardy handshake and a brotherly hug.

"I'm glad that work is slow this time of the year. Let's go in the house and talk."

Most of their talk centered on the war. They swapped military stories, good and bad. They drank coffee. Time went fast. Before they knew it, it was dinner time, and Laura had a meal ready for them. Roberto told Salvo and Laura that Tessa had broken up with him, and that he planned to return to Boston after Christmas. They were disappointed but understood his decision. On their way home, Roberto took Anthony to the cemetery to show him their father's grave.

An early Christmas card from Anna awaited Roberto at home. In the enclosed letter she wrote that she, like everyone else, was glad that the war was over. John was coming home, Eddy, the chauffeur, had died in the Spanish flu in Europe. The influenza pandemic had spread to America. Although it was not yet official, it was estimated that one hundred thousand American soldiers had died in the war. Her Cousin Ethel's husband, Gordon, was one of them. He was a pilot, and his plane had been shot down by the enemy in France.

Roberto knew that the European causalities of war were much higher than the American. Germany had suffered nearly two million deaths; yet, no foreign soldiers had fought on German soil. France, Austria-Hungary, and Russia each had suffered in excess of a million deaths, the British Empire almost as many, and Italy and the Ottoman Empire about seven-hundred-thousand men each.

When adding the injured, the imprisoned, the missing, and those who had died from disease and hunger caused by the war, the figures multiplied. It all seemed senseless and unworthy of humanity. The world map would change, but would it give lasting peace?

Roberto was thankful for the American intervention. He had no doubt that it had shortened the war. He had written it all down, and it would be included in his articles about the war.

The two brothers enjoyed a few days together before Anthony had to depart.

"You should continue to write about your war experiences," Anthony told Roberto. "I think you'll be well paid."

"I'll do that until it's time for me to leave," Roberto said. Roberto accompanied Anthony to the train.

"I'll see you in Boston then. Merry Christmas Roberto! The new year should be happy now that the war is over."

"Merry Christmas to you and your family. Sophia and Collette will be glad to have you home for the holidays. Can't wait to see you again, but I don't want to arrive in the winter time if I can help it."

Anthony laughed and waved. "I'm used to it. It isn't so bad."

Roberto was surprised to see a letter addressed to him from the *Boston Globe* It must be about his articles, he thought as he eagerly opened it. His eyes widened as he saw that it was signed by Julia Nicolo.

Dear Roberto,

The chief editor has asked me to write to you. He wants you to submit more articles about the war in Europe and how it finally ended. Our readers have commented positively on your articles so far. I will explain why I'm working at the paper. In college, I volunteered at the college bulletin office and found that I liked that kind of work. So I majored in English and Journalism. After my graduation, I secured a job at the Globe. As you know, many of our men were in the service, and there was a shortage of reporters. Mr. Foster liked my work, so he asked me to stay and be in charge of the reports from our foreign correspondents. You are one of them, Roberto. I hope that you are well and can send us more articles. Photos are also welcome if you have any.

Sincerely,

Julia Nicolo

The letter excited Roberto. He felt happier than he had in a long time. Julia had contacted him. Apparently, she was still single, and she wanted him to send her articles about the war. The request couldn't have come at a better time. He had several articles ready to mail. Best of all, he could keep in touch with Julia, and he would have a reason to see her when he came to Boston. But would she want to see him? She might have a boyfriend returning from the war.

Between Christmas and New Year's, a registered, insured parcel arrived for Roberto from the Navy. Numerous postage stamps and seals made it seem important. When he had signed for it, he opened if with care. It contained a blue box covered in velvet. Inside the box, there were three medals: *Madaglia Al Valore Militare* (Military Medal for Valor) one in bronze, one in silver, and one in gold, each attached to a ribbon. Roberto turned them over and read the inscription:

"GUERRA DI, 1915-1918, ROBERTO COSENTINO."

He felt proud, but what good would they do him? The king had signed the accompanying proclamation. He hoped that Salvo had received at least one medal. Salvo deserved it for sure.

Mama wanted a photograph of Roberto to remember him by. She insisted that he dress in his Navy uniform wearing his medals. Feeling guilty about leaving, he complied.

After New Year's, a letter arrived with the *La Gazzetta* logo on the envelope. Roberto's anxiety rose as he opened it. Mr. Parini wrote that he would be happy to give Roberto a job at his newspaper. He also suggested that he might want to delay his trip until the Spanish influenza had subsided in the United States. Roberto planned to arrive in the spring.

The Italian soldiers were coming home and looking for work. Roberto predicted that there would be another mass emigration to America. He was lucky to have a job on Uncle Carlo's fishing trawler.

Every day, he searched the harbor for a freighter going to New York. When he found one, he presented his credentials from the Navy and asked if there would be a position for him aboard. The ship needed a wireless operator, so Roberto took a test and was hired. He crated up his desk, put extra clothes in the desk drawers, a few more in his suitcase, and hired a hack to take the desk to the freighter. Last, he said goodbye to Mama, family, and friends. Once aboard, he wired Mr. Parini and Anthony that he would be arriving around the first of April.

Chapter 39

Three weeks later, Roberto arrived in Boston ready to welcome spring. Teamsters and cabs waited at the train station. He hired a teamster to take him and his crate to Anthony's address, where Sophia greeted him with Collette on her arm.

"Welcome to Boston," she said. "Anthony has rented an apartment for you. It's not far from here." She looked at the large crate and said, "I don't think we have room for that big thing."

"Then we'll take it directly to my apartment."

"I'll get the key and the address," Sophia said. "You can come back here when you have unloaded. Anthony will be home soon."

The teamster stopped outside an apartment house, and Roberto helped him unload the crate and carry it inside. Roberto's eyes scanned the furnished apartment. It was good to have a place that he could call home. Having paid the teamster, he unpacked his suitcase and placed the contents in a chest of drawers. He would have to borrow tools from Anthony to uncrate the desk. It felt good to wash off the travel dust, shave, and change clothes. Now, he looked forward to an evening with Anthony and Sophia. He'd missed the bantering with his younger brother.

The next day, Roberto headed for *La Gazzetta*. He had no trouble finding his way. Mr. Parini welcomed him like an old friend.

"Our readers liked your articles, Mr. Cosentino. You can continue to do reporting work as needed, but be prepared to assist in the office, selling ads, or working in the print shop, if necessary. I'll pay you a living wage, and we'll see how it goes. If you're doing well, you could get a commission. Does that sound all right to you?"

"Yes, it does. I'd like to learn the business, and I'll do my best, sir. When can I start?"

"You can start on Monday at 8:00 a.m."

"Thank you very much, Mr. Parini. See you Monday morning then."

Roberto's next stop was the *Boston Globe*. He recalled how anxious he had felt the first time he faced Mr. Foster, the chief editor. Now, he felt nervous about meeting Julia again. He had no idea how she would receive him. The receptionist called her and gave Roberto's name. After just a few minutes, Julia appeared, looking beautiful and professional in a grey suit. She greeted him with a hand shake and a glint in her hazel eyes.

"Welcome back, Roberto. Please follow me to my desk."

Roberto admired Julia's shapely body as she walked ahead of him. He recognized the big room where all the reporters sat clicking at their typewriters. Julia's desk was behind a partition. She motioned to a chair for Roberto to sit down. His eyes went to her left hand, and he was relieved to see that she didn't wear an engagement ring.

"I was thrilled to get your letter, Julia," he said.

"Mr. Foster asked me to write it."

"Just the same I was glad to hear from you."

She praised his articles about the war as being informative and realistic.

"That's good because I brought some more."

"I can go with you to Mr. Foster's office and see if he'll take them."

"I appreciate that."

Mr. Foster recognized Roberto and welcomed him back. "I see that you brought something. May I look at it?"

"Yes, it's about the war."

"Actually, Miss Nicolo is in charge of foreign correspondence, so you can leave them with her. If you have something else, you can bring it to me."

"All right. Thank you very much, sir."

"Then we can go back to my cubicle," Julia said. When they were seated again, she looked at the articles, but said that she would read them later.

"May I ask you something personal, Julia?" Roberto asked.

"All right, if it's not too personal." She fingered a pen while looking at him.

"I was wondering if I could show my appreciation for your kindness by taking you out to dinner. If you're available, that is?"

Julia smiled. Oh, how he loved that smile with those dimples in her cheeks. "Let's see." She looked at her calendar, and said, "Sometimes, I work late, but as a matter of fact, I'm free tonight. We could have a business meeting over dinner, couldn't we?" Her smile told him that it was just an excuse.

"Yes, if you want to call it that?" He smiled back.

She wrote down her address and phone number on her business card. "Is seven o'clock all right?"

"Yes." Roberto looked at the address. It was her parents' home. So she still lived at home.

"Do you want me to come inside and say hello to your parents?"

"Yes, I think it would be nice. They'll be glad to see you again."

"Until tonight then, Julia. I will walk myself out."

That went well, Roberto thought. He felt that he still had a special connection with Julia and couldn't wait to see her in the evening. Spring was in the air. It was a perfect time to fall in love all over again. He thought that Julia's beauty and bearing could have made her a movie star. He was lucky to have a date with her even if she called it a business meeting. Were his clothes nice enough? He might splurge and buy something new like he had done that time long ago.

Dressed in a new, navy blue suit, Roberto rang the door bell exactly at seven o'clock. Julia had a big smile on her pretty face as she opened the door for him.

"Good evening, Julia."

"Good evening, Roberto. Please come in. My parents want to see you."

Roberto admired her light blue suit that she wore with a narrow belt around her tiny waist.

"You look lovely, Julia." She smiled again and so did he.

He stepped into the living room, where Mr. Nicolo came toward him with outstretched hand.

"Good to see you again, Mr. Cosentino. I've read your articles. They're excellent. You've come a long way in your writing."

"Thank you, sir."

Mrs. Nicolo came from the kitchen and greeted him in a friendly way.

"How is your family in Italy?" she asked.

"My father died shortly after I arrived, but my mother and siblings are all well. Thank you for asking, Mrs. Nicolo."

"So sorry about your father. It must have been hard to lose him."

"Yes, it was."

"We're not going to keep you. Go out and enjoy the evening. Julia can show you what's new in Boston."

"I'm looking forward to it. Good night." He put his hat on and opened the door for Julia. It all seemed like yesterday that he had picked her up for their first date.

"I told my parents that I was going to show you what's new in Boston," Julia explained.

"I thought so." Roberto gave her arm a squeeze.

"The city hasn't changed that much since you left. Everything stood still while we were at war."

"It's the same in Italy. You haven't changed either. You look as young and pretty as you did five years ago, or could it be six years ago?"

"It's six years since we parted ways. I'm sure that we've both matured."

"I know I have. Would you mind if we go to the restaurant where we met?"

"No, I'd like to see it again. It's under new ownership, and they don't serve pizza anymore. I think it's a steakhouse."

"That's all right. I'm looking forward to a good steak. We had a shortage of meat during the war."

"We did, too." So far their conversation was going well, he thought.

"Julia, I'm sorry I didn't contact you those last few weeks before you started college. Some unfortunate things happened to me, but I've never forgotten you."

"I'm sure you've had other girlfriends since then."

"I had a girlfriend in Genoa, but the war separated us and she's going to marry someone else. What about you? A pretty girl like you must have a long row of admirers."

"I try to keep them at a distance."

"You certainly did that with me. Do I stand a chance at all?"

"We'll see," she said.

At the restaurant, Roberto ordered steak and a bottle of wine. While they waited for the food, they sipped the wine.

"Tell me about your family. All I know is what you wrote in the articles about your brothers. Do you have any sisters?"

"Yes, I have three sisters. Perhaps we can talk about them some other time. I'd like to learn more about you. How was college?"

"I lived at home the whole time, so I didn't have a sorority life."

"I suppose your father liked that. He could shield you from the boys."

"Perhaps... Now that I make good money, I could afford my own apartment, but it's customary that unmarried girls live with their families."

"I know. It's the same in Italy. Julia, I'd like to propose a toast to Boston in the spring time. It's so much better than winter."

"To Boston in the spring time then."

Julia met Roberto's gaze and held it, and he took it as a promise of more.

"You're so beautiful, Julia, and I like everything about you," he said.

"That's a lot of compliments in one evening."

"I can't tell you how much I appreciate that you accepted my invitation to dinner."

"For old time's sake," she said

"For old time's sake," he said and raised his glass touching hers.

Roberto was afraid of scaring her by being too forward, but he felt that they had reconnected in a good way.

"Now that I've met you again, it feels like we've never been apart."

"I have to admit that it was hard to lose you six years ago," Julia said.

"It was hard for me to lose you, very hard, because I truly loved you," Roberto said.

"I felt it, but I was determined to get my education."

"You were right even though you had to break up with me twice."

"We had some wonderful times together."

"Do you remember when you came out to the Cape?"

"How could I forget? My parents found out about it, and they forbade me to go there again.... But it didn't matter when I didn't hear from you." She lowered her eyes, but her voice revealed how disappointed she had been.

"Do you know that my beach house was destroyed in the hurricane?"

"No, really? You could have told me."

"I broke my leg in the rubble and was in no shape to date."

"But then I didn't hear from you until Christmas and when you sent me that postcard from Italy. Something else must have happened that made you go back there."

"Yes, I came down with an illness. My intention was to stay in Italy for a few months to recuperate, but then my country entered the war, and I couldn't avoid the service. So I joined the Navy and served on the hospital ship until the end of the war."

"If it hadn't been for your articles, I wouldn't have known that."

"I've changed, Julia. The war made me realize how precious life is. I've changed a lot."

"We've both changed."

"That letter you wrote from *Boston Globe* gave me hope."

"Is that why you came back?"

"It gave me an extra incentive. I hoped against hope."

The food came and Roberto told himself that he must try to keep his feelings in check. When they had finished the meal, Julia asked, "Do you need many things for your apartment?"

"Not right now."

He told her about the desk that he had brought all the way from Genoa. "My father made it, and I wanted to keep it."

"I can understand that."

"Otherwise, my apartment is furnished. I guess it's not the most economical way to rent, but it's a start. Later, I might want to have my own furniture. My father and grandfather were both furniture makers."

"But you're not following in their footsteps?"

"No, it doesn't pay anymore to make furniture by hand. It takes too long."

"I'm sure you're right."

She looked at her watch and said, "It's getting late, and tomorrow is a workday."

"I'll take you home then."

They walked quietly, arm in arm, until they stood outside her home. That's when Roberto kissed her. To his delight, she kissed him back. A wave of happiness went through his body.

"When can I see you again?" he asked. When she didn't answer right away, he said, "I'm falling for you all over again and I think you feel the same."

"I do, Roberto. It's a wonderful feeling." They kissed again and the feeling became more intense.

"Will you go out with me on Saturday night?"

"Yes."

"You're wonderful." They kissed again, and again. Roberto was sure that she liked it as much as he did.

"I have to go in now," she said. "If we're going out on Saturday night, I have things to do."

"Where do you want to go?"

"You decide. Call me at home tomorrow evening."

"All right then. I'll let you go."

"Thank you for dinner."

"My pleasure. Thank you for a wonderful evening. Good night." He tipped his hat to her and waited until she was inside the door before putting it back on.

He felt like the luckiest man in the world. Julia had put the spring back in his step.

Chapter 40

When Roberto called Julia the next evening, he told her that the two of them were invited to his brother's for dinner on Saturday. "Please come with me. Anthony and Sophia want to meet you," he said.

"All right, I'll be glad to. Will you pick me up?"

"Yes, I'll come and get you at five o'clock. They have a little girl, so they want to have an early dinner."

"How old is the girl?"

"I think she's four."

"Then I could bring something for her to play with."

"I suppose that would be all right."

Julia brought a little doll for Collette. Roberto watched how good she was with the child. She would make a good mother, he thought. The brothers talked about the war, and Anthony mentioned Roberto's medals.

"Medals, I'd like to see them," Julia said.

"They're at my place," Roberto said. "We could stop there before I walk you home."

Sophia looked questioning at Julia, but she did not say anything. Instead, she turned to Collette and asked if she had seen Uncle Roberto's medals.

"No, I don't think so. I don't know what they look like," the girl said.

"They're beautiful, and Roberto received them for his bravery during the war in Europe," Anthony explained. "The Italian King signed the letter."

"Well, many other men deserved the recognition more than I did." Roberto said.

"I think that Collette is a little too young to understand all that," Sophia said. "Dinner is ready, so please come to the table."

"Nice family," Julia said as they had said their good-byes and left.

"It means a lot to me that they're here."

"I have so many relatives that I can't imagine what it would be like not to have any," Julia said.

"Do you want to stop at my place? I promise to be a gentleman."

"In that case, we could make a short stop."

Roberto showed Julia his desk and his medals.

"What did you do to earn these?" she asked.

"For the gold one I took a shot in my leg."

"Oh, dear... you should write a story about it."

"I don't want to write about myself."

"Someone else could."

When Roberto put the medals back in the drawer, Julia saw his picture.

"Let me see that," she said.

She took it out of the drawer and looked at it. "You look so handsome in your uniform, and you're wearing your medals."

"My mother insisted that I get my picture taken in my uniform before I left."

"Do you have an extra one for me?"

"No, but you can have this one. I don't need it. I've rather have a picture of you."

"I'll give you one. Thank you, Roberto." She put it in her purse and said that she would frame it.

"Come here, sweetheart." He pulled her close. "A gentleman can kiss his girl, can't he?" She didn't protest.

"You mean so much to me Julia," he said, "but I'm afraid that I'm not good enough for you."

"But you are, Roberto. You are a war hero." He had his arms around her waist, and she had her hands on his chest, looking up at him.

"I love you, Julia. I can't help it. I want to be with you."

"Let's go outside, and I'll tell you how I feel."

Roberto smiled. She was not only cute as a button, she was smart, too. When they were outside, he asked, "So what do you want to tell me, sweetheart?"

"That I'm still attracted to you."

"I like that. That means that you're falling in love all over again."

"It seems that you're the only one who can make me feel this way." Roberto's heart almost jumped out of his chest.

"Do you like the feeling?"

"I feel warm all over. I feel it in every fiber of my body when we kiss."

"That's love, darling. That's love you are feeling."

"I'm 24-years old, but I still feel like I'm doing something forbidden."

"It's because of your strict upbringing. I'm 27, and I'd say that we are old enough to act like adults in love."

"Does it show that I'm in love?"

"Yes, darling, it shows. I think that your parents will notice." Her hands went to her face and she looked a little scared.

"Will it show at work, too?"

"You might smile a lot."

"You're teasing me, Roberto."

"No, I'm not. You'll see. Don't try to fight it, darling."

"My parents think that I'm an old maid already and that I'll never get married."

"We'll show them that they're wrong."

Julia skipped rather than walked. Outside her home, Roberto asked her, "Are you happy, darling?"

"Yes, I'm ecstatic."

"You're making me euphoric." They kissed like they would never want to part.

On Easter Sunday, Roberto noticed that Julia's parents looked at each other and nodded in agreement as Julia beamed with pride while telling them about his medals.

"I have a picture of Roberto in his Navy uniform. He's wearing his medals." She took it out of her purse and showed it to her parents.

Roberto had to explain once again what the medals were for and why he had received them. He felt like he had gone up a notch in the eyes of Mr. and Mrs. Nicolo, but would they agree if he asked them for their daughter's hand in marriage? He told them about his new job and how much he liked it.

"I think that the newspapers business will be my career," he said.

"We subscribe to *La Gazzetta*," her father said, "and I've read all your articles, both in Italian and English. It's a gift to be bilingual like you are. You'll do well. Perhaps, one day, you can take over the paper. Mr. Perini is getting old."

Roberto registered Mr. Nicolo's comment as a vote of confidence, but humbly confessed that he had much more to learn about the entire production.

"You'll learn fast. The question is how long the ethnic newspapers can last."

"I think that the ethnic newspapers might switch to English eventually, but that they will continue as special-interest papers," Roberto said.

"You might be right," Mr. Nicolo said.

Roberto wanted to show Julia and her parents that he could succeed. He worked one week in each department to learn the newspaper business from the bottom up. Before long, he was Mr. Perini's right hand and was rewarded with a raise. He continued to see Julia and envisioned his future with her.

Chapter 41

It was summer and Julia had promised that she would go with Roberto to Cape Cod the following weekend. He told her that he wanted to see what Anna's and John's new beach house looked like. They would take the train to Falmouth early in the morning and come back the same day. He told her to bring a bathing suit.

Julia felt excited about going to the Cape again. Too many years had passed since she was there to visit Roberto. The weather was perfect, and they walked to the beach. Roberto loved swimming in the salt water. Julia still swam the breast stroke, and couldn't keep up with him.

"I should teach you the crawl," he said. "You should be flat in the water with your face below the surface. See here, look at me, honey."

"I can't breathe that way."

"You turn your head to the side to catch your breath. Don't be afraid."

He pulled her close in the water. No one could see what they were doing. He held her in a tight grip. It was as close to satisfaction he had come with her. He would let her go for now, but they would get in the water again.

Julia went to the changing rooms and put on a dry suit with daringly short legs. The sun warmed their bodies and Roberto had to hide his lust.

"Let's see who can hit the water first, darling." He threw the towel aside, took her hand and led the way.

"I want to see if the sandbar is still there," he said.

It was—although it had shifted some.

"You remember this place don't you, darling?"

"Yes, I do. The water is warmer here."

As they faced each other, he slid her bathing suit off her shoulders, and she didn't seem to mind. He stroked her bare shoulders while she stroked his chest.

"I like your touch," he said while slowly slipping one hand inside her bathing suit and cupping her breasts. It surprised him that she let it happen.

"You're so soft and wonderful. I adore you." Reluctantly, he removed his hand. "I've been waiting for your love for six years," he said, "I love you more than ever, and I want you to be my wife. Please marry me, Julia."

"Yes, I'll marry you, Roberto. I love you so much."

"But you have to promise not to break up with me again. I couldn't stand it."

"I promise."

"You've made me the happiest man in the world." He hoisted her in the air and cradled her in his arms. They played in the water; they laughed, kissed, and were happy. Roberto dove between her legs and hoisted her to his shoulders. He dove again and they were both under water.

When they surfaced, Roberto said, "I'll ask your father for permission to marry you. Do you think he'll give me his blessings?"

"Yes, I'm certain."

"Then I'll buy you a ring, and we'll make it official."

"Yes!" She shrieked with joy.

"Are you as happy as you sound, darling?" he asked.

"I'm in seventh heaven," she said.

"I'm on cloud nine. It must be close to seventh heaven."

They were overjoyed with love as they walked to the train station. Roberto took a little detour to the Whitmore beach house.

"This is where my beach house stood," he told Julia. "The one you saw when you visited me. It was completely destroyed by the hurricane. John and Anna Whitmore bought the lot from me and built this house. It's so much bigger. I was in Boston when the hurricane hit, and when I came out to check on the damages, the house was flattened. I had nothing...."

"Then I didn't hear from you until you were in Italy."

"I'm sorry, darling. Now, that I know that you love me, I'll tell you what happened after that. I caught the tubercle bacillus and had to go to a sanatorium. I didn't want you to know. When I had recovered, I decided to go home to Italy and stay there for a while.

"Now, I understand," she said. Her eyes were full of sympathy and love.

"I sent you a postcard from Genoa."

"But with no return address."

"Then I sent you a Christmas card."

"But with no return address. I didn't have your address until Mr. Foster gave it to me."

"I'm sorry."

"It doesn't matter now that we're together again."

They held hands the whole time while walking and also while riding the train. Roberto couldn't wait to talk to her father.

"I love your daughter, sir, and I'm asking for your permission to marry her," Roberto said as he faced Mr. Nicolo.

"We've seen this coming. Julia is old enough to decide for herself, but you have our blessings. My wife and I will be glad to make the arrangements for your wedding," Mr. Nicolo answered.

"Thank you, sir." It was a load off his shoulders even though Julia had said there would be no problem. Now, he was thankful that Tessa had married someone else. Julia was the one he had wanted all along. They could plan for their future together. If she wanted a big wedding, it would be all right with him. Anthony would stand up for him.

Mr. Nicolo called his wife into the room.

"We've a wedding to plan," he said.

Mrs. Nicolo smiled and hugged her daughter.

"So what would be a good date for you two?" Mr. Nicolo asked. Roberto looked at Julia.

"As soon as possible," she said while looking at Roberto.

"Will August be soon enough?"

"Yes, Papa."

"Well then, Mother, you've plans to make."

"Yes, we all do. A church wedding seems appropriate," Mrs. Nicolo said.

"I understand that you don't have many relatives here, Roberto," Mr. Nicolo said.

"No, I don't. It's only my brother and his family. My brother could be my best man. I would also like to invite John and Anna Whitmore, sir. They're important to me, as is Mr. Perini. I would also like to invite a few colleagues and friends." He thought of Gretchel and Marius and wondered if he had their address.

"Well then. We'll speak with the clergy and see when we can have this wedding," Mr. Nicolo said.

"And you need to select the fabric for your wedding gown, Julia," Mrs. Nicolo said. "We also need an official announcement of your engagement."

"I haven't given Julia a ring yet, but I will. We could make it official next Saturday."

"You should go to a photographer, Julia. The announcement should have a recent photograph of you," Mr. Nicolo said.

"I can have the photographer at the newspaper take a picture of me."

"Well then, now, you two can leave, so that Mama and I can talk some more."

"Thank you, sir." Roberto shook hands with Julia's father and bowed to her mother.

Julia followed him outside. She had a new shine in her eyes.

"See, I told you they would be happy to see me married," she said.

"Not as happy as I will be. We'll have a very special date next Saturday. Where do you want to go?"

"Back to the Cape."

"I'm all for it. I know a good restaurant there. That's where we'll have lunch and celebrate."

They hugged and kissed in full daylight.

"I can't wait to give you a ring, darling."

"I can't wait to see it."

"Would you walk with me for a bit?"

"I don't think my parents will mind if I disappear for a while now that they are busy planning our wedding."

"Wonderful. I'll be walking on air with you."

She walked with him half way. He stroked her hand and had an idea. "May I borrow the ring you're wearing so that I can buy the right size?"

"Yes, of course." She took it off and gave it to him.

He put it on his little finger, and they kissed goodbye— several times.

Roberto went to his brother's and told Anthony and Sophia the good news, and as expected, they were delighted.

"Will you be my best man, Anthony?"

"Of course." Roberto looked at little Collette and had an idea.

"You could be our flower girl," he said and lifted her up on his arm.

"What's a flower girl?"

"Your mother will explain, sweetheart."

Chapter 42

The train ride to the Cape seemed longer than usual. Roberto carried the box with the diamond ring in his pocket. At long last, they walked into the restaurant. Roberto asked for a secluded table. "We've something to celebrate," he told the waiter. First he ordered a bottle of champagne. Then he went down on one knee and took out the box with the ring.

"Julia, darling, I love you. Will you marry me?"

"Yes, I will marry you. I love you, Roberto."

She stretched out her hand, and he slid the ring on her finger.

"It's beautiful, and it fits."

"I selected it a little tight so that you won't lose it in the water when we go swimming."

She blushed, and they hugged and kissed.

When the waiter came, he said, "I see that you're ready for a toast. Congratulations!"

"Thank you. Please pour," Roberto said.

Their eyes met as they drank to their future. Julia looked at her ring. The diamond sparkled in the sunshine from the window.

"You've spared no expense," she said.

"You're worth everything to me."

They dined on seafood. The waiter brought two pieces of cake for dessert.

"It's on the house," he said. "Come back again."

When they walked out of the restaurant, they met Anna and John, who were on their way in.

"Roberto," Anna said, "What are you doing here?"

"I'm here with my fiancée. This is Julia Nicolo."

"What a nice surprise. I'm happy to meet you, Miss Nicolo, and congratulations to the both of you."

Roberto introduced Anna and John Whitmore to Julia, and John bowed to her. "My best wishes on your engagement," John said.

Anna turned to Julia and asked, "When is the wedding?"

"In August. We'd be honored if you would come? I've heard so many good things about you and your husband."

"We'd love to," Anna said. "What are you two going to do now?"

"We're going swimming," Roberto said.

"Would you like to come for a drink after that?"

"We would, wouldn't we, sweetheart?" Roberto looked at Julia.

"Yes, we'd be delighted," Julia said.

"See you later then," John said.

"That was a pleasant surprise," Roberto said as they walked toward the beach. "I'm really looking forward to seeing their house on the inside."

"Me too."

"But now we're going to enjoy the swim that we've been waiting for all week." Roberto put his arm around her, and they quickened the steps that would take them to the beach.

Being in the water seemed to wash away Julia's virtue. The champagne had done its part. They laughed out loud and splashed water on each other. She turned away from him, so that he would chase after her. It was their little game before surrendering to their desires in the shallow water on the sandbar. The ocean was their witness.

Looking tanned, happy, and relaxed, they walked to the Whitmore beach house, where Anna and John welcomed them with drinks on the porch. Anna wanted to know everything that had happened to Roberto since she saw him the last time. Roberto asked her about her family, and he and John talked about their military service.

Roberto told them that he worked full time at *La Gazzetta.* "I wanted to be a reporter, and now I am."

"We're happy that you're doing well, Roberto," John said.

"I've some good news to relate," Anna said. "Now that the war is finally over, my father and brother, Erik, are moving to Boston. My father has sold his flower shop in Sweden and will probably buy another one here. They're coming in late August, so that Erik can start high school. I can't wait to see them again."

"I'm happy for you, Anna. But I was sorry to hear that your mother died. Anthony told me."

"And your father died, Roberto. It's hard to lose a parent."

When the nanny brought the children, Roberto bent down to Henry's level. "You're a big boy now. I haven't seen you since you were a little baby, and I haven't seen your sister at all."

"This is Mr. Cosentino who made your sailboat," Anna said to her son.

Henry looked at Roberto and asked, "How did you do that?"

"I carved it."

Roberto patted the boy's head first and then the girl's. "You are beautiful children," he said.

When the children had left the room with John, Anna said, "Kristina was born with a drooping eyelid. She's had one surgery so far. After the next one, the doctor says that she'll be able to open her eyelid all the way. She's doing well."

"She's a beautiful girl," Julia said.

"How's Irene?" Roberto asked.

Anna explained to Julia who Irene was, then said, "Irene is going to school and she's a bright and pretty six-year old girl. We now know who her birthmother was. Let's go outside, and I'll tell you how I found out."

Anna said that what she was about to reveal was confidential. She spoke in a hushed voice.

"A woman came to my door and asked if I would hire her as my laundress. I had placed an ad in the paper. She said that she could work only while her son was in school. I didn't consider that a problem, so I hired her.

"One day when the woman was having coffee with the cook in the kitchen, Mrs. Anderson told her about the baby we had found on our doorstep five years earlier. Before Mrs. Anderson had said that it was a girl, the laundress asked a lot of questions about what had happened to her. She hadn't washed any clothes belonging to a five-year old girl, she said.

"Mrs. Anderson suspected that the laundress was the baby's biological mother and told me about it. When I asked the woman, she confessed. She said that it was her husband who had placed the baby on our doorstep. She broke down and told me the whole story. If it's true or not, I don't know.

"She said that she had a son with her first husband. When her husband died, she was employed as housekeeper for a widower who let her keep her son. But the widower wanted more than a housekeeper. He wanted her to sleep with him. She didn't have much of a choice if she wanted to stay in the home. When she became pregnant, she didn't tell him because he had said that he was not interested in marrying again. That's when she'd gone to the pawnshop to buy the suitcase, your suitcase, Roberto. She said that she planned to go home to her parents, but her parents said that she should stay where she was. She feared that she would not be able to support two children alone, so she began a relationship with another man and hoped that he would marry her. When she told him that she was pregnant, he assumed that he was the father and married her. But when the baby was born earlier than he had expected and still full term, he became suspicious. He said that the baby could not be his and gave her an ultimatum: She would have to give it up if they were to stay married.

"In the middle of the night, he pulled out the suitcase to pack the baby clothes and found Roberto's name and our address in one of the pockets. He then demanded to know if Roberto Cosentino was the father of her child. She told him that she had never met the man, but that he was probably the former owner of the suitcase. Her husband said that the address was to a mansion and that Cosentino could be the gardener there. He assumed that the owners were Americans and that they would take good care of the child."

Julia looked at Anna with her eyes wide open. Roberto leaned closer.

"He put the baby in the basket and placed it inside his truck, threw the suitcase in the back, and took off before daylight. The mother said that she cried for days after that. Her husband left her two months later, and she had to support her son by doing laundry work."

"It's a sad story," Julia said.

"So that's what happened," Roberto said. "Did you tell Sally and John that you had found the girl's mother?"

"No, I did not, but I gave her name to our church…just in case Irene should be searching for her birthmother in the future…. I know that I was glad to find my biological mother. Of course, the information will also be on the birth certificate if Irene knows how to look it up." Anna wiped a tear from her cheek. "Irene doesn't know that she has a half brother," she added.

"So now we know how the baby basket and my suitcase both ended up on your doorstep," Roberto said.

John came outside to say goodbye. He turned to Julia and asked, "Are you the Julia Nicolo who writes for the *Globe*?"

"Yes, sir, I am."

"So you're both reporters then."

"Yes, we are."

"By the way," Anna said turning to Roberto, "Bill Drake would like to see you if you have time to stop at his house."

Roberto told Julia that Bill Drake was the father of Sarah and Jane. He looked at his pocket watch and said that they could visit with Bill for a few minutes.

The visit with Anna and John had almost made Roberto feel like they were equals. Anna had said that they had read about his war heroism in the *Boston Globe*, and John had told him to call him by his first name. They were both veterans, but John said that while he had only served at a desk in the nation's capital, Roberto had risked his life overseas and been injured.

As they walked the short distance to Bill Drake's house, Julia asked Roberto, "How many lives have you saved from drowning? I know of Anna, Olivia, and Jane. Then there were several while you were in the Navy. Were there others before that?"

"I didn't keep count of all the foolhardy swimmers I rescued while I was a lifeguard in Genoa. Some of them might have made it without me. But personally I also have people to thank for saving my life, for instance, the passengers in the lifeboat who pulled Anna and me from the icy waters, my fellow sailors who helped me when I was shot, and the doctors that operated on me. And I can't forget all the assistance and favors that have come my way. I think that I've been rewarded more by actions than by honors. Anna and John got me on my feet when I was down on my luck, and Bill Drake and John helped me when I had broken my leg."

Julia squeezed Roberto's arm. No words could describe how proud she was of him.

Bill Drake stood on the front porch when Roberto and Julia approached. Having congratulated them on their upcoming marriage, he turned to Roberto.

"Mrs. Whitmore told me that you're a war hero. It does not surprise me. You've been a hero to me ever since you saved my daughter's life."

"How are your daughters?" Roberto asked.

"Sarah is married and living in New York. Jane still goes to college. She works in our furniture store over the summer. My wife and I want you and your fiancée to go to our store and select your living room furniture."

Roberto began to protest, but Bill waved his hand, saying, "It's on the house. It's the least I can do for you for saving Jane's life. Please sit down, and I'll go inside and write something on a piece of paper. My wife is ailing, so she's not up to visitors."

Roberto and Julia sat down on the porch. They looked at each other like they couldn't believe their luck. "We should invite them to our wedding," Julia said, and Roberto nodded.

When Bill came back he handed Roberto an envelope that carried the logo of the furniture store.

"Thank you so much, Bill, and please convey our thanks to Mrs. Drake. Hope she feels better soon so that you both can come to our wedding."

"If my wife and I can't come, Jane will be happy to attend. Be sure to ask for her at the store."

"We will, and thanks again."

On the train back to Boston, Roberto opened the envelope and showed the gift card to Julia. They were both astonished at the amount that Bill had allowed for their living room furniture. Of course, they knew that he didn't pay retail prices, but still that's how much the furniture would be worth to them.

"We should look for an apartment before we select the furniture," Roberto said.

"Yes, we should. I'm sure that my parents and my other relatives will give us all the household goods that we need, so we don't have to buy much at all."

Roberto thought of his family in Italy. He would write to them and tell them about his engagement. They might even put a notice in the local paper. In a letter from his sisters, he had learned that the furniture maker who rented the shop was interested in Mama. Why not? She was young enough to marry again. It would be a good solution for them all. He also learned that Tessa had married her doctor. Their picture had been in the paper. *Thank you, Tessa, for breaking up with me. Now, I have the right girl.*

Roberto thought of how nice it would be to have a honeymoon on the Cape. In mid-August, most of the summer guests had returned to the mainland, but it was still warm. The hotel would have reduced rates. They could afford to stay there for a few days. He asked Julia what she thought about the idea.

"I'd love it," she said. "We'd have to take time off from work, though."

"It shouldn't be a problem. Our bosses can't deny us a honeymoon."

Chapter 43

The wedding date was set for August 16. Julia's engagement photo had been published in the *Globe* and in *La Gazzetta*. Her fiancé was listed as Petty Officer First Class in the Italian Navy, a war hero, and a newspaper reporter for *La Gazzetta*. She was listed as a graduate of Boston College and reporter for *Boston Globe*. Her girlfriends and college friends sent their congratulations, and Julia added them to the list of wedding guests.

"With all our relatives, we'll probably have one hundred people at the wedding," her father said. "I'll order the invitation cards."

With the wedding date set, Julia went to Mr. Foster and asked for one week off before the wedding and a week after.

Mr. Foster looked surprised. "So I won't be losing you after you marry?"

"No, I'd like to continue working here."

"That would be unusual."

"As long as we don't have any children, I want to work."

"Well, we're going to make some changes in the staffing. Since the war is over, we don't have as much to write about in your department. But as long as you want to continue working, I would like to move you to the editorial department. You have a college degree and a major in English. You'd be perfect for that."

"I appreciate that, but then I wouldn't be writing anything myself."

"You could do that, too. You're one of my best writers. Then if the day comes that you don't want to work full time, I can always use you part time, or as a free-lance writer."

"It's a good offer, Mr. Foster. I'll accept."

"I'll mark down that you'll be off two weeks in August, Miss Nicolo. Congratulations on your marriage. When you come back you'll be Mrs. Cosentino."

Julia had her first fitting of her wedding gown. It would have pearl embroidery and layers of lace. Together with her parents, she decided on the menu, the drinks, the cake, and the flowers. Everything pointed to a traditional Italian-American wedding. She contacted her cousins and got as many bridesmaids and groomsmen she wanted. Roberto's sister-in-law, Sophia, was pregnant with her second child and wasn't interested in being the Matron of Honor, so Julia's best friend from college would do the honor. Sophia's and Anthony's daughter, Collette, would be the flower girl. Anthony had already promised to be Roberto's best man. The wedding party was complete.

Addressing wedding invitations in the evenings after work, Julia didn't have much time for Roberto. He yearned for her full attention, and she couldn't give it to him. She gave him her engagement photo and told him that he would have to be satisfied with that until they were married.

"It will make me long for you even more," he said.

She hunted for an apartment, and when she found one, she showed it to Roberto. People still lived there and they had paid rent until August 15.

"It's all right," Roberto said. "We won't need it until after our honeymoon. I'll call the hotel in Falmouth."

Their close embraces and hot kisses had to sustain them for a while longer.

Together, they selected the furniture that the Drakes had gifted to them. Roberto let Julia select the rugs and drapes.

Julia thought of how the roles of women had changed. The suffrage movement would perhaps give them the right to vote in 1920 if all the states had ratified the constitutional amendment by then. She could continue to work after she married. She also wanted to be a wife and mother. She wanted it all.

Julia knew that Roberto was impatient. She had neglected him, but she wanted to abstain from love making before the wedding, so that their wedding night would be special. Roberto had reserved a room at the hotel in Falmouth, and she could hardly wait for their honeymoon to begin. She was certain that Roberto felt the same way.

Roberto spent his evenings with Anthony and Sophia. He told them that Anna and John were coming to his wedding. Anthony asked questions about the Whitmore beach house and the family. Roberto told him about the girl's drooping eyelid.

"The rich people have their problems, too," Anthony said.

"Anna has had her share of them. Her sister died on the Titanic, her mother in Sweden died, her butler died, her son was kidnapped, and at one time, she found a baby girl on her doorstep, grew found of her, but unselfishly gave her up so that her childless friends could adopt her. Then while John was in the service, she gave birth to her own daughter and still managed all the affairs of the estate," Roberto said.

It was August 16, and Roberto stood at the altar with Anthony and waited. Collette looked shy and cute as she carried her flower basket, spreading the rose petals in the aisle. The bridesmaids and groomsmen walked up next. Roberto recognized Jill among the bridesmaids. He waited for Julia to enter the church. The guests all stood up when they heard, "Here Comes the Bride." There she was—a breathtaking sight on the arm of her father. Her face was covered by a veil. When she came closer, he could see that she smiled, and he smiled back. He would get through this day, and then they would be alone. That's all he could think of as the priest went on and on and the soloist sang. Finally, they were ready to say their vows. They repeated what the priest read, and promised to love and obey.

Finally, he could lift her veil, see her face clearly, and kiss her as his wife. She looked like an angel in all that white. He was sure that her bridal dress was the best that money could buy, but he could have married her in the nude on the beach if it had been up to him.

"You are beautiful and I love you, Mrs. Cosentino," he whispered in her ear.

"I love you, my husband."

They turned around and faced their guests. Walking out was easy, but to stand in the reception room for two hours and greet the multitude of the Nicolo relatives was a challenge. He would never be able to remember them all. Roberto felt relieved to see Anna and John come forward.

"Finally, people I know," he said, as he kissed Anna and shook hands with John, who, in turn, kissed Julia. It was also good to see Bill Drake and his daughter, Jane. But Roberto was even happier to greet Gretchel and Marius and introduce them to Julia. Gretchel hugged them both and told them that she was expecting her second child. "We're way ahead of you," she said. Mr. Perini and the employees at *La Gazzetta*, all men, paraded by and kissed Julia. Roberto felt that his bride had been kissed enough. When would it be his turn to kiss her? People were still standing in line to congratulate them.

Reporters from the *Boston Globe* and *La Gazzetta* were there to take pictures. Julia had insisted that Roberto wear his medals, and again he had to explain to the reporters what they were for. A little later, the bridal party would go to a studio and have their official wedding picture taken. Then there was the dinner, the speeches, and the cutting of the cake.

Anthony read telegrams from their relatives and friends in Genoa. He also translated for those who couldn't understand the Italian language. On a personal note, he expressed his happiness about having his older brother back in Boston and congratulated him on his marriage to the beautiful and intelligent Julia. "Welcome to the Cosentino family, Julia," he said. "*Salute* to the bride and groom."

Roberto saw that Julia just pretended to drink from her glass. He sipped a little for each toast. He wanted to be sober when he could finally be alone with his bride. They would stay one night in the same hotel where the wedding dinner was held. Julia's parents had paid for it all. In the morning, they'd take the train to the Cape for their long-awaited honeymoon.

After the wedding waltz and the obligatory dances with the relatives, Roberto took Julia to their room. The dancing would go on for hours.

Once they were in their room, Roberto lifted his bride and swung her around so that her legs dangled in the air.

"Darling, this is the fulfillment of my life," he said as he put her down.

They looked at their marriage bed and hurried to get undressed. Julia's dress took time, but he helped her. Roberto then carefully removed his medals from his rented tails and placed them in the blue box that he still had in his suitcase.

"I want to wash off all the lipstick and tobacco juice from my face," Julia said. "Then I want only your lips to touch me."

"I'll be happy to comply, darling. I've already washed up." He made quick work of his suit, studs, and starched shirt.

She came back dressed in a pretty negligee. Her shiny, chestnut-colored hair was brushed and hanging down to her shoulders.

"I've never seen you looking more beautiful, darling. Not even in your wedding dress. Thank you for becoming my wife." He swept her up in her arms and laid her on the bed.

"I'll kiss you from top to bottom," he said.

He began with her lips, her face, and her neck. She ran her fingers through his black chest hair. He looked up at her and asked, "When do you want to start a family, darling?"

"I know that my parents are anxious for grandchildren, but I'd like to wait a while if it's all right with you? I've studied the cycle of women's fertility, and it should be safe right now."

"Oh, darling, I don't have words for how much I love you." His voice choked with emotions.

While the newly-wed couple slept, Julia's colleagues wrote an article for the social page headlined, "Hero of the Titanic and the European War Weds his Boston Sweetheart."

About the author:

Lilly Setterdahl was raised in Sweden, a country steeped in folklore and sagas, and where almost every community had its own local poet. Swedish authors, such as Selma Lagerlöf, Astrid Lindgren, and Stieg Larsson have caught the interest of readers around the world.

Hero of the Titanic is Lilly's fifteenth book and her second historical novel. She has received many awards for her research and writings. As this book goes to press, she is working on a nonfiction manuscript about the Swedes on the Titanic.

Residing in the Quad Cities, Illinois, Lilly travels often to participate in various events and to visit relatives both in the U.S. and abroad.